'*Little Boy* is an extraordinary novel, audacious and poignant and superbly well-written. It imagines the unimaginable, finds innocence in awfulness. This is what the literary novel is capable of, and so rarely pulls off.'

—Andrew Cowan, author of *Your Fault*

'Bold, audacious, written with surgical precision, quiet lyricism and incredible assurance. Provocative and surprisingly moving. This novel hurt my feelings, and made me think deeply. As Little Boy says, "All the time he had spent in institutions, sheltered from the world, when in reality there was no greater threat to him than the institutions themselves."'

—Sharlene Teo, author of *Ponti*

£12.99

LITTLE BOY

LITTLE BOY
BY JOHN SMITH

BOILER HOUSE PRESS

PART I

1

One morning a small boy was found buried in the ground in the Belgian Congo. He was buried up to the scalp. A tangle of filthy weeds encircled his head. Nothing could be seen of him but a little dome, hard and hairless, fixed like a rivet in the wild grass. The boy was not dead—not quite dead. The sun had singed the dome, deepening its cracks, raising its carbuncles, and it was now an unpleasant shade of yellow.

The man who found him was an Englishman named Robert Sharp. He had been walking in the tall grass with his guide, rifle in hand, on the lookout for roan deer. It was now late morning. The year was 1935. A buried boy was almost the last thing this gentleman had expected to find in this plain, far from human habitation—but such things were not unheard of.

Mr Sharp laid down his rifle and began uprooting flowers and weeds and tufts of grass. After some time he had unearthed a good part of the head and shoulders.

The boy made his first observations of the sky, and Mr Sharp went away. He was gone for what seemed to the boy like a very long time. Then he returned with his guide, a wiry man with heavily lidded eyes. They leaned over the boy and gazed at his head.

It was not a large head. It was small and narrow, predominantly gray in color, yellow on top, veined with sickly reds and greens. His scars, of which there were many, had not faded into the skin as scars usually do, but had swollen to great sizes, cracked asunder in festering gulfs, twined together, branched and sprouted into curious shapes. Tumors covered his face. The biggest and most bulbous of these embellishments lay above the eyes and below the mouth, which would have been advantageous to the boy, had the face remained in any salvageable state. But the nose was in a pulp, and the mouth lay open, like a doll's mouth. Only the eyes were immediately recognizable as belonging to a living creature. Lidless, dilated, they stared out of the twisted mass of tissue, staring without fear or pleading or desperation or accusation or even confusion. His facial expression—to the extent that one could be observed—was one of mild dissatisfaction.

'Hurry up, old boy,' said Mr Sharp. 'Quick.'

The guide plunged his hands into the dirt either side of the boy's skull, applied pressure to the temples and lifted, without result. The boy wondered what was happening.

The guide made a groaning sound.

'Let me at it,' said Mr Sharp.

He scrambled down onto his knees and began

squeezing and pulling at the boy with all his might. But the boy would not budge.

'What shall we do?' said the guide.

Mr Sharp stood up, reached into his breast-pocket and withdrew his pipe and a few shreds of tobacco. He was a tall man, slender, a little knock-kneed and yellow-haired. After a brief silence he instructed the guide to get the mattock. The guide went to the pack, which he had left a short way off, and untied the mattock. Mr Sharp, having sat down on a stone, placed his pith helmet on the ground at his feet and began to light his pipe. As the guide began to dig, Mr Sharp wondered why the child's face did not stir, why it stared silently ahead, no matter how much they pulled and prodded it. Mr Sharp was no great judge of the ages of children, but he estimated the boy to be about six, or perhaps six and a half.

To extract a child from a shallow grave seems at first, to the casual observer, a ludicrously simple matter. And in most cases it is. But in the case of the boy there were several complications which revealed themselves gradually and unpleasantly to his rescuers. The first being that his shoulders, which they had expected to be roughly symmetrical and equal in size, were all crumpled over to one side and fused together in places. His arms, which they thought reasonable to assume would be connected to his shoulders, were nowhere to be found. A few yards from his head they found a long rigid limb which they took for a leg. And a little further on, tinged with the telltale yellow, was something small and hard, resembling a finger, or thumb. They were unable to extract any of these pieces, for they were wedged among the rocks, and at a certain depth the ground became too hard for the mattock. The guide identi-fied a number of gleaming strings, perhaps of ligament.

'They keep going up the hill, Mr Sharp,' he said, stumbling up through the rank grass towards the top of the bluff. 'Look, here.'

Mr Sharp made no reply. He did not rise from his stone, nor look at the guide, nor look at the boy. One could not even have been sure that he was listening. He gave a few thoughtful, distant jerks of the head, sending puffs of smoke from his mouth, and squinted at the sky. He sat a while in this manner, listening to the heavy breathing of the guide and to the tick tick of the mattock, slower and slower. Then he turned his head and watched the mattock for some time, moving in repeated arcs over the savannah.

'Carry on, Malupenga!' he said gallantly. 'That's the ticket—sweat out the toxins.'

After a tranquil pipe Mr Sharp went down into the ditch for a look. He cleaved to the sides, fearing that he would stumble and break a limb. They lay scattered, all still embedded, partially unearthed, sticking up out of the floor of the ditch. In the center was the greater part of the boy— the lurid bald head and shoulders, stiff and motionless, like a damaged marble bust.

It was impossible to say with any certainty what each of the other scraps was. Perhaps they were merely rocks that looked like body parts. It was difficult to tell. Even the face, the more he looked at it, seemed less and less to resemble any face he had ever seen. He could not even be sure that all the body parts, if they were body parts, belonged to the same child. The situation seemed to him very unusual.

A wind blew and the distant thorns began to convulse.

'Try socking him one,' suggested Mr Sharp.

The guide drew back his foot.

'Lightly,' said Mr Sharp.

The guide socked him one on the back of the head, but it was to no effect.

'Tricky business, this,' said Mr Sharp.

He got out of the ditch, went back to the stone, put his helmet back on and dabbed at the bristles of his moustache with a small handkerchief. Soon he became weary of the sound of the mattock. He came up with a plan, which he described to the guide. They would mark the place, he said, and return together to Jadotville, some twelve miles away. They would notify the mining corporation there. They would tell them a boy of six or six and a half was buried here, buried discreetly and discretely, dismembered, strewn underground across a great area, so that it was impossible to remove him by hand. Then it would fall to the corporation to bring the infant to safety—an operation for which it would be far better equipped, he explained, than they were. The hour was late and he was thinking already of his tot of rum and quinine and of curling up in the twilight underneath his mosquito-curtain.

The guide stood a while in the ditch. There were ants on the little digit. He looked at the head and there too regrettably he saw that spiders and safari ants were crawling, hastening in and out of the mouth and nostrils, up and down the swirling philtrum and over the long weals of the forehead. Bending, he scattered them with his hand, but they returned, and the guide said to himself that as long as the boy lay exposed in this manner in the ground it was inevitable that vermin should come and feast on what edible matter they could find, and for a moment his mind was full of spiders and other creatures, the beasts and birds of the plain, that would come creeping out of the jungle and whirling down out of the skies—each in their turn, or simultaneously—to devour the face.

Mr Sharp cried out that it was time to go. He had his rifle slung over his arm and his helmet on his head and he was brushing the dirt from his puttees. The guide knew all too well Mr Sharp's little fits of impatience. He got out of the hole and heaved onto his shoulders the pack—the towering, wobbling, sixty-pound pack, laden with tools and wicker baskets and bottles and Swiss pedometers and boxes of ammunition—and they set out.

The boy stared dumbly from his ditch. He had paid little attention to his rescuers. Everything was strange to him— the sky, the smells, the wild savannah stretching for miles, the shadows of the stones and of the termite mounds crawling eastward over the frantic grass. The boy did not know he was a foundling, did not know into whose hands he had fallen, nor did he know what enormous asperities lay before him. His thoughts were simple. Finally freed from the dark, he attempted to shut his eyes. But he could not shut his eyes. To execute the command that would have lowered the lids over his eyes was beyond his abilities. His body would not listen to him. And in any case, he had no eyelids.

After a while he stopped trying. He watched the sky fade until it was dark, then he observed the stars. He heard the men beating through the grass. He listened to their steps until they were quiet, and there was no sound but the wind and the birds and the hiss of the trees.

2

Mr Sharp dutifully reported his discovery to the mining corporation. Some men came—very fat men, dressed in white—and examined the boy in his ditch, standing around him and talking in low voices, setting up theodolites, putting stakes into the ground and tying pieces of string between them.

Larger and larger groups began to arrive in the plain, more and more of the earth was dug out, and more and more body parts were placed carefully aside. Simple shelters were erected, with timber posts and grass roofs, to accommodate the great number of men who had been recruited for the effort. But soon these shelters, in their turn, were outgrown by the operation, and as the ditches and trenches grew larger and deeper and the excavation became more extensive, they were cleared away and replaced with more permanent structures. After a few months the whole region had undergone an extreme alteration in appearance. The hole had grown into a gaping pit, several hundred feet in depth, and the hill had vanished, and a russet haze darkened the air, and everywhere was heard the chatter of hydraulic drills and the thunder of dynamite.

The rescue of the boy was an operation of the utmost intricacy, due to the depth and distribution of the scraps. The enormous quantity of these scraps was quite in excess of what one would expect from one child. The reason for this curious anomaly was not clear, and the corporation did not like to speculate.

The main piece of the boy—the one comprising his head and trunk—had been successfully extracted and set aside, in a shed. With this action the corporation could well have given up, abandoned the site, and left the rest of the scraps buried out of view. There were some within the leadership who advocated this course of action. But since it had been discovered that his plot coincided with rich natural deposits of various minerals, such as cobalt, silver, nickel, bismuth and arsenic, the argument was made that if the corporation carefully calculated and defrayed its expenses, it was possible to continue extracting the boy's fragments without adversely affecting its business. So the corporation persisted, and even profited, maintaining a record of what it had recovered of the child and including him each year among the tables and inventories of its annual reports. It did not comment on the nature of the abnormality that enabled him to survive in his most unusual manner, though it reported accurately on his physical condition.

The reports were largely ignored by the general public. There was some small interest outside the Congo, in medical circles. Certain obscure journals advanced the hypothesis that the boy was not the only one of his kind. Other cases were presented and debated—all male, all paralytic, all pre-pubescent, in similar states of survival, all panting on like him in spite of catastrophic injury to the musculoskeletal, digestive, circulatory and respiratory systems. Theoretical models were proposed to account for the persistence of his consciousness, his extraordinary resilience, his extreme limbic and cortical malleability, his absence of motor control and various other features of his condition.

But the corporation paid no attention to such specula-tions, and soon the interest waned, his novelty as a medical curiosity began to fade and the medical profession found other things to talk about.

3

For the next four years the boy lay in an open-sided shed, in
a state of dazed discomfort, while the rest of him was being
retrieved. They had placed him on his left side, facing out
of the shed. He was small in stature, no more than three
feet from top to bottom, but very heavy. Though he had no
arms or legs, he was in possession of a fine solid pair of
stumps, projecting from below the flitters of his pelvis.

The shed was his home. From the day he was placed on
its concrete slab until the day he was removed he did not
stir an inch. His eyes remained open. His mouth remained
open. Every part of him was fixed and still. He had a large
part of the mine to gaze out on—one half of the gaping
pit, the precipice, the road curving around its edge, the
buildings on the other side, the headframe that towered

above the buildings, and the vast hazy sky. Far off he could even see a part of the workmen's camp with its few jacaranda trees and its little narrow church and the elderly Belgian nuns going in and out in their white habits.

He was seldom disturbed. Each day the workmen brought in cartloads heaped high with scraps and emptied them around him, one shovelful after another. A white gentleman in a white uniform came now and then to check on him, before hastening away, by means of a hammock supported by two guides, to one of the other sheds under his supervision. From the perspective of the corporation it was an ideal arrangement. The boy asked for nothing, nothing was provided.

He was a simple-minded boy, prone to fits of brooding. Deprived of a mother and a father, of company and motion, of affection and attention, of anything resembling the natural concomitants of childhood, he found it difficult to make sense of the simplest concepts. When he tried to think of the time before his rescue, to recall for instance the loss of his first leg, or the loss of his second leg, or of his arms, or the onset of his tumors, he drew a blank. He knew something was wrong with him, but he did not know what it was.

He was in pain—this at least admitted of no ambiguity. His left shoulder and his left hip ached from supporting him in his position on the filthy floor. The dry, itching crusts of his scabs were extremely unpleasant, particularly on his face. This dryness also affected his mouth and eyes, which were perpetually open. He felt the puffiness and the tightness of the infections, the weight and pressure of the foreign matter that clung to him. But he could not scratch these itches, nor summon anyone to scratch them for him. All he could do was lie still, staring unblinkingly in the one direction, with the same idiotic expression on his face.

As the months went by there was little change in the condition of the shed. The limb heaps grew. The young simpleton found ways of growing accustomed to things. He ceased to fear the harsh sounds. He grew accustomed to the flies moving about on his head, his tumors, his face, his eyes, scuttling across his corneas, buzzing overhead. He listened to them and soon ceased to worry about them. He grew accustomed to the workmen, their loud boots and voices, and the rattle of the limb-carts and the constant scraping of their shovels. He listened to them talk about the mine, and the bosses, and various other things he did not understand.

Thus he passed the first years of his melancholy existence, scarcely expecting that things would or could be any different.

4

In January 1939, a medical conference was held at George Washington University. It had been a most exciting few months in the field of prosthetics. Some doctors in Berlin had just discovered a process for converting neural impulses directly into electrical signals. The news had spread across Europe and was now being discussed for the first time in America. It was widely agreed that it had enormous implications for the creation of prosthetic devices.

The conference was now over, and its organizer, a young Hungarian doctor named Edward Teller, had just sat down for what seemed like the first time in several days. He was in his living room with his wife, slumped in a low armchair, his legs crossed in his usual manner, his necktie loosened, his head resting on his hand, when the telephone rang.

It was late. Their guests had all departed and Mrs Teller was tidying the living room. The house was in a state of ruin. Some of the doctor's music books lay open on the piano. The Waldstein sonata had slipped down over the keys. The ashtrays were overflowing. All about the room there were dirty glasses, plates, medical papers, coffee cups and crumpled napkins.

Mrs Teller watched her husband rise with difficulty and go into the other room to answer it. Then she went on bustling about the room, taking up stacks of plates, pouring into the trash the gnawed knishes and the wrinkled cigarettes and the fine gray dust of ashes. She took from the table the report of the celebrated German experiments and looked at it. In the photograph a man sat calmly in a chair, a thin man with a shaved head, dressed in white pajamas, an array of electrodes connecting his scalp to a large machine. The German doctors stood on either side of the man, their indifferent faces in profile.

She heard Dr Teller speaking in Hungarian in the other room.

'I'll—yes, I realize that—I'll come and pick you—We can discuss it when I see you. Alright. If you will stop talking a moment—Yes, indeed. I'll see you soon.'

After a moment he came back into the living room. Dr Teller was a greasy, large-nosed, round-shouldered, awkward-bodied, black-haired man of thirty-one, with a limp. His eyes stared out of hollows beneath his large dark eyebrows. He looked gloomy at the best of times, but now he looked especially so. Before she could ask he said: 'Leo Szilard.'

Mrs Teller had dared to hope for a moment that it had been something about her family.

'What does he want?'

'He's just arrived in Washington.'

Mrs Teller put down the medical report. 'To hell with him,' she said. 'Doesn't he know the conference is over?'

Dr Teller shook his head and stared at the floor.

'It's important,' he said.

He went into the hall, took his coat from its hook and began rifling in his pockets for his car keys.

'If it's about the German experiments,' said his wife, 'you ought to have told him we have heard everything there is to hear about the damned German experiments.'

Dr Teller was silent in the hall. He had found the keys and now he was holding his coat, looking down at his feet. He was thinking about the boy. He had not thought about the boy for some time, but as he considered him now in the light of the latest medical advances, his case seemed suddenly much more urgent and much more interesting than it had before.

Mrs Teller came down the hall after him. She was a short woman with black hair and a wide flat mouth. To her neck, which was a neck of extraordinary thinness, her fingers were inclined to stray, in times of mild concern.

'I'd better go with you,' she said.

'If you like,' he said. 'I'm just going to pick him up.'

As she put her shoes on, Dr Teller stood in the doorway and stared.

'You know, he may be right this time,' he said.

'About what?'

'You remember that boy of his? The African case?'

Mrs Teller held a lambskin glove before her face with one hand and made a series of tentative parries at its open end with the other.

'It's always something with Szilard,' she said. 'If you

invite him to stay I will hit the ceiling. We can take him to a hotel. Really, what a nerve he has to drop on us like this after the conference. And if he is right, well, he's picked a fine time to finally be right about something. Why is he in Washington anyway? Just to keep us awake?'

'He's meeting with some government people. About that boy.'

Mrs Teller wrapped a scarf around her neck.

'What nonsense,' she said. 'The boy is miles away. He's never even seen him.'

Dr Teller's eyes darted back and forth across the carpet.

'Let's go,' said Mrs Teller.

They went out into the night, got in the car and drove to the railway station.

For a while they sat waiting, staring through the windshield at the steps. It had rained that afternoon and on the pavement the water lay in broad gray tranquil puddles, cradling the evening lights. The streetlamps were illuminated and through the narrow cones of fog people passed in varying states of flight and pursuit.

At length a figure appeared on the steps. It was a fat man in a badly crumpled trench coat, with a suitcase in each hand. He moved with extreme inefficiency. He kept turning back towards the colonnade like one who thought he had forgotten something. When he reached the car he fumbled for a few seconds with his bags and the door handle. It opened with a blast of cold air.

'Well,' he said. 'Didn't I tell you? Didn't I tell you the Germans would do it? Everybody said I was a fool. Help me with this door—I think I am running a fever. How do you do, Mrs Teller.'

'Fine, thank you,' said Mrs Teller.

Dr Leo Szilard was forty-one years old, ten years Dr Teller's senior. They had been colleagues in Germany, before the Nazis.

As they drove northwest along Massachusetts Avenue, the doctors entered into a pathological discussion. Delicately they touched upon the various features that made the boy an irresistible experimental candidate for the Germans. They considered and debated the feasibility of treatment according to the German method, the theory Dr Szilard had been advancing for some years, the implantation of electrodes, the mechanism of electrical intracranial stimulation, the possible benefits of isolating or concentrating by surgical means the active tissues, the practical difficulties of such a process, and the predicted resultant increases in energy output—in a word, all that concerned the boy in a medical capacity.

Dr Szilard was sweating, wiping his forehead continually with his sleeve. 'It's troubling,' he kept saying. 'Exceedingly troubling.'

'Surely they wouldn't,' said Dr Teller.

Dr Szilard shook his head.

'Don't be an imbecile, Teller.'

'But really—military applications? It is far too early to speak of—'

Dr Szilard blew his nose into a handkerchief. 'I'm sure I'm coming down with something,' he said.

Mrs Teller leaned her head against the cold window and listened to the men debating. The car swept round Dupont Circle and she thought again about the photograph of the German experiments. The seated man, the white pajamas, the bald head, the wires. Though not a doctor herself, Dr Teller often spoke to her about his work, and she understood. She had to admit that Dr Szilard's theory was sound, mathematically at least. To the extent that one could probe at a cerebellum of a boy who was miles away, it was sound.

They came to the house. Dr Szilard paid no attention to the state of the living room. In fact, with his travel-rumpled coat, his messy hair, his scuffed shoes and luggage, he formed a part of the general disorder. Dr Teller's tiredness had left him and was gradually being replaced by something else—a creeping feeling that somewhere in Germany, somebody was having this very same conversation, or perhaps had already had it.

'I just don't believe they would do it,' he said as he sank into his armchair. 'Would they really—I mean, it is a child we are talking about. It would be totally unethical.'

'There is no such thing as ethics in Germany anymore,' said Dr Szilard.

'Think of the sterilizations,' said Mrs Teller.

Dr Teller put his face in his hands. Mrs Teller made some coffee and brought it out on a tray.

'Have a little coffee,' she said.

'No thanks.'

'Come on.'

'Did you hear me? I said I don't want it.'

Dr Szilard paced the living room, laying out his plan of attack.

'We must get everyone in the field working on this. And we must not publish. That's very important. Total secrecy. Teller, I want you to come to Columbia in the summer. New York, you understand, to work with me and Dr Fermi.

You know Fermi already, of course. Fermi is a good man. And we must track down the other boys—'

'Other cases?' said Dr Teller. 'How many are there?'

'Not many. The others are less certain. One in Czechoslovakia, possibly. Very troubling. One in Canada. Nothing is confirmed. The African boy is the one I'm most concerned about.'

'Why?'

'He is the most promising. He fits the diagnostic model in every particular.'

Dr Szilard was indefatigable. He did not stop pacing until he had persuaded Dr Teller to go to New York in the summer and join his team. They would not yet be working on boys, of course. These were merely trial experiments. Proofs of concept. But boys could be quite easily found, he said. Yes, once the medical community began to catch on, Dr Szilard said, there was no doubt that more boys would be found.

It took some time for the theory to sink in, for Dr Teller. But once it did, it presented itself to his mind with remarkable precision. All of a sudden, everything he and his colleagues had discussed at the conference seemed unimportant—child's play. The floor had fallen out from under him. The closer he looked at this idea of Dr Szilard's, the more its implications swelled and grew, the more wild and uncontrollable it became. And he sensed for the first time, in the midst of this little academic discipline in which he had built his career, something brutal and true. It cut through all he had known or thought he knew about the medical sciences. It was a strange, primal feeling. He smelled blood. He felt the tremor of the shifting of epochs. He felt the danger of what would happen if it fell into the wrong hands. Control over life—that was what it was.

Pure control over human life. For the very first time in his career, Dr Teller perceived some external confirmation of a notion he had long held: that he was a person of significance, destined for great discoveries.

'I'll do it,' he said, 'I'll go to New York.'

And with renewed energy they went on talking about the boy for almost an hour more, until they were interrupted by Mrs Teller. 'Dr Szilard,' she said. 'You must stay the night.'

A look passed between the Tellers, during which each seemed to blame the other for this state of affairs. They took him to the guest bedroom. He shuffled in and sat down on the bed. There he remained for a moment, his face stern, blinking occasionally, staring at the wall as though in a trance. The Tellers looked at him and wondered if they ought to say something.

'The mattress is too hard,' said Dr Szilard, getting up. 'I am sorry. You will have to take me to a hotel.'

Dr Teller began to protest.

'If he wants to go, let him go,' said Mrs Teller.

'It's for the best,' declared Dr Szilard. 'I will be up early—meetings, you see. The things I have to do, Teller. The revolting people I have to meet! It's much simpler to stay in a hotel. Thank you, Mrs Teller, thank you! I must be on my way, Teller. There's no time. Let's go.'

Mrs Teller gave him directions to a hotel which was within walking distance from the house. He thanked her and Dr Teller showed him outside. The doctors shook hands on the steps.

'I shall see you in New York,' said Dr Szilard.

Then he hesitated a moment. He considered asking Dr Teller if he had received any news from Hungary. But he decided against it. If the news was good, he thought, they would have told him already.

When they had said their third or fourth goodbyes, Dr Szilard went down the brick steps, heard the door close behind him and hurried off into the night.

5

Arduous and intricate were the efforts in which Dr Leo Szilard was engaged over the next few months.

His primary goal was to contact the mining company or the Belgian government. But his letters and telephone calls and telegrams fell on deaf ears. He spoke to doctors at all the major American universities and urged them to secrecy, he made inquiries in Canada and Czechoslovakia, he identified facilities where he thought the boy or boys may receive treatment, he combed the newspapers and the medical journals in search of new cases, he appeared before research foundations, private benefactors, philanthropists and all the relevant government agencies, all of whom were impressed by the gravity of the situation, but regretted to inform him of the inevitable limits of their charitability, especially in matters in which the science was not settled. It did not help that Dr Szilard was sometimes late to his meetings, that he sometimes lost his way in Manhattan, that he tended to forget names, that he entered and exited through the incorrect doors, that more than once he left his scientific papers in diners and on park benches, and that he gave little thought to his personal appearance and almost never took off his trench coat.

Every few days he went to see Dr Fermi at the University. Their laboratory was a small, cluttered room in the Prosthetics Department. In the center of the room was a wooden table. The subjects—all adult volunteers—would lie prone on this table, their scalps stuck with electrodes. The wires of the electrodes led to an assortment of boxlike machines, which measured the energy output, ticking, clucking and blinking. Dr Fermi would hasten back and forth in his white coat, checking the connections, calibrating the machines and writing in his notebooks. Sometimes he would experiment on samples of brain tissue (normal brain tissue)—peering at them through a microscope or placing them in vacuum chambers or in test tubes containing various liquids or heating them or boiling them or cooling them or shaking them or stirring them or stimulating them with electricity.

Dr Fermi was a hands-on fellow. He was small, balding, Italian, thirty-eight years old, highly respected in the field, frank in agreement and disagreement, and always good-natured. Dr Szilard, unlike his colleague, did not perform experiments—such busywork was beneath him—but spent his time in the laboratory pacing before the blackboard and talking. The experiments confirmed what they had feared for some time—that the thing was possible. With normal human beings, of course, the signal was diffuse, the energy output was very weak. But if the tissue of a living subject could be reorganized, Dr Fermi said, it would be a very different matter. All that was needed was a living brain that they could take apart and put back together in a more efficient formation. Then the signal could be concentrated. The increase, he said, in the energy output would be exponential. And this meant—but here Dr Szilard always stopped him, for they both knew what it meant.

In March, Czechoslovakia was annexed by the Germans. Dr Szilard and Dr Fermi waited for word about boys, but heard nothing. Spring passed. Summer descended upon the city—windows were cracked in the tall buildings, women removed their nylons, bodies dripped in the airless streetcars, gray crowds filed through the clean pavilions of the 1939 World's Fair. Dr Teller arrived in the city and brought with him a brilliant doctor named Hans Bethe, from Cornell. Dr Bethe, a good friend of the Tellers, was a German man with an overbite and an enormous forehead. At first he was resistant to the idea that they must keep their work secret, rather than publishing it. But soon they convinced him that the information was too dangerous to be waved about where the Nazis could see it.

While Dr Fermi, Dr Teller and Dr Bethe worked on the experiments, Dr Szilard took long walks in the city. Walking helped him to think—and nothing was more important to Dr Szilard than the clarity of his thoughts. He would go for a few hours aimlessly through the neighbourhood, down Broadway, far from the university, or up into Harlem. His route was never the same, as far as he knew. He loved to walk. Even in the winter months he walked, in the snow and rain, buttoning his trench coat about his neck. He did not walk to admire the city so much as to gouge his presence into its streets. He wore it on his senses for hours on end, tried all evening to exhaust it, failed, then took it to bed. Like all men who live alone in a great city, he was its lover, and it breathed in his ears as he slept. Cars blared at him in the streets where he paused to think, birds excreted on his trench coat, dogs found themselves and their long leads and their owners tangled beneath his feet. Sometimes, on a fine day, Dr Szilard would go into a park, or onto a lawn, and simply stand there. For a joy it is, and a great joy, to stand among the blades, on the fallen blades, still, and feel, head uplifted, the sun's passage through the gulf between two banks of cloud. And to deduce, with eyes closed, that it is there and that it is moving, moving through the azure emptiness, brightening all below. In such moments the boy was clearest to Dr Szilard, and he best understood the way to help him.

He continued to meet with people about the boy. In July he met with a banker from Lehman Brothers named Alexander Sachs. When he had finished explaining the boy's predicament, Mr Sachs spent a long time in deep consideration. Then he leapt up out of his chair and declared that the child must be transported at once from the squalor of Africa and deposited into an American institution, such as Harvard, or if that was not possible Yale. He was, he explained, an intimate acquaintance of President Roosevelt. He was, he explained further, an architect of the New Deal, a patron of the arts, a friend to welfare recipients, an opponent of the homeless, a proponent of a Jewish homeland in Palestine, extremely broadly read, and a scholar and popularizer of the sciences. It was no use, Mr Sachs said, bothering with the private sector. He promised him he would take the matter directly to the president, and Dr Szilard left his office with renewed confidence.

6

Dr Szilard returned to his hotel room, intending to write some more letters and telephone Dr Teller. But first he ran himself a bath. It was late, almost nightfall. He took off his suit and put on his hair net. Then he got into the cast-iron, claw-footed bathtub and lay on his back in the water.

He gazed a moment at the ceiling. He closed his eyes. He imagined himself to be a head, a head only, with a face, and a little hair, floating bodiless on a shoreless sea. All became flat and calm, calm and humid. He perceived for miles about him the softening, warping, twisting of the million girders of the city. The sky reddened, buildings wilted. He waited for his thoughts to coagulate, sink, dissolve. For a moment all was silent, then the silence broke, gradually, carefully. Or rather, it parted, opened, to be filled as by a muted gong—a deep, full, womb-muffled echo. The sound slowly opened and slowly closed, a plain plosive. The edgeless body murmured, wavered as one, wavered and was still again, silent again, its last ripple faded.

Dr Szilard came very close to relaxing, but he did not relax. He could not relax. He could not stop thinking about the boys, and the African case in particular. It was his mathematics—his idea. Before anyone else he had predicted this particular manner of exploiting the latent energy of the neural tissues. He had simply neglected to put it into practice. Now he felt that his idea was slowly acquiring a life of its own. Somebody had their hands on his idea and was toiling away with it—calmly, practically, methodically, efficiently.

He opened his heavy-lidded eyes and looked at the pale islands of his knees, the spots of the pores, the fine stray hairs. The water was cooling. All was cooling. His skin was wrinkling. The laws of thermodynamics were having their way with him.

What would the boy be like, he thought. The prosthesis, the artificial body—what would it look like? What would be its dimensions? He tried to picture it physically rather than mathematically. What shape would it take? A perfectly reorganized brain—a mind stripped of its superfluities, perfectly primed and concentrated to a single purpose, precisely calibrated—a machine for the manifestation of the pure, undiminished, undiverted will?

He could not see it. Mathematically he could see it—but not physically. The machine itself. He could not conceive of it. It could look like anything, he supposed. That was what made it so dangerous. There was no limit. No need to correspond to the human form. No needless appendages. Round? Square? Stout? Slim? Pyramidal? An isosceles triangle? He did not know. It would depend on the boy himself. His neurology. All he knew was that the boy would be vast, imposing, impressive. In fact Dr Szilard had always had a much clearer sense of the way people would respond to the prosthesis once he had finished inventing it, the things people would say about the prosthesis, the esteem he would derive from the prosthesis, than what the thing itself would actually be like.

He got out of the bath. He did not drain it—the draining of bathtubs was maids' work. Naked, straight-backed, he presided over himself in the mirror. He looked plump and grave. He combed his hair back. He observed his florid cheeks, his straight nose, his low pursed lips—an imperious countenance. He glanced at his desk, which was littered with books, medical journals, papers, torn envelopes and drafts of letters and memoranda.

In their stillness and silence they struck him as meaningless objects. What value, he thought, had any of these papers? They were just rectangles of cellulose pulp. None of them had accomplished anything. Were any of them worth more than the lamp shade, or the curtains, or the wallpaper? He heard footsteps in the hall—sharp, efficient footsteps. Tick tick. A cockroach scuttled across the papers with clambering legs and fidgeting antennae.

Dr Szilard had long ago decided it would not be sufficient for him merely to direct the course of the child's treatment. He would also take a personal interest in his care. He would improve him, detach him from the gross physical and intellectual disadvantages of his present situation, and introduce him into a life of comfort, sophistication and society. He would influence his opinions and judgments of the world, improve his manners, imbue him with sensitivity, and raise his situation and standard of life to a higher plane.

For some reason, having surveyed his desk for a few minutes, Dr Szilard felt the distinct sensation of having done something productive. And as he put on his blue cotton pajamas, he told himself that despite the clarity brought on by the act of bathing, it was too late to begin the other tasks he had planned for that evening. The next day he would complete the letters he had been meaning to write and he would speak to Dr Teller and soon the trustworthy man from Lehman Brothers would speak to the president. One could not hope for much more than that. Action would be taken. The boy would be safe. This was how progress worked, he told himself—each day a little closer.

Before he went to bed he checked his suitcases. They were the way he always left them, the way he had been leaving them each night since 1933, in his various hotel rooms—by the door, fully packed, the keys in the locks.

The next morning he took another bath. It was two in the afternoon before he came downstairs into the lobby. He felt primed for action. He had successfully distilled the events of the previous day into their clearest possible for-mulation in his mind and was now perfectly ready to write his letters and telephone Dr Teller at the first available opportunity. The more he thought about what Alexander Sachs had said to him, the more he agreed that it made sense to go through the government, rather than a private organization. He would telephone Dr Teller, then he would take a walk, then he would write his letters.

He called Dr Teller from a telephone in the lobby. As he

spoke to the operator and waited for the connection, he gazed about the hotel with its white wainscoting, its green carpet, the pinewood mailboxes over the reception desk, and the door thrown ajar to admit the summer air. There were a few other guests in the waiting chairs—an elderly man with a newspaper, a woman in a camel hair coat, the clerk with his horn-rimmed spectacles. They had the listless, suspended look that people acquire in hotel lobbies.

'Leo,' said the voice of Dr Teller. 'I was just going to call you.'

'You remember this fellow Sachs?' Dr Szilard began, forgoing the greeting, as was their custom. 'I told you abou—'

But Dr Teller was trying to speak over him.

'What?' said Dr Szilard. 'I can't hear you, Teller, start again.'

There was a pause. The line was silent.

'Can you hear me?' said Dr Teller.

'Yes, go ahead.'

Dr Teller began to speak. He spoke quickly. His voice was low, less animated than usual. 'I have just managed to get through to a colleague in Germany...'

Dr Szilard raised a plump hand to his brow and exhaled slowly.

'It's confirmed,' said Dr Teller. 'The Czechoslovakian case. The Nazis knew about it.'

'Are they experimenting on him?'

'We don't know. They've cut off all communications. All we know is they have him.'

Had this news come a few months earlier, Dr Szilard may have reacted with anger, throwing the telephone, or kicking the wall, or indulging in one of the many other things men are accustomed to do when they are angry. But as it came now it struck him with a sense of banal inevitability. The prospect of a poor outcome, of various poor outcomes, had hung in the air for a long time, and now it had happened, the day long feared—one of the days long feared—had arrived. He stood a moment with the telephone pressed to his ear, knowing that Dr Teller was doing the same. He heard the slight rustle of the surrounding world—the rearrangements of pigeons, the cars, the swell and seawash of their exhausts, the cluck of their horns, the shudder of a train passing below in the subway.

'They're doing it, Szilard,' said Dr Teller. 'They're after them.'

7

Strange men were at the mine. The boy had never seen them before. There were three of them. They were standing near the shed, partially obscuring his view of the pit. The boy was in his usual place, his body and his face in the exact position as when he was first placed there.

The day was bright and clear. The rainy season had just ended, and the mine lay outspread below a cloudless sky. The air was quiet but for a low rumble, and the occasional cries of birds. The scent of acacia, borne on a gentle wind, was mingling, in the shed, with the odor of the boy's necrotic tissue. The high terraced cliffs of the pit looked clean and gray. On the pit floor, of which he could see only a small part, were great heaps of pale cobalt ore, and here and there a little pile of darker matter—limbs and body-scraps.

On the ledges the workmen moved in silence at their tasks, seeming to have little effect on that vast stillness, and the boy felt the sense of equanimity that accompanies the sight of tiny people at a distance who do not know they are being watched. High above them, on the opposite rim, the buildings too were calm and still. On the tall headframe the wheel turned, raising and lowering its iron chain. He knew nothing of its function or of the network of tunnels that lay beneath it—rather he assumed that it had been placed there purely for his entertainment, a mere ornamental feature. The pit was wider and deeper than in earlier years, the grass was longer around the shed. But little had changed at the mine with the lapse of the years.

One of the strange newcomers leaned against a doorpost of the shed, half in the shade, smoking a cigarette and glancing occasionally at the boy. The two others stood further off, speaking to Mr Cousin in voices the boy could not hear. Their backs were to the boy and they looked out over the mine.

Mr Cousin was one of the most senior men at the mine. He had never spent this long at the boy's shed before. The strangers seemed to be taking an undue interest in the boy. They had been here for almost an hour, talking quietly and gesturing and smoking their cigarettes. It was all very unusual. Their uniforms were similar to that of Mr Cousin—white, with high black boots, and flat caps with a pretty gold braid.

As they were talking there was a blast in the pit—a common occurrence. The dust leaped on the slab. The pit shook. A part of its wall burst, a small torrent of rocks came tumbling down the cliff and an elegantly shaped cloud of red dust rose above it. Then, at a slight delay, the sound came, deep and clear.

The men went on talking as before. But after a moment they turned, came towards the boy, and inspected him more closely. One of them even stooped and reached out, with his index finger, towards one of the boy's protuberances, and wiped away a little of the dust that had accumulated there. The boy found it strange and wanted to recoil, but of course he could not.

The murmuring of the men continued. The boy understood nothing of what they said. A few more minutes passed of quiet and calm. In the pit the tiny workmen shifted and stirred. There was another blast. They all watched it. The cloud faded gradually from the air. Then the strange men went away.

Such is what passed for an event, at that time, in the life of the boy. He thought about the men for several minutes and wondered what interest they could have in him. But soon new sights emerged to entertain him. A steam excavator came creeping into view in the pit. And for a while the boy watched it fumbling along and gleaming in the sun with its long steel arm and the great bucket swaying and teetering on its cable. Around three o'clock there was a beating, and the boy quite forgot about the strange men. That is not to say that a beating was anything unusual, and therefore more worthy of the boy's attention than the question of the strange men, for it was not. It was rather that the boy was easily distracted, and he applied his attention not to those things that seemed personally to affect him, as he perhaps should have done, but rather to any event that took his fancy. He was under-stimulated, after all, and eager to forget his pains. And so the quotidian rituals of the beating, which he had observed on countless occasions, on different days, and in different areas of the pit, now fully commanded his attention. And he wondered, as he always did, in his simple way, about the various procedures associated with the beating, such as why the trousers had to be around the ankles, and why the chicotte made its particular whooshing sound, and so on, until, all having been put right again, this piece of entertainment came to an end, in its turn.

The wheel turned on the headframe. The shovels ticked faintly, tick tick, and the engine of the excavator rumbled. The shed creaked. The shadow of the pit edge crept towards the workmen, met them, overtook them. They went on working in the shade. Then the workday ended and the pit was empty.

At evening the bell of the angelus, which was the bell of the curfew—for they were two and the same—sounded wearily. The cry of the hoopoe was heard across the mine and the nuns came out of the church and locked its door, with the wind in their habits. With the churchyard just visible from the slab, the boy liked to watch them, to watch their white tunics rising in wild wind-shudders, disclosing the small black shoes at the ends of their legs. And he watched them go, as they sometimes did, into the lee of the church, in their white hoods, in the midst of the dimness overspreading the earth, and light a cigarette and pass it between them. The grass had grown long at the verge of the slab, and the place to which the nuns went next was obscured behind the fretting stalks. They went with slow and halting steps, penitential steps, their hands always clasped before them, with the exception of the one who held the cigarette. He watched their habits moving, the wild moves of the white cloth, lifted and wafted, the waves that traveled along the hems. The boy felt night beginning to fall, and sleep beginning to rise upon him. And to ease somewhat his usual pains, he imagined, for a bit of fun, that his tiredness was rising up out of the bottom of the pit to enfold him, and to take him away from his life.

8

The next morning a truck stopped by the shed before
dawn. It was loaded with workmen and empty 55-gallon
drums. The workmen had long thin legs and their bony
knees click-clacked together as the truck wobbled to a
stop. Mr Cousin got out of the cabin with one of the other
bosses. The workmen hopped down in twos and threes
and came towards the boy. Their eyes gleamed in the
dark. Some of them began rolling the drums down out of
the truck, while others took up their shovels and began
hacking at the limb-heaps.

'That's the way!' said Mr Cousin. 'Get it all in, gentlemen, and roll them out.'

The air was filled with frenzied scraping. Up went the
little boy, armless and legless, on the end of a shovel, on

the flat steel, wobbling and trembling, and down into a drum with a crash and an awful pain. Helpless to break his fall, he had landed right on the crown of his yellow head, in the dusty dark. He felt chunks of his own hardened flesh raining down on top of him, clattering around him. Then a flat lead lid was brought down over the top of the drum, sealing him in.

Mr Cousin deposited a little snuff into his nostril.

'Very good. Excellent, gentlemen. Roll on, boys. Easy now, mind your fingers.'

The drums rolled and bounced and skidded on the wooden ramps and clattered against one another as though with contempt. So long had he spent in stillness that the boy's immediate experience of movement was a feeling of nausea, which was not at all improved by the violent rolling of the drum and his tendency, being very heavy, to smash against its walls.

'Did you ever play at hoop-rolling?' said Mr Cousin to the other boss. 'When you were a bonny boy? With a bicycle rim? Nothing is more pleasing. Driving it along with a stick. Keeping it upright.'

Mr Cousin was a short man, bald-headed and barrel-chested. He smiled to himself at the memory. When he opened his mouth to smile, as he did now, its whole interior unfolded itself into the light of day, the tongue, the tonsils, the front teeth that seemed to flee from one another and even the little yellow points of the rum-soaked molars.

'Never,' said the other boss.

'Gentlemen,' said Mr Cousin. 'We are going to the railhead. Your dossiers, gentlemen. Your dossiers. Your stabilization cards, your re-engagement cards, control cards, equipment cards, hospital cards, prison cards, leave cards, your documents for inspection. Mr Fidere of Kamungu, thank you, Mr Louis of Makonko, thank you, Mr Matepo of Kaniama, thank you...'

They drove out of the mine towards the railhead with the headlights on, for it was still dark. Mr Cousin and the other boss sat in the cabin and had a long conversation bearing upon the future of the mine and the European war and the manual training programs for the workmen's children and the excellent rate of marriage in the camps. A few workmen sat in the back on top of the drums. They too talked of the war. They were worried about being sent to fight. There were stories that all the unemployed men in Jadotville and Kolwezi had been conscripted. Belgium had fallen. The boy heard their words but was far too caught up in his own situation to wonder about their meaning.

A train was waiting at the railhead. Mr Cousin watched with satisfaction the drums being rolled up onto the flatcar in the dawn. He inhaled for the last time the dusty scent of the boy's body parts, sucking it deep into his lungs. He did not know precisely where the boy was going or what was to be done with him and these were not questions to which he gave his consideration. He eyed the workmen carefully, his chicotte tightly clenched in his left fist. In one direction the railroad stretched into the distance and in the other direction was the end of the line, the wooden posts overgrown with weeds and behind that a wall of jungle, green and sap-spewing, that revolted Mr Cousin and made him feel that he was at the end of civilization.

'Roll on, gentlemen!' he cried. 'Keep it moving!'

A metal drum can be an unpleasant and tedious means

of travel. But fortunately these were old drums, and very damaged. The one that had been selected to contain the boy's head and trunk boasted the amenity of a patch of tiny rust-holes along one of its sides, which provided him not only with a dappling of light, but also, when properly positioned by the forces of gravity, the ability to see out. Such was the case when his drum came to rest and was stood up with the other drums on the flatcar. Slumped against the rust-eaten side, he found himself overlooking the view to the right of the train. He could see then a fragment of a wild untended field and a few thorn-trees swaying in the wind, growing paler and paler in the morning light. And as he watched the swaying boughs he was able to collect himself, to straighten his troubled thoughts in spite of his fresh injuries, and to consider dimly what was happening to him. But having scant experience to draw on, he did not get a long way in finding a solution to this problem. It startled him somewhat to hear, when the drums were all loaded, the voices of the workmen drawing away and falling silent. For in spite of his feebleness of mind, he was able to deduce from this that he was alone.

The whistle blew. The boy heard the hissing of the steam and the air brake, the strangled inflow and outflow, and the crash of the couplings. The train began to chug, and then to thump, to which the drums thumped in response, and his small body thumped and vibrated, and his tumorous forehead thumped once more against the drum, and the train moved off. The steam gushed from the chimney and around the engine. It blew in veils all about the drums, obscuring his pinpoint of vision. They began to move faster, the thumps quickening, echoing, like enormous human hearts, and when the steam clouds cleared, he saw that there were trees gliding past him.

In the dark of his drum, the boy rocked back and forth with the rhythm of the train, his face impassive, his mouth agape as ever, his eyes observing the passing scenery. Hours passed. The wheels thundered on the rails and he grew accustomed to the sensation of the earth sliding under him, slipping away. At the first water stop there were rockfowls on the water tower. They peered down at the train with catatonic eyes. The boy watched them through the rust-hole.

The train moved off again. Aside from the rattling and the occasional banging of his head there was nothing particularly unpleasant about it. The countryside confused the boy. He gazed out at plains profuse with tall, fat baobab trees. They did not seem real. He kept waiting for the moment when he would see the headframe again, or part of the pit, and could thereby determine his location, but he did not see them.

After some hours the train passed the town of Dilolo and crossed into Angola. When night fell the noises mingled together—the beating and thumping and the jostling of the drums on the flatcar—and the breeze, which brought a fresh scent from the passing orange groves. The train pressed on, threading through the night, through the morning, making its slow ascent out of the declivities of the sandy country, into regions of rivers and high bridges. Great cliffs and chasms appeared, wider and deeper than the pit he knew so well, and the train wound around them, past the roaring Cuemba Falls, into regions the boy had never before seen or imagined, ever climbing, charging towards the veld and the great plantations.

On the second day of the journey, the train stopped a while in the town of Silva Porto. The platform was a jumble of bicycles and hats—straw hats, pith helmets, panama hats—and a crowd of black faces, women, men and children. The porters were shouting. Animals went clattering and braying past the train in the dust. He saw goats, calves, chickens, an ox wagon. Mail bags were thrown onto the flatcars. Dusty women went by with bundles on their heads, dressed in batik cloth.

In all this bustle and scramble, an inconvenient thing happened. The boy's drum moved and he slipped down within it, finding himself in a position that was much less agreeable than before. He was deprived entirely of his view through the rust-hole, and when the whistle blew for the train to move again, he was in darkness, with only a tiny point of light remaining at the upper verge of his vision.

He watched it for hours. It turned mauve, violet, rose red, brown and finally, gradually, went out. Then he could see nothing. And in the dark there came to the boy a faint sense of the vastness of the world, and of the terrible extent of his solitude within it. He could not understand why they had decided to send him away, and who had decided it, and why he had been sent away in such a great hurry, and he did not know where he was going. He was frightened. For the line had steepened, their course had slowed, and he could hear the howl of the wind in the great gorges. Suddenly he wanted the train to stop. But the train did not stop.

9

Time was moving too quickly for Dr Szilard's liking, and Mr Sachs was moving too slowly. The banker had promised that he would speak to the president—and indeed, he had proved to be a man of his word. What Dr Szilard had not realized was just how carefully Mr Sachs' words were chosen. A meeting had certainly occurred, words pertaining to the boy had undoubtedly passed between Mr Sachs and the president, but beyond that nothing whatsoever had happened.

It was now several months later, and there had been no communication with the Belgians, no commitment of funds for the experiments, and no indication that the government had the slightest concern for the welfare of the young paralytic. Things were just as before.

Dr Szilard determined that the best response to this problem was to continue pestering Mr Sachs by calling on him as frequently as possible. One day he was leaving the laboratory to do this, when a telegram arrived from somebody named Dr J. Robert Oppenheimer, of Berkeley, California. It commented briefly on the boy, and then rather abruptly asked if Dr Teller and Dr Bethe could be spared for a few days for a meeting with various prosthetists in California.

'Oppenheimer?' said Dr Szilard. 'Who the devil is Oppenheimer?'

'I have heard the name,' said Dr Fermi.

'He is very intelligent,' said Dr Bethe. 'I have met him once. He talks like—well, you must hear the way he talks. He's quite a striking person.'

'Striking, how?' said Dr Szilard. 'Is he an American?'

'Oh, yes. But I believe he studied in Europe. He seems to have been everywhere. Speaks a thousand different languages. Though he's quite young, I think. A remarkable fellow.'

'You are sure he did not ask for me?'

'Yes.'

Dr Szilard sniffed.

'I have no time anyway. Does the telegram say anything specific about the boy?'

'It says the boy is quite something.'

'What?'

'Quite something.'

'What does that mean?'

'An American expression,' said Dr Fermi.

Dr Szilard was anxious about splitting up the team, even if just for a few days. He had felt for the last few months that they were moving up and down in one place, treading water, that nothing was being accomplished. It was as though every day was the same day, masquerading as another. And yet he could not deny it was a good thing that word of the boy was spreading, and if this Oppenheimer fellow was willing to take a look at it, where was the harm? He pondered the matter for a second, and said:

'Well, perhaps at Berkeley they are finally coming to their senses. Still, I don't know if conferences like this are a good idea.'

'We can't succeed without collaboration,' said Dr Bethe.

'Yes, well. It will be good to have some help from the Americans.'

Dr Szilard went to see the banker and tried to think no more about the telegram. But it troubled him somewhat, for reasons he could not explain, to reflect upon Dr Oppenheimer and the audacity of his intrusion. Though there were few things that did not trouble Dr Szilard, at this troublesome period.

The office of Alexander Sachs was a mess and his desk was piled high with papers. The air was stale and thin. The clock ticked faintly and the jostle of Wall Street could be heard at the open window. Mr Sachs sat with his legs lightly crossed and his hands clasped together, the fingers interlaced, upon his knee. He wore thick round spectacles and a tan suit with extravagantly long lapels. His left brogue tapped in the thin air. A section of his argyle sock was visible.

'We're making progress,' he said.

The latest of Mr Sachs' slender assurances was that the matter would be brought before a government committee in the near future. The boy would be investigated in all relevant physiological, political, administrative and material aspects.

'When I spoke to the president he was very sympathetic,' said Mr Sachs.

'So you have told me. I—'

'He is a paralytic himself, you know. Oh not a total paralytic, but lame, quite lame. Yes, he's confident it will all be taken care of. Now we just need to prepare ourselves for the committees.'

'We don't need a committee, we need immediate action.'

'The committees are not going to abide that sort of talk, Dr Szilard.'

'I don't know what else I can say to you, Mr Sachs. You have our letter. It makes our concerns very plain. For the safety of the boy, and the safety of ourselves, it is absolutely urgent—'

'The wheels are turning, doctor. The cogs and wheels are enmeshing. Washington, you have to understand, is terribly bit-a-bitarian. If I may—' Sachs bent forwards, his chair creaking, to his shambles of a desk, and extracted, with two fingers, the letter Dr Szilard had given him '—let's take a look at the letter. In Washington it is the order in which you present the information that makes all the difference.'

'Mr Sachs,' Dr Szilard began.

But he was quieted by the raised finger of Mr Sachs, which proceeded to press the intercom. 'Judith,' said the banker, his eyes glued to Dr Szilard, 'would you bring us some coffee?'

Mr Sachs released the intercom and took up the letter once again. 'Now then,' he said, 'and I quote. "Some recent work by E. Fermi and L. Szilard," et cetera, et cetera—Passable, passable. But here—' he lowered his spectacles and angled his elastic face towards Dr Szilard '—the terminology. Are we thinking lexically, Dr Szilard? Do you say for instance that he can be cured, treated, rehabilitated, fixed, tell me, what do you say?'

'It says what it says,' said Dr Szilard, at length.

The coffee was brought in and deposited, with extreme care, on Mr Sachs's desk.

'Thank you, Judith. Very lovely. Is that silk? That's nice.' Mr Sachs retrieved his spectacles. 'You say here, doctor, paralyzed. Merely, paralyzed. What are the proportions, what is the weight, Dr Szilard, of a word such as paralyzed, in the intelligence of a congressman? You really must ask yourself what you will need to convey to the committee. Paint a picture, sir, of the little wastrel. Let us see him, really see him before us in the cobwebs and the dust, in articulo mortis, unable to walk, unable to crawl, to raise his arms. He wants to move, he wants to reach out, cry out. Everything is out of reach. The joys of groveling on the floor at his father's feet, sniveling for his mother's breast, the thrills and pleasures of rolling on the floor—rolling, Dr Szilard—every operation of the human apparatus is denied him. Arouse our sympathy. Do you catch my drift?'

Mr Sachs puckered his lips and drank some coffee.

'I know what the facts are,' said Dr Szilard. 'So do you. That is all we need. The thing is getting so chewed out of shape that soon we shall not even remember what the facts are.'

Mr Sachs smiled. 'Everything must be chewed sooner or later.'

'Mr Sachs. As we speak, the child is languishing, the Nazis are working. Perhaps they have got him already. We have heard of other cases. There is a promising case in Colorado we ought to look at.' Dr Szilard leaned his weight against the back of his chair.

Mr Sachs was nodding thoughtfully.

'We are running out of chances. And you know, the Nazis, they will not hesitate. While we pause to ask questions, they will act. I must insist that you deliver the letter. The facts are there. It reads well. President Roosevelt needs to do something about this now.'

'Let's take a step back,' said Mr Sachs. 'If it reads well it means you have read it insufficiently. I assure you that I have some familiarity with these things. If there is one thing I know, it is that our president is a good man. He has a good hard head on his shoulders. He's one of the hardest headed people I've—'

'Tell me this,' Dr Szilard interjected. 'Where is the boy?'

There was a pause.

'Where is the boy right now, Mr Sachs?' said Dr Szilard, realizing this man did not have the slightest idea where the boy was, nor the slightest inclination to find out.

Mr Sachs continued to smile.

'Let me tell you something about this complicated sport we call lobbying...'

10

In the laboratory, Dr Fermi stood on a step-ladder before one of his experimental apparatuses—a great square thing covered with black wires. Through the long windows, the sky was dark pink. It was time to pack up for the day, and Dr Fermi was covering the apparatus with a large cloth.

'Give me a hand with this, would you?' he said.

Dr Bethe and one of the graduate students hastened to the other end of the cloth and they pulled together as Dr Fermi raised it, until the apparatus was covered. The cloth made a short, sharp sound, like an exhalation.

Dr Fermi came down from the ladder, wiping black graphite dust from his hands on his laboratory coat. Dr Teller was leaning against a desk, contemplating the blackboard, a great mess of equations.

'Come on, Edward,' said Dr Fermi. 'You'll wear yourself out thinking.'

'What would be to stop them,' said Dr Teller, 'from combining two boys in one prosthesis? I mean hooking up two—two of them. Doubling the energy release?'

'Let's not get ahead of ourselves,' said Dr Bethe. 'One is complex enough.'

They passed out of the laboratory, down the stairwell and through the hard-floored, echoing, urine-colored foyer of the science building, talking in their various accents of technical matters. Outside, in the square, the graduate students fanned off on their own trajectories, talking of the war.

'No more word from the government then?' said Dr Fermi.

'No,' replied Dr Teller. 'Szilard is still pushing them.'

'If they don't give us something soon, we'll run out of money.'

Dr Bethe went slightly ahead of the others, to follow some pigeons in their small circles. His hair grew in a frizz around the great bulb of his head. A pen protruded from his chest pocket. He shuffled along with his hands behind his back, chewing his bottom lip. From behind there was something imposing, almost threatening, about him, his broad shoulders, his powerful body, but then he turned and revealed his strange small face, with his calm and gentle eyes.

'You have still been making calls?' he said.

'I will make calls until there's no one left to call,' Dr Teller replied.

'Our trouble is, for a lot of them, as soon as they hear an accent, that's the end of it. They don't want to know.'

The lights in the university buildings were going out one by one. The cleaners were going into the buildings with mops and buckets. The doctors could see, in certain windows, the tops of people's heads moving back and forth. How late were they working, Dr Fermi wondered aloud, at the Kaiser Wilhelm Institute? They walked out of the university and onto Broadway, where they stood for a moment before a crosswalk. Dr Bethe remarked on the grid, the Manhattan grid, which had always instilled in him a sense of calm and precision.

The doctors gazed northward along the steaming street. At its vanishing point the little lights of cars and street-lamps and crosswalks converged and trembled together and for a while the whole living city was tapering before them, with its millions of irreversible exhaustions. They crossed the street. Then, after walking on a short way, Dr Fermi bid them goodnight, and headed for Riverside Drive where he lived with his wife and daughter. They watched him go, moving in his quick and efficient way, the low sun shining on his bald patch.

Dr Teller and Dr Bethe went on at a leisurely pace, the former limping along with his dark, oily head bowed and his face turned to the pavement, and the latter gazing up at the windows as they passed, his hands thrust into his pockets. They spoke, as they had done for all the years they knew one another, in German.

'This is all very strange,' said Dr Teller.

'Yes,' said Dr Bethe. 'It will be quite a feat, if it turns out to be possible.'

'That's not quite what I mean. It feels rather like none of it is really happening. Do you ever get that feeling?'

'What do you mean?'

'As though it's all much too big for us. Therefore it can't be true. You know, I have had this feeling at other points.

When I proposed to my wife, I felt something like this. We were surrounded by geese.'

'Geese?'

'Yes—unmistakably.'

'In Hungary?'

'In Buda, yes. Just as I turned to ask her to marry me, they began making that sound they make. That laughing sound. Gá-gá-gá. You know it? The more I spoke, the more they did it. Gá-gá-gá. And so she began to laugh too.'

'Would things have felt more realistic without the geese?'

'I'm not sure.'

There was another silence as they walked, and Dr Teller reflected on the green sodden sweep of the Buda Hills and his wife and the domes and spires of the old city, where it was no longer safe.

Eventually Dr Bethe turned the conversation back to the boy. 'You know there are many who still say it's impossible,' he said. 'The scale of the thing. The number of people who would have to agree to work on it. I don't think Oppenheimer is convinced yet.'

'It *must* be possible,' Dr Teller insisted. 'I am sure of it. I feel it. I wish I was wrong. But I am more sure each day the thing is doable, and the Nazis know it. That is their great advantage—they know it. And we remain in denial.'

Dr Bethe lowered the big square dome of his head and squinted.

'There are, however, things we have that the Nazis do not have,' he said. 'We have Leo Szilard.'

Dr Teller laughed.

'And Fermi!' he added. 'You can't win without Fermi. We always used to be racing Fermi. Remember in London? We were going to publish a paper with Dr Peierls, but then

Fermi got to it first. Now he's on our side.'

For the last few blocks of their walk they reminisced again about the days before the war. Night had fallen finally, there were no cars, no sun, none of the stifling heat of that humid summer, no wind, no sound, except the perpetual sounds. It was like a world made purely for their conversation, a world without conditions, and it was almost surprising to them when passing a window they heard a radio— 'and it's a line drive right over the short-stop Rizzuto's head between Keller and DiMaggio in the left center field, Reece is rounding third—'

They came to Dr Teller's street and parted.

'Well. So long,' said Dr Bethe.

'Goodnight, Hans.'

Dr Teller was alone. In his mind's eye that baseball, flung by the long line drive, was still passing overhead, over Keller and DiMaggio and over the city streets, like a comet. He was the youngest of the group, though Dr Bethe was only two years older than him. As he hobbled back to his apartment, he began to think of his youth for the first time as an advantage. Did he not, more than any of the other doctors, possess the energy and vision to take charge of the child's case and see him to full recovery? Though he would not dare to say it, the notion of Dr Szilard heading this project seemed to him totally impractical, and he was confident that when they began to receive proper funding, the greatest level of responsibility would reasonably fall to him.

Mrs Teller was still awake when he came into the bedroom.

'Typical!' she said. 'Typical. Home late. Wake your wife. No consideration.'

The enmity that existed between Dr Teller and Mrs Teller was the foundation of their excellent relationship.

Had there been no institution of marriage when they met, it would have been necessary for them to invent it, for it provided them with a reason to continue running into each other, in spite of their arguments.

She flicked on the bedside lamp in order to frown at him. He took off his clothes and shoes, drew the belt out of his trousers, carefully curled it around and around itself into a small circle, and put it away. Mrs Teller adjusted her position for him to lie down, for he slept always in the same pose—prone and sprawling. Dr Teller sat on the bed beside his wife, reached down, fumbled for a few seconds, removed his foot and set it on the night table. Then she reached for the lamp and switched it off.

11

The train having reached the port of Lobito, famous for its long spit, the boy was transferred, without being removed from his drum, onto a ship, and put to sea.

It was a long journey—several weeks on the open ocean. He remained in the hold, in his drum, seeing nothing. The indignities of this marine expedition—the nausea, the noise, the stench, the immaculate blackness— were beyond anything he had experienced before. When finally the ship arrived at its destination, after so many indistinguishable days and nights, the boy was eager to see where they had brought him.

The drums were rolled off the ship onto the dock. The air was full of shouts of men and birds and the stink of spice and seawrack. He bounced and bumped on his wounds and growths and tried to catch a glimpse through the perforations. He saw it only for a moment—the skyline of a city, enormous and pale, its thousand razor-sharp spikes and spires crowding to the ashen sky. And for a moment, across the water of the harbour, the city returned his blank and childish gaze. Then he rolled on and his view was gone. And the drums, shuttled by the dockworkers, were formed into a line along the concrete quay. The dockworkers, oblivious to the fact that there was a boy and his body in the drums, rolled them about with excessive force. They rolled the drums into a warehouse on the quayside and closed the doors and went away.

The posture in which the boy now found himself was not wholly unpleasant. During his time in this warehouse, his discomforts complemented and counterbalanced each other, abating and intensifying as though in shifts, and preventing him from becoming fixated on any one in particular.

Almost perfectly upright, he leaned against the curved side of his drum. His twisted shoulder was also just tolerably supported. His stumps were embedded in a fine crush of pummeled scraps. His face—thin, tumorous, gaping, gray and goggle-eyed—had not changed in the slightest, nor had his expression. In the side of the drum, roughly level with his right eye, was a hole of considerable size, which gave him a view of his surroundings.

He had no idea where he was. He could see down an aisle between rows and rows of drums. The warehouse was large and negligibly decorated. Dust floated between the wooden floor and its high wooden rafters where rats scampered, from time to time. He counted twenty drums to the far wall, which had a row of dirty windows along its upper half. The city could not be seen, but he could see the water of the harbor, and a part of the lean steel sweep of a bridge, and the sky into which there drifted silently, at rare intervals, a tiny airplane.

For several weeks nothing happened. Things were even less eventful than at the mine. Some men came once and left without a word. The weather, in the warehouse, was very different from the Congo. The light was different, and the cold was unlike anything he had known before. It made icicles hang from the windows and made everything quiet. One day he heard steps. Then he saw a small fat furry body, on the filthy floor, gazing up at him.

For the next several months, rats were the boy's chief interest and entertainment.

They were common rats, slow and placid of movement, with fat greasy tails. Their fur was matted. They stalked up towards him timidly, ticked along the concrete with their claws and paused before his drum, never attempting to scale or breach it, but simply looking, with their sparkling black eyes.

In periods of tedium, that is to say during most of his waking existence, he sometimes imagined the rats to possess special jobs. He knew these to be false, they changed according to his whims, but it didn't matter. He was playing. They had wars against other rats, rats he did not see, from other warehouses. When they all fell silent in the morning he fancied it was because they had gone out to fight them, to make raids. And during late after-noon or at night when one or two of the rats drew near to his drum, it was for a briefing or a debriefing, or to make a report of their day's reconnaissance, whose details he also imagined. Much time could be absorbed by watching and thinking about his rats, in this manner.

In mid-spring his rats became afflicted with diarrhea, flaxen in color, frothy in constitution and copious in quantity. The smell filled the warehouse. While not as potent as some extant smells, it was remarkable in its pervasiveness and obstinacy. After a week they began to chew at their fur. The boy could do nothing but watch and smell these gradations of indignity with silent horror, send them mental messages of support, and apply his mind, with what efforts he could muster, having only the mind of a child, to the intricate subject of rat excrement. Perhaps, he thought, if they ran less, or lay down, or stood on their front paws— and so on, vain fancies. By summer Fortune was smiling again on the rats, and they began slowly and warily to return to their old caperings. By the month of July he could observe with relief that they were wholly recovered.

To keep track of a single rat, let alone a great many, is a task of enormous difficulty. It was necessary for the boy to monitor their incomings and outgoings. It became such that any alteration, however small, real or merely perceived, to his rat collection, was of paramount importance, in this chapter of his life. At night he could not rest until the last rat was asleep. To this purpose his inactivity again proved a formidable obstacle. For his visual field was restricted greatly by the drum, granting him access to approximately six thousand square feet of the warehouse floor, which could not have been more than thirty percent of its total area. When they scuttled out of this visible area, towards the many tempting and entertaining areas beyond its bounds, he had only the faculty of sound by which to track them. The rats unseen, in stillness, were as good as nonexistent, to the boy. The result of all this was that he could be sure of their location only when they were all directly in front of him, and he could have a vague idea only when they were all either in front of him or in motion. And what is more, the rats were insolent, and did not obey his orders, though he pretended that they did.

The truth is, though the boy thought of himself as a rat-keeper of the highest order, in reality he had only a negligible command of their locations, and frequently erred in his predictions of where he would next hear a scuttle. If somebody had come into the warehouse, put a revolver to his head and demanded he answer the simple question of how many rats lived in the warehouse, he would not have been able to answer. It was a task far beyond his years and expertise. But the boy was stubborn, and with nothing to do and having been cooped, literally cooped, for month upon month in his drum, and never having stirred, never ever having stirred, he needed some task by which to pass the time and distract himself from his pains.

Moreover, his setbacks in record-keeping were offset by the other benefits he derived from his observations. For it is not only entertainment that a little boy gains from the sustained investigation of rodents. It was through watching his rats that he became acquainted with his first inklings of animal tenderness, of social and amorous relations, of that want of a connexion that daily paralyzes and deranges the good sense of living beings. He observed, for example, the way the tiny long-tailed pups cleaved to their mother. He imagined what it would be like to have one, a figure he could perhaps blame and execrate for having produced him, for having left him, for poisoning him with tumors, for burying without first murdering him properly, and for various other infractions. He tried it for a while, raging in his mind against a rat of a mother. But finding that it did not materially alter his situation, or even make him feel better, he gave it up.

There were two of the rats that he particularly liked to observe, one big and one small. It is very likely that one was a male, and the other a female. But one can never be sure. From time to time he would see one of this pair plod into the aisle. It would stop. Then it would wait. Then the other would emerge from the shadows, sidle along for a few paces, then pounce, and the two would be entangled—stumbling together, in the act of love, in the event of love, humorless and stolid, and their bodies would cleave together and he would cease to distinguish between the two bodies and it would be as though each limb, and each hand, was owned in common by the two, and that new limbs were growing from their old limbs, and they would form, in their inexplicable union, one monstrous organism, jerking and twitching, on the floor. So he watched them performing this strange act, with their black eyes glancing about them, at various sights, blinking. And he asked himself—why did the rats do that? As he considered these matters he began to acquire some understanding of the principles of venery. The little hands in the midst of the fur, holding on, the pelvis moving, curling, the fat rolls, the noses and whiskers quivering, and the sun's faint glow on the fur—all stirred his mind with ideas and made him wonder at the great complexity of relations into which creatures seemed naturally to organize themselves. And naturally he thought of himself and his own place in such a scheme, which gave him no end of further questions.

12

The government had long lain dormant on the question of the boy. The committees had considered his case and had expressed serious concern about his predicament—about the terrible things the Germans may do to him, and the terrible ends to which they may steer him. But although they were more or less in agreement on the gravity of the situation, the committees were hesitant to take action. For they were not convinced that the child's welfare was relevant to the national interest.

In December, 1941, the Japanese attacked Pearl Harbor, and the United States found itself at war with Nazi Germany. All at once, the committees altered their position. They agreed suddenly that the boy was their business—and that all possible cases needed to be tracked down immediately.

At last, in all its terrible weight and grandeur, the government rose from its slumber and began to act. Orders were drafted, vast sums of money began to flow from the black budget and entreaties were made at last to the mining corporation in the Congo.

A meeting took place between the government's agents and the chairman of the corporation, who was—by some curious stroke of luck—residing in New York.

It was a very short meeting. It took place in a nondescript office building. The chairman was a small man, Belgian, greatly aged, with a white moustache and a vascular anomaly over his right eye. He spoke rarely, and with the greatest reluctance. As he listened, at the desk, to the proposals of the government agents, his jaws moved silently, like one who was chewing an oyster, or wobbling a loose tooth, by means of his tongue. At times he did not even reply to their remarks, but stared down at his own sleeves, with confused, sorrowful eyes.

When the agents had finished describing their proposal, the old gentleman scratched, with one white finger, the port-wine stain on his forehead. Then he sniffed a long sniff that caused certain bristles of his moustache to tremble. The agents interpreted this as a sign of unwillingness to part with the boy—even of personal attachment—and the chairman, though he had never seen the boy in his life, allowed them to draw this conclusion. Finally he replied, in prolonged and distorted English, that he may be open to the idea of granting them custody of the infant, provided they could straighten out certain necessary questions of compensation and reimbursement.

The government was prepared to comply with these

conditions. And after a few minutes, having reached an agreement that satisfied the chairman's concerns, they began to draw up a contract. The chairman did not ask them what they planned to do with the boy. He did not mention the letters of Dr Szilard, which he had been carefully reading for some time. He did not tell them of his ingenious order to dispatch the boy from the Congo. He did not disclose how long he had been waiting—patiently, stealthily—for the government's call. He mentioned none of this. When the agents inquired where the boy was, and how many weeks it would take to bring him to America, the chairman simply smiled, and said:

'He is here.'

'What do you mean?' said one of the agents.

Whereupon the chairman took a cigarette from an ivory case which he kept in his pocket and smiled again.

'He is here. You may have him at once.'

The agents were silent for a moment.

'You mean—in New York?'

'No, no, my good man,' the chairman said. 'In Staten Island.'

A short missive, typed on yellow paper, arrived at the Prosthetics Department at Columbia, addressed to Dr Szilard. It was winter, snow was falling on New York, Dr Teller and Dr Bethe had gone to meet with Dr Oppenheimer. Dr Szilard was alone in the office and he sat down to read the letter by the window. It explained the basic details of the purchase and assured him of the child's safety. Arrangements were being made, it said, to place the boy at the first available opportunity into an appropriate institution of care. The treatment would be implemented, it said, exactly as the doctors recommended.

This letter did not calm Dr Szilard. He was weary and knew he was only at the beginning, and that the uncertainties before him were orders of magnitude greater than those he had surmounted. So much time had passed already, so many boys were still unaccounted for, and there was a line at the end of the letter that raised a whole new series of concerns, in the doctor's mind.

The boy, it said, was now officially a ward of the United States Army. From now on, it said, all inquiries concerning all patients would be directed to the office of General Leslie R. Groves of the U.S. Army Corps of Engineers.

13

Just fifteen miles from Dr Szilard's office, the boy was gazing through the hole in his drum, patiently awaiting the return of his rats. It was almost the hour at which they normally came back into view. The snow was falling faintly on the harbor and reaching the gray surface of water and vanishing. The warehouse was cold. The drums stood where they had always stood, now dressed in a layer of dust, in their still and silent rows.

Two days earlier he had received a visitor. A gentleman with a hunched posture and a trembling Adam's apple had come, cleaned the windows, and then gone around the warehouse with an object whose purpose the boy did not understand. It was a kind of metal tube, painted red, with a nozzle and a tin can fastened to one end. The hunched man had shuffled through the aisles, working the little pump-handle of his device, then he had departed.

As the boy sat there in his drum, drowsing at the sight of the snow before all went dark, the roller door of the warehouse began to open. Behind the boy a pair of men in military uniforms widened their legs, threw back their torsos and entered. One was tall, the other fat and box-headed. They walked together down the aisle. One of them was holding a clipboard. When he saw them, the boy wondered briefly, foolishly, if they were the same strange men who had visited him at the mine. But they were not. One of the men lifted the lid off a drum and they gazed into the mess of limbs and ligaments. Thinking they were unobserved, they made no effort to hide their looks of disgust. The man dusted off his hands on his khaki trousers. They stood beside the window and talked. At one point the square-headed man took out a piece of yellow paper and read aloud:

'Transportation of patient by Thursday no later. Ensure drums are accounted for and in adequate condition. Transfer with minimum of public notice. Now what kind of chumps does he think we are?'

'That's two days.'

'We'll be hard pushed to make it to Canada in two days.'

'The general's a hard pusher.'

'I think he's sore they haven't sent him overseas.'

'Did I tell you what I said to him last week? I said, General, I said, they didn't build Rome in a day, you know.'

'Uh huh.'

'He says, Merritt, he says, maybe if they didn't waste their lunch hours playing post office with the local floozies, they could have.'

'I think he's got a screw loose.'

They were silent a moment. They looked around the warehouse.

'Well, looks like it's all here.'

'If only we knew what the hell it was.'

'What you don't know don't hurt you.'

The boy understood none of this. It was the longest conversation he had witnessed in more than a year. He longed to report these developments to his rats. But they were still away on their expeditions. The tall soldier cracked his knuckles.

'Let's do it,' he said.

The fat soldier rested his clipboard on one of the drums and began filling out a form with a pencil. To the boy's surprise, a crowd of soldiers streamed into the warehouse as if from nowhere and, beginning at the far end, near the windows, set to work rolling out the drums with a great clamor. As each row was cleared, a soldier came pacing slowly into the empty space where they had been, pushing a pile of dust and garbage before him with a long broom.

The first drums were rolled out of the warehouse. The snow was falling thinly. Down past the bridge, that darkening curve of steel, in the orange sky, came gray fat birds, not moving their wings. The time had passed for the rats to return. But they had not. Where were they? Were they staying away because of the soldiers? The boy tried to picture his rats, to communicate with them, to encourage them. There was nothing to be afraid of, he said, and would they please hurry up?

He knew that his time in the warehouse was coming to an end, he knew the drums were being taken away again and soon he would be taken too. The soldier went on scratching and ticking at the form, breathing through his mouth, his cheeks flushed, clasping the pencil in his fat fingers. One by one the drums thundered heavily down and were rolled out. Row after row disappeared. The warehouse began to look empty and bare. The men who pushed the drums, scrawny and pale, unwarmed by their work, shivered in their green T-shirts. Silver dog tags hung over their chests.

The boy concentrated on his view through his rust-hole, searching for some sign of the rats. Surely they could not be hiding. Perhaps it was a trick. Perhaps they were really all there after all. Could they all be standing motion-less behind his drum, outside his view? But why would they do such a thing? He could see the soldiers, the drums in motion, the drums yet to go, the windows, the wall, the man with the broom, the little piles of dust.

Then he saw something very unpleasant. It was a rat, dust-pale amid the heap of dust, its small front paws stretched out before it, its mouth ajar, its small eyes closed, as though fast asleep, being borne rapidly along the floor, by the broom. And as the crashing of the falling drums drew closer and closer, the boy began to feel a great apprehension, a very sick feeling, deep down inside him. He was not sure which rat it was. He had checked his rats a few days earlier, pretending as he always did that he was calling their names and pretending that they heard him, pretending even that they responded to him, in their various voices, and making sure the main ones were there—the big rat, the mother rat, the pups, and all the other main rats. All had been accounted for.

The drums kept crashing to the floor. The man with the broom came by again, but the boy did not look at him, nor at his broom, nor at the little gray weightless pile he pushed ahead of him. He focused instead on the window, the fading winter sky, the birds. He told himself there was some reason he had to look there, and only there, and not at anything else. He concentrated every atom of his being on the window. An airplane passed—the airplane. He watched it shrink and pass beyond the limit of the window and kept looking at the white smudge it left on the sky.

Then his drum was roughly taken in hand and banged down onto the hard floor and he was taken out of the warehouse. By the time they rolled him up into the truck it was dark and the snow was falling heavily again. The truck took him to a train station and the drums were loaded onto a train.

He was traveling again. The trip was long, there were many delays—hours spent waiting on platforms and in railyards. The carriages were all closed boxes—freight cars. It was cold. He had hoped to see the city on his way out, but he did not. He felt no anger at this. He did not even try to see it. He was not able to muster any excitement about anything, for he was thinking of his rats. The train was quiet. There was only the rattling and chugging and the cold wind howling and rushing in through the boards.

The boy, simple as he was, did not know it, but a new era in his life had begun. He was in the care at last of the United States Army, and his days of idleness were over.

After many hours, the train arrived in Canada. The lid was taken off his drum and the light fell full at last on his narrow face, his gaping mouth, his taut swollen growths, his twisted shoulders, his scarred chest, his rigid stumps. The lights were very bright. There was a large sign on one wall, which said PORT HOPE, in gold lettering. With apprehension he gazed on the group of people that stood assembled to welcome him. They wore blue boiler suits and long rubber gloves. Some of the women wore handkerchiefs on their heads. He was weary and frightened, but as he grew accustomed to the light, and their faces came into focus, he felt some relief. For they were old people, pale and old, and their faces were serene and kind.

They took him inside, where it was warm, and then they fed him, taking care to follow every detail of the instructions they had received from the Army, into an enormous machine.

PART II

1

General Leslie R. Groves was in a difficult position. He had no interest in little boys. He was a soldier—an officer—and longed to be in the war. But he had his instructions, and his instructions came from the highest echelons of the United States government.

His secretary knocked on the door. He permitted her to enter. She told him the boy had begun his treatment.

'Good.' he said. 'Get me Nichols on the phone.'

He sat in his office in silence for a while with his hands on the desk. He wondered, with a vague sense of loathing, if the Canadians could be trusted. His office was brand new—bare walls, clean carpet. They had just moved in a few days ago.

The telephone rang and he spoke for a few minutes with one of his corporals.

'The Canadians have started the treatment,' the general said. 'Soon as you get the other boys I want them sent up to Port Hope—understand?'

The corporal told him they had identified another case in Colorado.

'Good,' the general said. 'We need more. I told the Canadians there will be more on the way.'

The corporal wanted to know how long the boy would be in Canada.

'That's none of your concern. He won't be there long, I can assure you of that. I expect those other boys within a month. Anything you need you let me know. Understand? Fine.'

General Groves put down the telephone. He was a very large man, wide around the middle. His hair had a streak of gray. He had a thick neck and a beefy face, with a carefully maintained moustache. His shirt, tie and trousers were all the same color—khaki. He wore two stars on his collar.

'Mrs O'Leary,' he said.

He sat up a little straighter at his desk. She entered.

'You see this wall?' he said. 'I want to have a painting here. Right there.'

She lingered in the doorway. He looked at her legs—the varicose veins.

'A painting of what, General?'

'What do you think?' he said. 'Mickey Mouse?'

She blinked at him. He smiled at his own remark, then he sniffed the air, and looked at the white mug in her hand.

'What is that?' he said. 'Mocha java? Keep it in the other room, would you? Don't take it in here, I don't want to smell it.'

She went into the other room.

'It's no good for you,' he said. 'Coffee, cigarettes.'

There was no response. She could not hear him.

'Mrs O'Leary,' he said.

Nothing.

Mrs O'Leary was an adequate secretary, though her understanding of the science of the boys' disorder was lacking. And in truth the general was not perfectly clear on this question himself. But this was the fault of the doctors, who refused to explain things fully and who struggled even to speak English. It was a matter of processing—chemical processing, a very big job—you had to reduce the boy down to the pure brain matter, then you had to make all sorts of measurements, then you had to design the body, and only then could you build it.

In the first drawer of his enormous desk, the general kept a store of number-two pencils, perfectly sharpened at his insistence. His itinerary allowed him a few minutes before his next meeting. He took out a pencil and a notepad, then he looked at the blank page and tried to envisage the boy. The boy was a monstrous thing, he was sure of that. He saw him as bug-eyed, for some reason, swarthy, with a perpetual grimace. He tried to envisage the prosthesis the doctors were going to make. Carefully he sketched a circle on the notepad. Would it be circular? Where precisely would the weaponry come in?

He would demand some concrete answers from the doctors. They spoke in riddles. They refused to tell him anything specific about the design of the prosthesis until they could examine the boy themselves, but they refused to do that until the basic treatments were complete. There were a great many doctors—their numbers were increasing by the day. He needed some way to organize them, to put them all in one place and impose some structure on their work.

General Groves glared at his drawing. Then he screwed it up violently. He rose from his chair and paced. The change jingled in his pockets. What he really wanted, at this moment, was to be on a battlefield, riding in a jeep—or even on a horse—along the edge of a trench, gazing down at squadrons of loyal men writhing in the dirt and the fleas and the gangrene and the shit and the spewing sandbags and the burst skulls and the spinal cords and the thoracic cavities, urging them on, inspiring them with the equanimity of his presence, then returning with satisfaction to his quarters, where he would have a large table, and a map, and chess pieces on the map—one chess piece to represent every thousand men. That was bravery! To instill respect and discipline in his inferiors, to be congratulated and praised by them, in service of his country, nothing would have pleased the general more.

The notion of babysitting an invalid child, like some kind of midwife, was not at all what he had foreseen for his career. And now, to be delayed by the dithering of eccentric doctors—it was an outrage.

But he had his instructions. He looked at his wristwatch. It was time for him to leave. He was going to the War Department to request more money, and he was certain he would get it. General Groves was an influential man, with many friends. He put on his freshly-pressed military blazer and exited the office, passing through the other room. He found to his displeasure that in addition to the smell of cigarettes and coffee, a radio was playing. Voices were raised in song.

'Over there!' the radio said. 'Over there! Over there, over there!'

Mrs O'Leary said something as he passed her but he did not hear her, for his mind was on other matters.

2

Port Hope was a modern institution. The United States Army would not have allowed its new protégé to enter an institution that was not, in its methods, thoroughly state of the art.

The routine at Port Hope was rather like that of a boarding school. The showers took place each morning, followed by the beatings, which continued until dusk. Everything was automated. There were conveyor belts to carry the patients, nozzles in the ceiling to release the fluids, metal arms to stir and turn the scraps and to pummel the flesh, and heaters to dry them. It all occurred in a large, drab brick building.

At first the boy was the only patient. But the General's men had been busy, and soon more boys began to arrive. They resembled the boy—they had the same blank stares, the same total immobility, the same mangled, tumorous, dispersed and disarticulated bodies. Some were even less pleasant to look at than he was, with heads split in two, or with cheeks swollen up like balloons, or with missing mouths, or with raw scaly skin. Soon their scraps became thoroughly intermixed.

There was little camaraderie between the boys, and of course no conversation. Their bond, if it could be called a bond, was that of mere proximity—a series of instances of eye-contact, some brief and fleeting, others sustained over long periods. Each day they rattled mutely along the conveyor belts, swerving and dipping, passing in and out of the machinery—showered, beaten and dried, each in his turn. They gazed out at the long benches that ran alongside the belts between the vats and machines where the old men and women sat in their blue boiler suits, and at the sun streaming through the windows, at the conveyor belts ticking along, and at the great vats spewing their slimes of coagulate boy-bits, and the bubbles that burst in the mud of the mingled flesh, and the rose-colored vapors that clouded the air. At night they were put back into the drums. And sometimes the boy would find himself crammed into the same drum as another boy, their bodies pressed together, their excrescences touching, their faces close, gazing indifferently into each other's eyes. As the weeks passed, they gradually lost their tumors, and their complexions yellowed. It was as though all but the yellow was being filtered out of them. And after a few weeks they resembled, from a distance, little heaps of millet or corn.

The boy had no interest in his peers. He had nothing in common with them, other than their ailments, and no hope of communicating with them. He did not wonder about the other boys, did not question where they came from, or if they were orphans like him, or if they were older than him or younger than him. He did not care. For he was occupied almost exclusively with the agony of being looked after. He disliked Port Hope. And he felt each night that his body was getting smaller, and tried to count the new lacerations and the new sores that the machines were inscribing on him.

He remained at Port Hope for only a couple of months, before the general ordered him brought back to the United States. Some soldiers came and took him away, just as they had done from the warehouse. He was not sad to leave.

A period of upheaval ensued in the life of the boy. Throughout 1942 he passed through various institutions, in various locations. This is a common story, for abnormal young boys—they move from place to place, staying no more than a month or two, growing up in a state of flux, never laying their roots. Each new institution poses for them a new set of problems and challenges to be surmounted, a drastic disordering of the constants of life in the form of new buildings, new routines, new rules, and a whole new set of people to wish never to see again. So it was for our diminutive hero.

Back and forth he went, from city to city, across America. He saw Cleveland. He saw Saint Louis. He found them largely indistinguishable. His world was a world of loading bays, roller doors, belts and vats and tanks and drums. It was the world of the railroads, of the engines and coal cars and cabooses, the steam locomotives and the diesel locomotives with their handsome curves, the rust-red freight cars, the shiver of the passing Pullmans, the stacks of pipes, pallets, timber and sleepers in the railyards, the swerves of the siding, the chimneys, the soot, the grating of the switches, the hue of the horns and the whistles and the bells and the wigwags. He came to know well the scampering sound of the filthy little boxcar men who would come singing and raving, or in silence, perching on the drums and smoking tobacco and reefer and passing bottles of wine back and forth in the long, howling nights.

The treatments he received in all these institutions resembled those of Port Hope in their basic focus on showering, beating and drying. The boy did not attempt to discern the object of his impositions, but accepted them as a necessity which all children, at some point, must endure.

3

In 1943 he was admitted into an institution for boys in Tennessee. The name of this institution was Oak Ridge. It was an enormous facility—a huge windowless building with a towering smokestack, secluded among the foggy ridges of Appalachia. At Oak Ridge the treatment for the boys consisted of being fired at extreme speed through curved tubes, several times per day.

It was in Oak Ridge that General Groves finally came to see the boy. He arrived in a chauffeured black car, with Mrs O'Leary, who carried a briefcase overflowing with papers, and a bald pale man in an Army uniform.

They stepped into the enormous exercise hall, and the general gazed about him. The machines were of an ingenious design. The tubes, through which the boys were fired, were contained within square vacuum-sealed metal tanks, which were fifteen feet high. The boys were fed through an opening near the bottom of the tank, then propelled through the tube, swooping around in a semicircle, at such an extreme velocity that the extraneous matter would separate from them, as in a centrifuge. The speed was achieved through a complicated system of electromagnets. The boys were then collected from a compartment at the top of the tank, and the procedure was repeated. It was necessary, of course, to repeat it several times. This is why there were so many of the tanks—ninety-six of them—in the exercise hall, all arranged in a great rounded rectangle.

It was a most impressive sight, with the boys being carried back and forth in large glass bottles and the workers hastening up and down ladders without rest, some riding bicycles to get from one end of the hall to the other, and the air filled with the hum of the electromagnets, the sucking and blowing of the huge vacuum pumps.

The director of Oak Ridge—Dr Ernest Lawrence—came walking with huge strides down the aisle beside the machines, his arm extended to shake the general's hand.

'Good to see you, General!'

'Dr Lawrence,' said the general. 'You know Mrs O'Leary, my secretary. And this is Captain De Silva, from Intelligence.'

'Good to meet you. How do you do.'

Mrs O'Leary freed one of her hands from the briefcase and Dr Lawrence shook it.

'Can I get somebody to take that case for you?' he said.

'No, no,' said the general. 'I may have to dictate something.'

'Thank you,' said Mrs O'Leary, 'I'm quite alright.'

Dr Lawrence was a tall, dashing fellow in the prime of life. He wore a gray sports suit and a pair of rimless spectacles. His blond hair was parted handsomely in the middle, and he had very white teeth. He looked everybody squarely in the face when he spoke to them and smiled almost constantly.

'Come this way, please,' he said.

The boy had just been freshly rebottled, and his bottle was resting on a metal trolley. He watched the group as it proceeded through the hall.

'Look around. Take it all in,' said Dr Lawrence. 'We can go up the top. Do you want to go up? The best view is from the top.'

A narrow iron stairway led up to the top of the assembly of tanks. They went up the stairs and the boy saw them moving for a time on the high platforms, Dr Lawrence pointing enthusiastically and the general nodding from time to time. Then at length they came down again.

'Feel that in your shoes, General?' Dr Lawrence said. 'Like walking in a ploughed paddock, isn't it? That's the magnets pulling on the nails in your shoes. Everything that is done here comes from the magnetic field.'

Dr Lawrence did not spend all his time in Oak Ridge—indeed, he spent most of his time in his office in California—but he was eager to demonstrate to the general his familiarity with the machines. The general examined everything carefully and nodded with satisfaction. As he introduced a few of his workers, Dr Lawrence thumped them hard on the back, and called them his friends. He was a great believer in teamwork and expected everybody else to share this view.

'How close are we, doctor,' the general asked, 'to having one of these boys ready for the next stage of treatment?'

'Closer every day,' grinned Dr Lawrence. 'You see, what we are doing here cannot be done overnight. We are getting the boys down to their essential neurological particles. Filtering out everything else. It's a slow process, General. Wheat from the chaff.'

Dr Lawrence led them over to the boy's trolley and picked up his bottle so that they could admire him. On Dr Lawrence's right hand, the end of the small finger was missing. The boy slipped down along the edge of the glass.

They looked at the boy. The boy was a little older now, and his appearance had changed considerably over the past year. His scars were gone. The machines had reduced him to a near-perfect cube. His yellow days were over. He was now gray and smooth, with a few pockmarks. He was not so much a body anymore, as a lump of highly-concentrated brain-matter. He could not be said to possess any recognizable human features at all, but for the dim, uneven, barely discernible pupils with which he gaped, unblinking, at the world. His basic facial expression, however, had not changed.

It was rare for so many people to pay attention to the boy, all at once. All of a sudden he felt very strange, very unpleasant, and he endeavored to understand what they were saying about him. He had by now acquired some mastery of the English language. But many of the concepts people described continued to elude him.

'All the way from Africa,' said Mrs O'Leary.

General Groves seized the bottle and, bringing it extremely close, peered into the boy's face.

'Does he see me?' said General Groves.

'Yes, sir, I'm sure,' said Dr Lawrence.

There was a pause.

'What is his opinion, do you think?'

The boy gazed blankly at the general.

'Awe and wonder,' said Dr Lawrence.

General Groves set the bottle back on the trolley.

'Small, isn't he?' he said.

He turned to Mrs O'Leary and asked her what time it was. She replied that it was fifteen hundred hours. They turned away from the boy and his trolley and began discussing technical matters—some minor problems with electrical overloads, rust, leakages, loose magnets, cracked insulators, metal in the cooling fluid, leaky vacuum tanks, problems with the bushings, and so on.

The boy stared at the enormous crumpled khaki seat of the general's trousers. Then he turned his attention to Mrs O'Leary, the glistening black braid of her hair, and her yellow dress, and her arms, straining with the suitcase. He felt, in addition to his usual physical agonies, a strange new discomfort. It was something about the way the general had looked at him.

'We're doing fine,' Dr Lawrence kept saying.

Captain de Silva—the bald man—now spoke for the first time, and all turned at once to look at him, as though they had forgotten he was there.

'Have you considered, doctor,' he said, 'that somebody may be tampering with the equipment? I mean somebody inside the operation.'

Dr Lawrence was not the sort of man to admit when he had not thought of something.

'Of course,' he said. 'But I would be very surprised if any of my workers—'

'Any man can be got to,' said General Groves.

'Do you look into the politics of the men you hire?' inquired Captain de Silva.

'Very closely,' said Dr Lawrence. 'Most extremely closely.'

'Could you tell me, for instance, how many communists there are in your outfit?'

'Not off the top of my head, no. But I'm sure the number would be very small. Possibly zero. Communists are just not my sort of workers. I can find that all out for you, of course.'

'Find that out, please, Dr Lawrence,' said Captain de Silva.

'Sure. No problem. We don't have any krauts here, you can rest assured of that,' said Dr Lawrence. Then he added quietly, 'And almost no Jews.'

The tour continued and the boy was taken back to the machines to continue his treatments. Dr Lawrence and his guests went down a corridor where young women sat on tall stools, staring at walls of knobs and dials. 'This is certainly the best-looking part of Oak Ridge,' Dr Lawrence said, with an ironical glance. He showed his guests the offices, the repair shops, the storage rooms, the lunchrooms, the various white areas and colored areas. Then it became time for the general to leave, and they passed back through the exercise hall.

'By the way, Lawrence,' he said. 'I have some news that may interest you.'

'What's that, General?'

'I have chosen our scientific director.'

Dr Lawrence kept his eyes to the floor, and said, 'Oh yes?'

'Dr Robert Oppenheimer. I understand you worked with him in California.'

'Oh!' said Dr Lawrence. 'Good... Good.'

He was silent a moment, then he went on: 'A little surprising, in some ways. He's, uh—unconventional, some might say.'

The general was absorbed briefly in the inspection of his green blazer, passing his hand over it, smoothing its few creases, picking specks of lint from its surface. 'Dr Oppenheimer is a genius,' he said. 'Everybody thinks so. Don't you think so?'

'I'm sure he'll do a fine job,' said Dr Lawrence quickly.

The general glanced at the machines as they passed and listened to the clatter of the boys, shuttling round at high speed, again and again. They stepped outside and saw that it was raining faintly.

'Christ!' said Captain de Silva, who hated rain.

The road was full of mud. Vehicles roared spraying through scattered pools, and people wobbled past with limp newspapers over their heads, plucking themselves boot by boot from the bog. Across the way, near the front gates, was a large billboard, depicting three monkeys, and the words:

What you see here,
What you do here,
What you hear here,
When you leave here,
Let it stay here.

The black car was waiting for the general and Mrs O'Leary. A chauffeur in army uniform emerged, holding an umbrella, and opened the door for them. Captain de Silva remained with Dr Lawrence. For he was going to stick around for a while—to keep an eye on things.

'You have a good tempo here, Lawrence,' the general said as he got into the car. 'But I want you to remember something. This war is killing three hundred people an hour. And the Germans are always working. Remember that, Lawrence.'

The doctor replied that he had several ideas for the expansion of the facility, which he declared he could do more cheaply than any other doctor in America, and he was still describing these when the general closed the door of the car.

After the general had gone and the day's treatments were over and the pain had subsided sufficiently for him to think, the boy thought, in his dim way, about some of the events of the afternoon. He thought about how he had felt when the general looked at him, and tried to determine what had so upset him.

For some time he had been growing frustrated with his paralysis—not merely annoyed at the discomfort, as he had always been, but angry at the idea of it. He had recently formed a foolish notion that all men began their lives in the same condition as himself, that all the grown men he saw about him must have passed like him through unpleasant mechanical processes when they were boys. And on the basis of this grave error, he had grown impatient to be done with his treatments and his paralysis and his hideous disfigurements, and to be a man.

He expected, in the future, to be different from his present self in almost every conceivable way. That was the cause of his frustration when the general had looked at him. He was simply not ready to be looked at, because he was not himself yet, not yet the self that he wished to be.

At present he was weak, silent, insipid. He did not want to be any of these things. He wanted to be bold, to be strong, to be—what? What to be? That was the question. He wanted to exert himself, in some manner, in a way that would cause others to notice him. He was tired of the institutions. He began to understand that his present life was not a life at all, but something that had to be endured before a life could commence. It was as though he was before a window, and could see life, but could not touch it. What he needed, he thought, was to be given the opportunity to live. For he would do great things, he thought, when he had the opportunity.

4

General Groves and Mrs O'Leary sat in their private car on the overnight train from Knoxville to Washington. With a cigarette in her mouth, Mrs O'Leary typed several letters on her portable typewriter and the general signed them. They were letters to the various companies now involved in the treatment of the boys—Stone and Webster, DuPont, Westinghouse, General Electric, Eastman Kodak. For security reasons they now referred to the patients by code numbers. The boy's number was twenty-five. Mrs O'Leary then reminded the general of his appointments, reading through his calendar.

Before retiring to their bunks, they briefly discussed a matter that had been irritating the general for some time—Dr Leo Szilard. Letters from Dr Szilard were piling up—letters full of ideas about treatments and organizations and councils of scientists and various other timewasting endeavors—clearly the man was trying to get in the way of the success of their operation. It was possible he was some kind of German or Soviet spy, but the general did not think so. It was more likely that Szilard was simply a know-it-all. Trying to make a name for himself. He was one of those men who knows everything and understands nothing. Such men were to be penned, General Groves always said—compartmentalized, at the moment they revealed themselves.

General Groves prepared his bunk in the train compartment. He smoothed the bedspread and tucked in the corners. When a bed is made to Army standards, a US quarter dropped onto the center of the blanket will bounce six inches into the air. If the coin does not bounce six inches you must remake the bed. The Groves family had always been a military family. His father had been an army chaplain. He had grown up on army posts—Vancouver Barracks, Fort Snelling, Fort Hancock, Fort Apache, Fort William Henry Harrison, Fort Lawton. His wife's family were military people too—good people. He had attended West Point. To his enormous displeasure the First World War had ended, right at the moment of his graduation. But he had been allowed to go to the battlefields of France, on an educational excursion.

After he had made his bed he lay in it and thought about the boy. He felt that his plan for the boys was beginning to take shape. Soon the preliminary treatment would be over and the doctors would be able to start designing the prosthesis. There would be no more gadding about for the boy—no more train rides—not until his body was finished. He had determined exactly where the prosthetic work would take place. He had worked it all out with Dr Oppenheimer. It was a boys' school in New Mexico. They would clear it out and devote it entirely to their special invalids. It would be the center of their operation. All the doctors would be there. They would have complete security, total isolation. The mind of the general demurred from the final questions of deployment, strategy, orders of battle, and so forth. For the questions of feasibility had to be determined before anything like that could begin to be done. One thing was for sure. If the thing could be done, he would make darn sure that it would be done by an American. And it would be a death blow for Hitler and all that he stood for. And if the general was entirely honest with himself (and he was not) he also had to admit that was some thrill in the thing. If the boys did what the doctors said they could do, they could change the nature of war itself. They could change everything. But it was too early for such thoughts.

The following morning, the train arrived in Washington and the general and Mrs O'Leary parted at the station. He handed her his blazer.

'Get this pressed,' he said.

She took it.

'Wait a minute,' he said.

He checked the pockets for change. The general was very particular about change. On his desk, in his home, he kept and maintained three ceramic pigs. There was a big black one for pennies, a small green one for dimes, and a medium-sized one, for nickels. Words cannot express the pleasure it gave General Groves to place, at evening, into each of the narrow slots, the appropriately sized coins. Whenever he bought anything, he would always use the largest bill he had, in order to get change. Then he would save the change, not spending it, even when he longed to do so, and bring it home, and put it in his pigs. He would even deny himself things in order to get change. When his children were young, they had watched him feeding his pigs each night. It was educational. It had taught them to economize. But now they were fully-grown, and he did it in solitude. One day General Groves would be gone and his pigs would be at sea in the world. He did not like to think about this.

He made a beeline down the station steps. Half an hour later he met his daughter at the tennis courts, dressed in his white cotton clothes and knee-guards. He beat her mercilessly. His knees were bad, but he was a good player.

They returned home together in his car. It was an apple-green Dodge sedan, a 1942 model. He listened to the radio as he drove, one of his favorite comedic programs, at the maximum volume. His daughter talked to him about her homework. She was seventeen, though she possessed enough sense to know that his work was classified, and not to ask him about it.

They drove through the leafy avenues of Washington until they came to a modest brick house on 36th Street. The yard was small, with a few shrubberies, no garden, and with a flag which the general raised and lowered punctually each day. It was a happy household, full of laughter, his laughter. He switched off the ignition and went inside.

Waiting in the living room was his wife. She was in a gold lamé blouse with a bow collar, blinking her black eyes, leaning on the big armchair with its inexpensive floral slipcover, as though she had been lingering there, just waiting for the moment of his arrival.

'Dick,' she said feebly.

He sighed and entered the living room. The general was known as Dick to his family and friends. He did not like to be called by his first name.

5

It was a quiet morning in February, 1944, when a man arrived to take the boy to New Mexico. A frost lay heavily on the ridges, in the hog-woods, on the wild laurel, on the pale amanita, on the smokestack and on the roof of the exercise hall. The man wore white gloves and carried a large briefcase. He removed the boy from his bottle and put him in the briefcase. Then he put the briefcase into the trunk of a car.

The journey—by car, train and car again—took several hours. The boy lay snugly and watched the light change in the briefcase. There was no apparent source for this light—no hole, no crack, as in some of his former receptacles. It was rather that the briefcase seemed to glow dimly from all sides, that all the sides were partially luminous, and he was conscious of the strange substance that seemed to line its interior, a diaphanous gold. He heard diverse sounds—ticking, roaring, tapping.

By the time the briefcase was finally opened, it was evening. He saw that he was in a small, crowded room with walls of army green. Someone set him down on a tabletop, on which a military officer was signing a piece of paper. The officer looked up from the paper, saw the boy, and nodded his head.

'Good,' he said.

The room was filled with doctors and soldiers. They swarmed, jostled, murmured. They all had white circular badges pinned to the lapels of their coats, which glowed before him in the dusk and the cigarette smoke. The lighting was insufficient. Shadows thronged on the walls. They pressed together, struggling to see him. There was a window in the room, but through the slits of the venetian blinds he could see only blackness.

The doctors were all talking about him. Some were saying he looked different to what they had expected, some were saying he looked the same. Among the doctors was Edward Teller. He muscled his way to the table, stooped before the boy, and gazed at him. Then he reached timidly forward and touched, with one finger, a little patch of blue oxidation above the boy's eyes.

'Do you see this, Hans?' he said.

Dr Bethe appeared at his side.

'Fascinating,' he said.

The boy observed the face of the Hungarian—the greasy hair and the thick, dark eyebrows, and the darkness that shrouded the eyes.

'Where did you say he was from?' said one of the other doctors.

'Africa,' said the soldier who had signed the form.

The doctor repeated the word as though it was an interesting but unpleasant dish of food.

Out of the crowd came Dr Fermi. He was holding in his hands a small metal instrument that made a ticking noise. The closer to the boy it came, the faster it ticked, sparse ticks at a distance, then drawing nearer—tick, tick, tick, continuously.

Eventually the crowd began to disperse. The boy noticed Captain de Silva was in the room, asking people if they were authorized to be there. The boy paid little attention to the faces that came, one by one, to peer at him.

'Move it out fellas, we have to lock everything up here,' said Captain de Silva.

'So this is number twenty-five,' said Dr Teller.

'Go on, scram, everybody,' said one of the other soldiers.

'We have a lot of work to do,' declared Dr Teller, in a cheerful voice, as he went out. 'Pardon me, Dr Oppenheimer.'

The man to whom Dr Teller had spoken was standing in a dim part of the room, by the door. He was a tall, narrow man. He wore a dark suit. Though all in the room were moving, he and the boy were still. At first, in the dim light, the boy could see only the Stetson hat, dust-colored and flat-brimmed, pushed low on his head, and the slender hand, in which a cigarette burned, which he raised now and then to his lips. Then he lifted his head and his handsome pale face came into view. It was his eyes, more than anything else, that made an impression on the boy.

They were as bright and blue as the horn of a gas flame. They lingered on him, searched him, pierced him. It made him very uneasy. The doctors shuffled respectfully past the director as they went out, some turning to take a final look at the boy. Dr Oppenheimer ignored them, went on gazing at the boy and smoking. Then finally, bowing his head once more, he turned and went out, leaving a faint, disembodied halo of smoke where he had stood.

6

In the belief that mountain air was conducive to the
healing and repose of young invalids, the Los Alamos Boys
School had been built on top of a mesa, in the high desert
north of Santa Fe. In the canyons that surrounded it, there
grew piñon pines and ponderosas and the cottonwoods
that had given it its name. In the distance, beneath the
enormous desert sky, the plains rose into alien undula-
tions, dotted with juniper bushes. To the west lay the Jemez
Mountains, to the east the Sangre de Cristo Mountains.

The buildings that now comprised the institution were
surrounded by a tall fence which closed them off from
the rest of the town. This handful of buildings was no
longer referred to as a school. Since the U.S. Army arrived
it was called the Technical Area, and it included offices

and warehouses and sheds and workshops. This area was further subdivided according to the various divisions of the staff. The Theoretical Division, for example, which included all the senior doctors, and was responsible for most of the fundamental prosthetic design, was housed in two large office buildings, which were connected by a narrow passage on the second floor. The boy spent most of his time, at this period, in the hands of the Experimental Division, whose leader was a friendly man named Dr Wilson. Soldiers worked among the doctors—members of the Special Engineer Detachment of the Engineer Corps, or S.E.D. men, as they were called.

At Los Alamos the demands on the boy were much less strenuous than at his previous institutions. At Dr Oppenheimer's insistence, there were no beatings. The boy was passed from doctor to doctor and measured by each one in a slightly different way. It was not with rulers or scales that they measured him, but with highly precise and specialized instruments, endeavoring to observe and chart each particle of his being, to determine his exact structure, with a view towards implantation, and to determine thereby the most practical design for a prosthetic body.

Sometimes he was laid on a rack, or put in a small bathtub, or in a cylindrical chamber, or fitted carefully into a compartment in a large vacuum-sealed machine. They tested their ability to stimulate his brain matter by means of special machines. Some of these had no effect on him whatsoever. Yet others tickled him faintly. For much of the time he did nothing at all, just lay around, thinking about his life, what it was going to be. Judging by the diagrams he saw on the blackboards and the blueprints that the doctors sometimes unrolled upon the tables, it seemed his body was going to be long, thin, oval-shaped, simple. His impatience was great, for in his own mind he was in perfectly good stead to begin his life, and he saw no reason for the delay.

After some weeks a second boy arrived at Los Alamos. Though the treatments of the two patients were similar, they were never treated together and were often taken away to be with different doctors for long periods. At night the boys were kept in the same storeroom in the Technical Area, guarded by soldiers.

Dr Oppenheimer's leadership gave Los Alamos the air of an academy. He was an eccentric, sometimes abrasive person. To him, the design of the prosthesis was as much a philosophical endeavor as a question of mechanics. He seemed to understand it as nobody else did. He went each day from room to room, assisting the various divisions with their work, standing before the blackboards, a cigarette in his mouth, disentangling their problems with furious swipes of chalk.

He smoked constantly, spoke very quickly, and never repeated himself. His voice was deep and precise. He instilled in the other doctors a sense of the solemnity and importance of their task. The word he used was 'duty'—pronounced with the yod, like an aristocrat—duty to America and to the Allies and to the advancement of medical science.

It was because of Dr Oppenheimer that they were all now in New Mexico. He knew the area from his youth. He had ridden horses in the mountains and camped out in the pathless canyons. It was he who had suggested the location to General Groves—some said he had insisted on it, that he attached to the mesas and deserts some kind of spiritual significance. And it was clear from the strange way Dr Oppenheimer sometimes spoke, from the archaic poems he occasionally quoted and the hours he sometimes spent in his office, reading the Vedas, that there was a certain mysticism in his approach to medical matters.

7

The doctors at Los Alamos respected their director. But
that is not to say that all of his decisions were unanimously
accepted. For instance, when he selected Dr Bethe to be
head of the Theoretical Division, there was some opposition
from Dr Teller. Dr Teller thought it an act of grave misman-
agement, and had frequently complained of the danger
that talented physicians, who he did not name, would find
themselves relegated to tasks below their abilities.

This came to a head one afternoon in early April. The
boy was in the Technical Area, in a large room onto which
many of the senior doctors' offices opened. Dr Wilson
was performing an experiment on him—he was lying
on a small irregular stack of metal bricks, on a table.
The doctors were making careful adjustments to this

arrangement. A little box was next to him, with a blinking red light. From another small machine came the constant sound of ticking.

'Bitch of a thing,' said one of the young doctors.

'Oh, it'll come around.'

Dr Wilson had the bright square face and the how-do-you-do manner of a Wyoming farmhand. He stood now at the helm of the table, moving with a gloved hand a few of the bricks, as required.

'Do you think the table could have something to do with it?' said the other doctor.

'How do you mean?'

'Right now we've got Twenty-Five on a wooden table. Well, that could be interfering with the reading.'

'Right.'

'Say we put him on a metal table—'

At that moment the door of Dr Bethe's office flew open. Dr Bethe's physiognomy always fascinated the boy—the strange high dome of the skull, as though the brain was trying to rise out of it, the small clockwork mechanism of the face, the cunning little eyes, the beaklike smile, and beneath it all a body of surprising strength and vitality.

'We will finish this discussion another time, Edward,' he was saying.

'Don't worry,' said Dr Teller, limping past him into the room. 'Don't worry, I am going.'

Dr Bethe threw an exasperated glance at Dr Wilson, which was returned with some sympathy.

'If you don't have time for me to speak,' Dr Teller went on, 'I will leave you alone.'

'You have made yourself clear, Edward. You don't want to do the calculations.'

Dr Teller halted. 'Yes. But you deliberately misunderstand me.'

'I understand you, Edward,' said Dr Bethe. 'But as I have said, they are complex calculations, and we need somebody with the skills to do them.'

Dr Teller's tongue was working in his mouth, turning and turning again a little weightless froth of saliva, spreading it, breaking it apart with alacrity. He considered for a moment Dr Bethe's calm, ill-distributed face. The little cud of sour spit began to bubble, now on the tongue, now on the palate, useless. Dr Teller's eyes swung round to the table where the apparatus was assembled. 'This isn't my area. If you force me to do this, you take away my ability to do more important things. There are others who can do these other things,' he said.

Dr Bethe sighed.

'We are going in circles. I have to find some way to divide the work.'

'And this is what you choose for me? This lug work, this bricklaying? This is not my type of work at all! Clearly you don't know what I am capable of doing, Dr Bethe.'

'Edward, I have another—'

'There is more I can do, that is all I am trying to say. There is more I can do. I have my own design, I call it the Advanced Design. If—'

'Edward. I have another appointment. You will have to excuse me.'

He left Dr Teller standing awkwardly by Dr Wilson's apparatus, and set off down the hall to his next meeting. Dr Wilson and his helpers had fallen silent, and by a series of gradual and imperceptible readjustments of posture and position, had managed to angle their faces in such a way that eye contact with Dr Teller was extremely unlikely.

Dr Teller looked at the blank smooth mildly dissatisfied face of the boy on his stack of blocks. His thoughts were not entirely clear to himself. This was all evidently a matter of principle for Dr Bethe, he thought, an attempt to assert his authority in the Theoretical Division. The pettiness of it was extraordinary.

'That's point three six seven, doctor,' said one of the young doctors in a low voice.

'What?' said Dr Wilson.

'You've written a five.'

'Do you think this is the way the Nazis are doing it?' said Dr Teller, turning to Dr Wilson.

This was a difficult question to answer under the circumstances. There was a silence.

'Here is my point!' he cried. 'We are slowing ourselves with all this regulation.'

'Don't shout, Edward. You are in a medical institution.'

'Why am I not allowed to know what everybody else is doing? This helps no one. I am supposed to sit there and do these brainless equations and have no idea what's going on on the other side of the wall. I cannot work like this, in a closed box. It's not the way I work.'

'Teller,' said Dr Wilson. 'I see your point, but I—'

'You see my point!'

'But we don't have time to be having this conversation right now,' said Dr Wilson. 'If you have a problem you ought to talk to Oppie.'

Dr Teller stood nodding for a few seconds. Then he raised his arms, dropped them to his sides—a curious gesture—and began battling the coat rack for his jacket.

'Oh, come on, Teller.'

Dr Teller went to his office with his jacket cradled in his arms and began to pack up his desk. He took a wad of pages—the pages of abstract differential equations Dr Bethe had assigned to him—threw them roughly into his safe and thumped the door closed. Then he pulled on his rumpled jacket and glared once more at the boy.

'Dr Teller,' said one of the helpers faintly, 'maybe you could take a look at the—'

Dr Teller shook his head and went out of the room. He limped heavily down the green corridor, in the haze of innumerable cigarettes, passing rooms where rows of women sat tapping at Marchant calculators, and rooms where S.E.D. men squabbled over plans and blueprints, past soldiers in garrison caps, past the office of Dr Oppenheimer, and emerged from the building, into the sun. He headed for the gate. He wanted to get home and put his foot up and play his piano. The wind was blowing his tie over his shoulder in a way that annoyed him immensely. He hoped he did not see anyone from the Theoretical Division, though he knew he would not, for they were all inside, at the tasks Dr Bethe had given them. He looked up at the barbs of the fence and thought of something he had been trying all day not to think of—Hungary.

A group stood lined up at the gate in single file, waiting to enter the Technical Area. They raised their security passes one by one to the guard. Dr Teller limped past them. He was the only one going out. The little town lay spread before him, the pond, the hospital, the apartments and barracks, and further off, beyond the mesa, the rolling, rising land, the green vast stillness of the Jemez Mountains.

The day was clear and unseasonably warm. The air had a clarity here he had encountered in only a few places in his life. In the High Tatras, and on his great American holiday, seven years earlier, in 1937, with the Bethes. He had known Dr Bethe for almost sixteen years. How easily they do it to you, he thought—your own friends, how clinically, when they are given the opportunity. He strayed with uneven step from the road, onto the dry dirt—there were no sidewalks—and cut between the rows of houses, where army-issue sheets were hanging on the washing lines.

8

Los Alamos was similar in many ways to other desert towns. It had its picket fences, porch lights, clapboard houses painted yellow and powder blue, lawn chairs in the dirt, oak trees and American flags in the front yards. It had, however, a rough and slipshod look about it, betraying the fact that it had sprung up in a very short time. And on its fringes one could see that houses were still hurriedly being built.

The closer one looked at Los Alamos, the more one saw little indications that there had grown, within the high fences that encircled the town, a rather strange kind of America. For instance, it had no street signs. Instead of policemen and crossing guards, there were soldiers. A tall fence surrounded the town, around which more soldiers patrolled on horseback—circling slowly, day and night.

There were no mailboxes, for all the mail went to one address, where it was read and censored by the Army. There was only one store, a commissary, and nobody ever paid for anything. All was provided. The townspeople seemed normal, though there was an unusual distribution of occupations. Everybody in the town worked for the Army, and whether they were a professor or a mathematician or a secretary or a laborer or a cleaner, their job was in some way related to the boy. Strangest of all, now and then, across the plateau, there came the sound of a blast, and in the midst of its long fading echo some of the women would pause at their washing lines or at their ovens or kitchen tables or piles of string beans, and stand for a few moments, listening.

It was not a long walk to the small government-issue four-plex in which Dr Teller now lived. He and his wife and his son lived downstairs and a couple named the Smiths lived upstairs. The house stood close to the edge of the mesa. A hundred yards from the back door was the tall fence, and immediately beyond that, the sheer drop into the canyon. He saw with annoyance that they had guests—a little crowd of women, gathered on the porch, some with baskets of clothes. Evidently they had come to use the washing machine. It had been Dr Teller's idea—Dr Teller's foresight—to bring the washing machine with them, along with the Steinway. They were the only household, other than the Oppenheimers, who had one.

His son, Paul, two years old, was playing with a few other children, swinging from the rails of the porch. The voice of Mrs Bethe could be heard across the yard. 'The prospects were magnificent,' she said. 'Very stimulating.'

'Really?' said Mrs Fermi, a small, squat Italian woman.

'You can drive up to the Valle Grande and walk from there. It's lovely. Just marvelous.'

'Look—a man before nightfall,' said Mrs Smith. 'The war must be over.'

Dr Teller accepted this veiled insult with a smile. The range of possible retorts available to him was limited, it being forbidden to speak about the young patients outside of the Technical Area. Placing his hands nonchalantly in his pockets he replied weakly, 'My job is to think, which is something I am able to do at home—from time to time.'

There was something ragged, ration-worn, tired, about these women—the way they stood jumbled about the porch, their kitchen-soap skin rawly glowing, the way they clasped their cigarettes between their fingers. Mrs Smith had curlers in her hair. Mrs Bethe was seated in the middle, a checkered handkerchief around her head. She was a handsome woman with a rosy-white skin, large light pale eyes, and a narrow nose with a high bridge—a picture of good health. Her wholesome face was tilted to look out over the rotted buds of the garden. One of her hands clasped the wooden armrest of her chair and the other was raised to her chin, not so much as a means of support but lightly, vaguely, as though establishing its continued existence. She turned to Dr Teller a polite, straight-toothed smile.

'Do you mind, Mici, if I go next?' said Mrs Fermi. 'I still have to go to the damned commissary and I'll be lucky to get home before curfew at this rate.'

'Not at all,' replied Mrs Teller.

'You'll be lucky to get anything there,' said Mrs Bethe. 'Oh how I miss pumpernickel!'

Mrs Teller came down to meet her husband, tightening

about her shoulders her tasseled shawl.

'Koko,' she said. 'Paul is being a nightmare.'

They glanced helplessly for a moment at the children, charging and swooping at one another.

On the porch a mousy woman named Mrs Bacher was talking in a low voice into the ear of Mrs Smith. '—she used to hobnob round the dinner table with Hermann Göring.'

'Surely not,' said Mrs Smith with a shudder and a ghastly look. 'She's the director's wife, for God's sake. The army would have to check these things. Why, the number of times they checked us at the gate when we came down from Chicago!'

'You think you had a rough time,' interposed Mrs Fermi. 'They held us up for three hours at the gate. And I'm sure there is more that goes on behind the scenes.'

Mrs Smith nodded her head at every word.

'Oh, I'm sure,' she said.

'It is necessary to make sure about everything,' said Mrs Fermi.

Dr Teller was striving to make sense of this conversation when one of the little ones, falling, began to siren at the top of his lungs. Mrs Smith, still interested in the piece of intelligence being imparted to her by Mrs Bacher, reached out her hand in a gesture of faint concern.

'Settle down now,' she said.

'Who is it?' cried Mrs Bethe, starting to her feet. 'Is it my little Henry?'

It was Dr Teller's son, Paul.

'Play nice, boys,' said Mrs Teller. She bent down after him, took him up in her arms and began to bop him. 'Ow! Right on the funny bone!'

'It's quite true though,' said Mrs Bacher, determined to

continue in her conversation about the director's wife. 'You wouldn't know it, but Mrs Oppenheimer is a German. Isn't she, Rose? She was born there, she's as German as you are.'

'Moreso,' said Mrs Bethe, reseating herself.

'Aristocratic stock,' Mrs Bacher went on. 'Speaks the language as well as anything. Tell Mrs Smith, Rose, the terrible thing she said to you.'

'I'm not going to say anything,' said Mrs Bethe.

'It was dreadful,' said Mrs Bacher. 'I'm not afraid to say it. She's a dreadful person. I'm not saying she'd have us wearing a yellow star, but then again...'

'She's not that bad,' said Mrs Fermi.

'Not that bad. That's what they all say. Everybody is not that bad, they say. Well, I tell you, some people are. Some people are that bad. This war ought to prove that.'

'But isn't Oppenheimer a Jew?' said Mrs Smith.

'Oppie is goyish.'

'What's this?' said Dr Teller. 'What are you ladies talking about?'

'Come now, Rose,' Mrs Bacher went on, prodding Mrs Bethe, entirely ignoring Dr Teller. 'What was it she said to you?'

Paul had begun to bawl louder in Mrs Teller's arms. He had his arm outstretched and was clutching at it, trying to twist the elbow around to get a look at it.

'Give him something to eat,' said Mrs Fermi.

'Come now, Paul,' said Mrs Teller. 'I'll take you in and give you an apple.'

'No!' he cried. 'No, no!'

This was his entire vocabulary—a fact on which Mrs Teller had often remarked with concern. But it did not bother Dr Teller, for he himself had not spoken until he was four years old.

'She said she was related to Hermann Göring,' said Mrs Bacher, 'didn't she, Rose?'

Mrs Bethe indulged in a slow shake of her head.

'I'm not sure that it was Göring. Perhaps it was Rommel. It made me very uncomfortable.'

'All of them should be hanged,' said Mrs Bacher.

'They are all as bad as each other,' said Mrs Bethe decisively. 'All thugs. Thugs.'

'Let's not talk about the war, girls,' said Mrs Teller faintly.

'I had better be going soon,' said Mrs Bethe. 'Hans likes his meals cooked at home. Come, Henry.'

'All I'm saying is, watch out. She isn't a nice person,' said Mrs Bacher. 'She uses people, she treats them like—it's as if she's a kid pulling wings off a fly. That's the way she treats people.'

'There's that cat again,' said Mrs Teller.

'Puss puss puss puss,' said Mrs Fermi.

'Looks like a suppurating jaw,' said Mrs Teller.

'I'm not sure. What do you think, Edward?'

The cat was hideous. Its hair had fallen out in patches and its tongue was all black and swollen.

'I could not say,' said Dr Teller.

'Something's terribly wrong with it all the same.'

'What could have done that?'

Dr Teller excused himself. He went inside to the living room, sat down before the piano and thought for a moment about the women's conversation. He doubted very much that the director's wife was a Nazi. In fact, he thought he heard somewhere that the Oppenheimers were somewhat left of center. But he did not feel like arguing the point with Mrs Bacher.

Over the keys of the piano a book lay sprawling, face down—*Darkness at Noon*, by Arthur Koestler. Dr Teller closed it and placed it aside. His Steinway was a beautiful object—a black glossy casket of hammers and strings. He played a C-minor chord and thought of his mother who had taught him to play the Pathétique, and wondered if she was safe, in Hungary. Then he thought of the prosthesis, and of the idea that had been gnawing away at him—his own design, the Advanced Design. Since 1939 this idea had hung in his head—two boys in one prosthesis. He was sure it was possible. It must be. It was horrible to think of—a grotesque thought. But someone had to think about it, or the Nazis would get ahead.

He began to play. He sank into a habitual posture, hunching over, sinking lower and lower in his seat, his long thin arms falling limp in their long gray sleeves, his hands on the keys, his eyes wide open, but seeing nothing.

9

It may be assumed, due to the demanding nature of their work, that the doctors at Los Alamos found no time to socialize. But this is not true. On the weekends when they were not copulating the doctors strayed into the wilderness. They drove out to the mountains, to the Truchas Peak, or Lake Peak, or the Valles Caldera. Or they went and admired the ruins in the hills—the abandoned houses and kivas, the caves carved by hand out of the cliffs, the fallen walls and the faceless statues. The prospects, as Mrs Bethe said, were stimulating—the endless junipers, the blue cacti, the deer, the mesquite, the mesas turning red at sundown, the windswept plains of grass in the caldera, the hidden creeks and the fields buoyant with mariposas and the choirs of white admirals that fluttered from the fringes of the trails.

There were quiet places where the canyons narrowed, where the ground was soft and sandy and the doctors made deep footprints. They would find jutting boulders and crawl beneath them and eat their lunch. And there, between high, bare, silent rock walls, they would talk, in contravention of the security regulations, about the boys.

One Saturday afternoon a party was held to welcome some newly-arrived doctors from England, and simply for the sake of having a party. The guests gathered in Dr Oppenheimer's house, in the large living room with its stone fireplace, its Navajo rug and its tall bookshelves. The mood was merry. Cigarette smoke hung overhead. Military officers mingled with the doctors, looking in their three-piece suits the way civilians look in their pajamas. The talk was of the war, and the American invasion of France that was sure to happen any day, and the terrible headache it would cause for Hitler.

All the senior members of staff and their wives were in attendance. Dr Bethe was there, and Dr Fermi, in his new blue jeans and his western shirt. Even Dr Teller was there, though he had been rarely seen in the Technical Area since his unfortunate disagreement with Dr Bethe.

Mrs Teller was glad for a chance to get out of the house. She mingled through the crowd with her husband, who seemed ridiculously uneasy. He kept looking about him, as though somebody was going to jump out and stab him. But nobody paid him the slightest attention, and this only seemed to upset him further. Nothing is quite so injurious to the sensitive intellectual, Mrs Teller thought, as the insult of continual inattention.

A telephone was ringing. Mrs Teller found this very unpleasant. She had always been funny about telephones. She looked around the room and thought how strange it was that they were all here for the same reason—the boy—and yet nobody mentioned it. She wondered how many of the wives knew about the exact nature of their husbands' work.

Mrs Bethe, in her coat of skunk pelts and with her glass of raspberry cordial—strong drink did not agree with her—had stationed herself in a large striped armchair and was presiding over one of her usual conversations. 'That's correct,' she said judiciously. 'It was not a pleasant winter. Los Alamos is very dry in contrast to Cambridge. The cold is even fiercer, but it isn't as disagreeable. In Cambridge Hans and I felt that we were freezing solid.'

'Chicago was perfectly wretched,' said Mrs Parsons, the admiral's wife, putting out her cigarette.

'I don't care for Chicago,' said Mrs Bethe. 'It doesn't agree with my eyes.'

'Your eyes, Mrs Bethe?'

'The wind, Mrs Parsons. The wind.'

'Have you been to Chicago, Dr Fuchs?' said Mrs Bacher, addressing a thin nervous young doctor, one of the newcomers, who was sitting somewhat awkwardly on the edge of the group.

'Er—Pardon me, what did you say?'

She repeated the question.

'No, not Chicago,' he replied.

'My husband was born there,' said Mrs Parsons.

'Wind can be nice sometimes,' said Mrs Wilson. 'Can't it, Mrs Smith?'

'Oh yes, it certainly can.'

There was a satisfied lull, during which Mrs Teller drifted into the group and, moving aside a few glasses and an ashtray, sat down beside Mrs Bethe. As she did so she found that her new red dress rose strangely about her shoulders, and she hastened to flatten it.

'What a lovely dress, Mici,' said Mrs Bethe. 'Is it a Hungarian style?'

'No, I bought it in Santa Fe.'

'Oh.'

'It is very—what is the English word?—vivid.'

Mrs Bethe's huge eyes lingered a moment on the creases of the bright tulle, connected a moment with the eyes of Mrs Bacher, then returned, placid and wholesome, to Mrs Teller's face. It was the same symmetrical smile she always wore. She gave no indication of the recent dispute between their husbands.

Dr Teller had of course described Dr Bethe's incompetencies at length to Mrs Teller. She was not so naive as to believe she was receiving the full and objective account of the facts from her husband. Naturally Dr Teller would tell her that he was a better doctor than Dr Bethe. But since he was her husband, she believed him, and supposed just as he did that some injustice must have taken place. Nevertheless she saw no reason for her and Mrs Bethe to be proxies for whatever professional disagreement existed between the doctors.

The telephone began ringing again.

'You must join us at our fourplex for dinner sometime, Dr Fuchs,' said Mrs Fermi. 'Mrs Peierls makes a lovely aspic.'

'Oh, yes. That would be nice.'

The young bachelor, Dr Fuchs, despite only having been in Los Alamos for a week, had acquired a reputation for the blandness and brevity of his conversation, the latter of which was a great impediment to social success. Though nobody could deny that he was unfailingly polite, he conducted himself with a nervousness, an awkwardness, that was not to their liking. Mrs Teller thought this somewhat unfair to Dr Fuchs, who was after all a mathematician. He kept his eyes lowered to the highball glass from which he sipped, timidly, listening to the conversation, looking up now and then to laugh when the others laughed.

'There'll be no dinner here, I suppose,' said Mrs Smith.

Food was a subject which never failed to arouse the general interest of this group. It was discussed for another few minutes, with many perceptive comments made on the recent quality of the vegetables and fruits at the commissary. Mrs Fermi described at length a fish she had eaten. Mrs Parsons made the controversial claim that she had not, in ten years, consumed a nut. Then, when Mrs Wilson happened to mention that Dr Fuchs was taller than one of the other doctors, they began to compare each other's heights, and to compare the heights of every doctor and soldier they could think of, which gave them great amusement. About five minutes of this had elapsed when Mrs Teller rose from her place and went to get some fresh air.

She went out onto the front lawn, where guests were scattered in small groups. Somebody remarked that the crows were out. And indeed they were—reeling in the desert air, throwing themselves in all directions from the writhing spruces. Mrs Teller strayed from group to group, and found herself at last in the company of Mrs Oppenheimer, whom she had met only once before, and very briefly, in the commissary. Mrs Oppenheimer was sitting in a lawn chair, talking to Admiral Parsons. Her reddish hair was tied up in a loose bun, and she wore a white shirt and cotton trousers. The sun was low in the sky. She gestured, with her martini, towards the mountains.

'Robert and I own a ranch there, in the Sangres. Over there, you see. It's *fine* country for riding. Hard of course'—she clenched her fist—'Tough. But that's the whole idea. No fun if it's easy. Don't you agree?'

'Oh yes,' said Admiral Parsons. He was a simple-looking man, balding, with a calm face—a plain face, Mrs Teller thought.

'You will have to join us on a weekend.'

'Sure. That'd be just fine.'

'Do you ride, Mrs Teller?' said Mrs Oppenheimer, turning to her.

'Not really,' Mrs Teller replied. 'Not since I was a girl.'

'You must continue,' Mrs Oppenheimer said, shaking her head. 'Stupid not to. You must.' Then, narrowing her eyes, she asked, 'What is it you do then?'

Mrs Teller felt several eyes on herself and her vivid dress. She considered the question, but before she could speak, Mrs Oppenheimer had bounded from her seat and was marching with impeccable posture across the lawn, towards the road.

'Spook,' she said, addressing a soldier who was standing with a pistol at the end of the drive. 'You are too close to my petunias. Stand over there.'

'No can do,' said the soldier. 'Orders.'

'Well for God's sake, if you are court martialed, you can blame me. Keep going, soldier, I am not going to argue with you. That'll do.'

Half an hour later, Mrs Teller and Mrs Oppenheimer happened to speak again. Mrs Teller expressed her regret that she and Mrs Oppenheimer had not previously had a chance to become acquainted.

'It's quite alright,' said Mrs Oppenheimer. 'I know very few people. And I can't stand large parties. And I forget everybody's names. I forget everything. Well, not everything, unfortunately. Ever since I had Peter I've gotten—loose in the head—'

And she tapped her skull twice. In spite of all Mrs Teller had heard of the director's wife, she did not sound German. Her voice had the same refined, brittle American phrasing as her husband's. She was a coldly beautiful woman, lean and angular. They talked about their lives before the war. Mrs Teller explained how she had studied mathematics and teaching in Budapest, then gone to study in America.

'By yourself?'

'Yes.'

'Well now! That takes nerve,' declared Mrs Oppenheimer.

They talked more and more freely, about education, and then about their children. The Oppenheimers had a son around the same age as Paul. Mrs Teller suggested the boys could meet one afternoon, an idea to which Mrs Oppenheimer seemed entirely indifferent. They talked about the countryside, which was, according to Mrs Oppenheimer, all ashes. 'All these cliffs and mesas. I am not sure when it was. Certainly more than a million years ago. There was a huge eruption that created the whole plateau. Can you imagine! Ash and cinders raining out of the sky, all the way down to the Mississippi River, supposedly.'

'Gosh,' said Mrs Teller.

'And did you hear about Vesuvius? Happening all over

again. The world is ending. No doubt about it.'

Mrs Teller found it increasingly difficult to believe that this woman could be a Nazi, or a friend of Nazis. Some time had passed, they had wandered down a little way from the other groups, and had reached the road, where the doctors' cars were parked, and the conversation had turned to their husbands. The Oppenheimers had a Cadillac—powder blue, very expensive. Mrs Oppenheimer complained about her husband, but it was in such a way that suggested a deeper admiration. She had known him, she explained, when he was all French-speaking and English-kissing. This amused her, she laughed—an icy shattering wave of a laugh. Now, she said, with all his work, she hardly ever saw him. With some hesitation Mrs Teller articulated the question that had been on her mind all evening.

'Does Dr Oppenheimer ever talk to you about it? I mean, does he mention'—she lowered her voice—'the boy?'

Mrs Oppenheimer seated herself smartly on one of the car fenders and lit a cigarette. She looked out through the dust to where the yuccas were flowering and the chaparral lay outspread on the slopes, in the reddening light. She gave Mrs Teller a brief glance and said, 'I have no idea what you mean.'

10

It was late in the evening when Mrs Oppenheimer and Mrs Teller returned to the house. The Bethes, who always went to bed early, were taking their leave on the porch. Dr Bethe kept turning back to Dr Oppenheimer, unable to resist continuing their conversation.

'But if Napoleon started the fires of Moscow—' said Dr Bethe.

'Impossible,' said Dr Oppenheimer, smiling.

'Come now, Hans,' said Mrs Bethe, grasping her skunks and descending from the porch.

'Rostopchin was in Moscow, was he not?'

'Yes, but—'

'No, no, allow me to finish. If Rostopchin—'

Mrs Bethe stood stiffly on the gravel path. She smiled at

Mrs Teller and Mrs Oppenheimer as they passed her. Mrs Teller slipped inside, while Mrs Oppenheimer, who took an idle interest in everything, opted to remain beside her husband, gazing from face to face with a blissfully indifferent expression. At last Dr Bethe gave up the conversation, and thanked Dr Oppenheimer for his hospitality.

'Go, Dr Bethe,' said Mrs Oppenheimer, drifting in behind her husband. 'Your wife looks as though she is going to have an aneurysm.'

The party went on. In the living room Dr Teller sat listing, in his usual style, in a low ottoman, surrounded by falling and sprawling and oscillating bodies. He received from the outstretched hand of Dr John von Neumann a bottle of gin.

'Queen A4,' he said.

Then he drank from the bottle and held it out to his companion. Dr von Neumann sat an instant with hands folded, quaintly brushed from an otherwise immaculate sleeve a speck of dust, took the bottle and said, 'C5.'

Dr Teller had avoided Dr Bethe all night, at first out of enmity, and then out of fear of increasing their enmity. Their opinions on the question of Dr Teller's role appeared to be polarized and irreconcilable, and Dr Teller had given up any hope that they could negotiate productively. He had resigned himself now to boardless chess with Dr von Neumann, an old favorite pastime. Their conversation had been long and full of reminiscences of Hungary and Germany. They had been discussing old friends, and they turned now to their countryman Dr Szilard.

'Poor old Leo,' said Dr von Neumann. 'Where is he? Columbia?'

'Chicago,' said Dr Teller. 'Queen A3.'

'What in blazes have they got him down there for? I suppose he would cause trouble here with all his ideas. He has no end of them, poor man.'

Dr Teller waited.

'Rook C8,' said Dr von Neumann.

'Bishop B5,' replied Dr Teller instantly. 'You are right. He has principles, and people don't like that. He would make a bother of himself wherever he was, but especially in such an isolated place as this, and where everything is done so strangely.'

'Strangely? How do you mean?'

'The leadership, I mean. And the regulations.'

'Well, my man, the whole thing is strange. The whole operation. Really cockeyed. Why, it's the old Indian rope trick—throw all the pieces in a box, say a magic word, and a living person pops out. When they first told me about this—how shall I say, about the boy—'

'Watch what you say, von Neumann.'

They looked at each other, and then at the crowd, to see if Captain de Silva was in the vicinity.

'A6,' said Dr von Neumann.

The telephone rang again and Mrs Oppenheimer answered it.

'How do you do, General? I'll tell him, yes. Oh, terrifically. Terrifically. Dr Baker is here too. Just fine. Thank you so much for calling, General Groves.'

The crowd waxed and waned. People walked aimlessly in pairs and trios. Hands went into pockets. Cigars went into mouths. Ice jingled in glasses. Dr von Neumann lost the game. The dancing began. Dr Teller demurred on the basis of his foot, and his wife danced with Dr Fuchs, who was, in spite of his nervousness, quite a tolerable partner. A woman's yodeling laughter filled the living room and began driving guests, in desperate convulsions, towards the exits. Around midnight Dr Teller met Dr Oppenheimer at the cocktail table and, having made the usual insignificant remarks that one makes at parties, began to broach the subject of his present problem. 'I must say,' he began. 'That is, I must say, the truth is, I am not entirely satisfied here.'

Dr Oppenheimer was stirring something in a glass. He spoke without looking up, his cigarette still in his mouth. 'You ought to have a drink,' he said.

'No,' said Dr Teller. 'I am serious.'

The director's blue eyes were all of a sudden upon Dr Teller.

'As I understand it,' said Dr Oppenheimer, 'you disagree with the way Dr Bethe is running the Theoretical Division.'

Dr Teller gazed down from under his thick brows at his hands, flat on the table edge. The stale fading flavor of gin hung about his back teeth and in the crypt of his throat. Unlike the American doctors he was not much of a drinker. Dr Oppenheimer seemed to be able to live off martinis without the slightest effect on his mental clarity.

'Here is my point about Dr Bethe,' Dr Teller began.

Dr Oppenheimer was looking among the glasses for his cocktail strainer.

'Where the devil—'

'I enjoy Dr Bethe's company very much. I have known him for a very long time. And there can be no doubt that he is a great and talented physician. He is, what we call in German a Geheimrat. But his work—you see, doctor, what Bethe does is he makes little bricks. You always know his work will be methodical and meticulous and—and—sturdy. But you see, that is not what I do. Of course, I have made some little bricks in my time, but it is not what I do well.'

'Uh huh.' Dr Oppenheimer had found the strainer and a martini glass and was pouring.

'I much prefer, and am much better at, exploring the various structures that can be made from the bricks, at seeing how the bricks stack up. Dr Bethe, you see, expects me to be a brick-maker like him. But that is simply not how I work, Dr Oppenheimer. It is unwise, I think, to expect me to work that way. These calculations—I mean, I can't speak about it here, but you understand.'

This metaphor of the bricks, which Dr Teller had repeated many times to his wife, was one that he considered particularly expressive. The director dropped his spent cigarette into an ashtray and, in a rapid and seemingly automatic movement, inserted another into his mouth, in its place. The martini lay glittering in its glass before him. Dr Oppenheimer rubbed his right eye with one of the knuckles of his right hand and began, in his careful baritone:

'I agree with you, Edward. I agree that a man of your ability ought to be doing what he does best. And I'm sure there are a few fine men who may be capable of taking on those calculations.' He lit his cigarette. 'I think with you, Teller, a new arrangement may be in order.'

'What do you mean?'

'I mean, you may be better employed as a sort of advisor.'

'Advising whom?'

'Why, the top brass. The leadership. Me, I suppose. It's only an idea at this stage, of course.'

Dr Teller paused. He had expected resistance from Dr Oppenheimer and was surprised by this. As much as he had previously disdained the decisions of the director, he could not deny the administrative logic of this sugges-tion. For it was true, he now realized, that while he was not suited to a subordinate position in the Theoretical Division, he would be equally ill-equipped to manage the bureaucratic humdrum of leading it. The notion of working outside of the Division and liaising directly with the director seemed, the more he considered it, to be the only one that made sense, for himself, for the boys. The only thing that he remained hesitant about was the thought of his Advanced Design, which he would be unable to pursue on his own.

'I would need to have some assistance, though,' he said, 'in my own research.'

'No man is an island,' said Dr Oppenheimer.

Was it possible, Dr Teller wondered, that the director did not dislike him? They stood for a moment watching the dancers.

'There is an idea, you know, in the Hindu Scripture,' said the director. 'A wise man—not quite a sannyasi, not a renunciant, I mean, in the full sense, but a wise man, who has partially renounced his worldly life. They call him a neighbor. He is a neighbor of the world. He still has his envelope of emptiness. Do you follow, Dr Teller? Here. Take a drink.'

11

Dr Teller seemed to be in a better mood when he departed that night. He and his wife were among the last to go. Dr Oppenheimer stood on the porch, his wife having retired to bed some time before. Beyond the limits of the little town all earth was at a halt—pitch dark, silent, for miles and miles, lightless as the sea. The last revellers reeled out at a slow amble, enfolding one another, staggering into the ciphers of their coats, their pearls and loose low neckties dangling, fumbling into the blackness. Dr Oppenheimer saw them off, married and single, soldier after sol-dier—'Good night, good night, good night'—and the door closed and he was alone with the stillness, the quiet, the simplicity of one of the simplest of all possible universes.

Dr Oppenheimer coughed. Out of the horn of the Victrola a slow voice, no longer human, intoned: 'There's a flaw in my flue...' He walked casually through the ruined living room, lifted the needle and put it away. His ears were ringing, a shrill constant sound. He was a little drunk, but it was the kind of drunkenness that causes one's problems to shrink, rather than expand. He felt that he was able, thus intoxicated, to perceive the shape of the great medical challenge that lay before him. He saw the prosthesis as a knot—a knot with an end somewhere that he must follow, discerning its loops and crossings and the kinks of its strands, untwisting and unraveling, from the great complexity, a little string. It was a problem of such elegance, of such technical sweetness, that he felt he would want to pursue it even if they were not in a race with the Germans.

It was his duty to solve this mystery. It had fallen to him and to no other. And he would find no consolation any-where but in the fulfilment of this task. D'altro non calme, he said to himself, as he moved through the kitchen, setting the chairs back on their feet, and sweeping into a heap a few shattered glasses. It felt right for him now to pledge in his heart, before termination of day, as though to invisible watchers, his commitment to this duty, in the words of the Italian poet. Life is straight—that was what George Herbert said, straight as a line. What an idea.

The ringing annoyed him. It was the sound of blood—Dr Oppenheimer understood this—in his inner ear, the alcohol having caused the vessels to swell. He passed the mantel-piece in which he kept, in a locked drawer, a few letters, recently received and recently answered, from a woman in California, to whom he knew he should not be writing.

He checked briefly on his young son, Peter. He was asleep. He went down the hallway to his room and found his wife awake, bolt upright, in a loose kimono, smoking and reading one of her mycology books.

'What's this stain?' she said. 'I don't remember—'

'My nose. The altitude.'

He undressed clumsily—long, thin, pale. Mrs Oppenheimer hummed and, lifting briefly before her face her side of the sheet, a lacework of cigarette-holes, inspected the stain.

'Terribly inconsiderate,' she said, 'seeing as I live in this bed.'

They lay down. Their arms, intermingled, clung and cleaved, below the sheet. He held her. They were at Planck's length from one another.

'What'll we do after the war?' said Mrs Oppenheimer.

'Hang up all our formal clothes,' said Dr Oppenheimer. 'No more suits and ties. We'll buy roller skates. We'll go together to the Himalayas, I'll keep you safe, you keep me sane.'

'Well'—she yawned—'That'll be something.'

He sat up.

'We will abroad!' he said. 'Alight out for parts unknown. Hell, I don't know. Our life and lines are free.'

His blue eyes, briefly, smiled at her in the dark. She lay on her back. Dr Oppenheimer felt again, or thought he felt, the acetic vapors, the vermouth-scented vapors, astir in his mind, and the words falling, troubled and wayward, tumbling to rest, wherever it is words fall, in the mind. D'altro non, and so on. And he thought again of the Vedas, and the envelope of—what had he said? Of emptiness. I have gone from thee, Pururavas, like the first of the dawns. I must read the Gita again, he thought. Once a year at least a man must read the Gita. He thought of Dr Teller and his bushy black brows—a very good doctor, very intelligent, but no Dr Bethe.

Then, sinking again into the bed, he laid his ear upon Mrs Oppenheimer's sternum, and listened, through the bones and tissues, to the leaking of her glands, and the beating of her heart, the closing of the valves, one after the other. He wondered. After the war. Something about that phrase struck him as strange, as though he had no place speaking about himself as he would be then. He thought of an old theory, one he had worked on during the Depression, that is to say, during his youth, and never quite made an end of. It concerned the deaths of stars, the collapse of their cores, their curious metamorphoses. The heaviest stars, his theory had predicted, would go on collapsing endlessly upon themselves. If a man could make it to the surface of one of these singular objects he would find himself in a state of perpetual free-fall. The rabbit hole. But why did he think of that now?

'Remember that time we were camping in the Frijoles Canyon,' he said, 'not long after we met, and you said—'

'Yes, I remember what I said.'

Mrs Oppenheimer was almost asleep.

'Let me finish. We were going outside, and you told me, something, I don't remember, I think you told me to put a hat on. And I said, As you like it, and you said—'

'I remember what I said!'

They lay still. The shudder of the southerly winds. Leaves, torn from the boughs of trees, came spiraling to rest. In the morning Dr Oppenheimer would wake his wife, and they would rise early, as they did most Sundays, and go riding.

12

The boy had reached that troubling age when one typically begins to fall prey to sensuous distractions. From certain windows, at certain hours, small groups of females were visible to him, most often at a great distance, vanishing into arroyos and stealing through the serried hills, or strolling through the Technical Area—though they never came anywhere near him or the other boy.

They were young—perhaps sixteen or seventeen. Most often they wore the khaki skirts and blazers of the Women's Army Corps. Yet sometimes they wore other things—dresses of mauve, orange, blue, gray, or other interesting colors. For a while this was little more than mere spectroscopic fascination. But after a few weeks of watching, an event occurred that altered significantly the nature of his inquiries.

There was a room in Building B, on the ground floor, where he was often left when not being measured by doctors. Depending on which of his six planes he was laid, and his orientation on the table, he found that he often had one, or even two eyes, exposed to the large window, which gave him a view of a path frequented by secretaries and stenographers and other lowly workers whom he did not otherwise see. Down this path came the girls one day in their bobby socks, with bundles of books in their arms, at a wild sprint. To see a long and golden female leg sticking out in its distinctive manner from a bobby sock and terminating at its other end beneath a restless hem is a peculiar thing for any young boy. It was, to our incapacitated hero, a thing of incomparable and excruciating strangeness.

'My God, I'm pooped, I'm gonna keel over,' said one of the young ladies, who was sandy-haired.

'Let's stop a minute,' said another.

'We'll be late,' said yet another. There were four in total.

'I don't want to go in there just yet.'

The sandy-haired girl dropped her books in the dust and another, who had dark eyes and dark hair, did the same.

'Oh, this wretched—' said the first girl, bending down and rubbing her knee violently.

'My heart is absolutely flying,' said the dark-haired girl.

'So's mine.'

'Give me your lousy arm,' said the first girl.

'What for?'

'For your heart rate. Look, it's the easiest thing in the world. Mind you don't use your thumb. The thumb has its own pulse, did you know that?'

Understanding very little of this, the boy watched as she snatched the limp white stem of the dark-haired girl's arm, twisted it and placed two of her fingers over its little wrist. Then she held up her watch and studied it. They bent to look, four little hooked noses.

'Isn't this the quietest two months you've ever had?' said a tall, freckled girl, who was still clutching her books to her chest. 'I didn't think it would be like this. When my father said we had to move because of the war I could never have imagined it would be so...'

'So what?'

'Well, so darned small.'

'You must have had a swell time back in Chicago,' ventured the dark-haired girl, her arm still imprisoned.

'I'm just glad Mother and I got to come along this time. My dad's always been moving around because of the Navy. Always away on a ship somewhere.'

'Shut your cake holes,' said the first girl. 'I can't count.'

The dark-haired girl waited. She was a little smaller than the others, narrower in the shoulders, and she held her head awkwardly. Her legs were somewhat strange, the boy noticed—bowed outward, just slightly.

'Not that it hasn't been a good summer,' continued the tall girl. 'Riding and hiking and swimming and everything.'

'Just you wait, when the winter comes we'll be able to go skiing.'

'Right, and then all anybody will talk about will be skiing.'

'One hundred and ten beats per minute,' declared the first girl.

The dark-haired girl drew her arm away in such a wild and carefree fashion that the boy felt a renewed pang of sadness for having no arms of his own.

'How did you figure that, Nella?'

'Arithmetic.'

'What do you say to a root beer after old Bacher turns us loose?' suggested the freckled girl, and the others assented, scrambling to recoup their books.

'We really are going to be late. Let's go!'

The mad patter of their shoes was heard again and the dust of the path went up in a cloud. But they did not all go. Three went, one lingered. The girl with the dark hair, with the dark eyes and the bow legs and the strangely hanging head, remained in her place. She looked around her, and said, 'Just a minute.'

She looked once in the boy's direction. But she did not do what people normally did, and turn away, and go on. In fact, she kept looking. Then, even more strangely, she took a few bandy-legged steps from the path, then a few more, each time drawing closer to the boy's window. He began to feel strange. Raising her hand to shield her eyes from the sun, she craned her neck and peered for a moment, through the glass, at the boy. To describe the look she gave him is no simple matter. It was not the look of indifference to which he was accustomed. Nor was it the inquisitive look he had come to expect from the doctors. It was not a smile of sympathy. It was not a grimace of disdain, of disgust, or of pity. It was not a look of approval, and it was certainly not a look of desire. No, this was something different. It was something new and unexpected.

The look she gave him was his own look. She looked at him in just the same way as he looked at her. Whatever ineffable combination of emotions had just risen up within him was reflected and reduplicated exactly in those dark eyes. The boy knew at once that he was looking at one who was a member of his own kind. She was beautiful, but he did not think about the fact that she was beautiful. His thoughts were overwhelmed by a sense of perfect comprehension between them, a pure consonance of minds that was suddenly more important to him than her beauty.

She turned to the side. Her skirt swayed. She cried to the scattering girls, 'Hold your horses! Hold your—Hey!' Her voice was high and trembling. The sunlight caught her beaming lips. She spun and took to the path again, her feet splayed and gangling, and slipped out of sight.

The boy felt for a moment as though his mind had gone with her. It had bounded out after her, uncoiled and left his body deserted and bereft of thought. Then thoughts began to come to him. He tried to settle the clamor of his soul, to return to a logical frame of mind, but the more he thought these new thoughts, the more he was deranged. His head was at once like a garden of newblown flowers. He, who had been largely indifferent to the human race, was suddenly seized by an entirely new set of feelings.

It was, to say the least, a baffling and interesting episode. But the boy did not foresee just how deep its bafflement would go, how it would possess him and grow within him over time. When night fell he was still thinking about it, replaying the moment in his mind and wondering if it had really been as he remembered it. But since it was not unusual for the boy to think continuously on a single subject for several hours, he supposed that it would pass.

The next morning, however, when Dr Wilson came to take him to be measured in the room with the Van de Graaff machines, it had not passed. On the contrary, he now felt a resolution that he must see the dark-haired girl again and verify somehow his version of the events. And it continued, as the days went by, to invade his thoughts, in a very annoying manner. Each day, as he was brought into the usual rooms to be examined, he hoped that she would appear, and though he knew it would not resolve this nagging in his mind, and would in fact probably increase it, nevertheless he wanted to see her.

On rare occasions, separated by days or weeks of longing, when all the variables of position and clarity of aspect and time of day were in alignment, then his wish, to be tortured with the sight of her, was granted. He resorted to the only method of courtship at his disposal: staring. He strained with earnest diligence, attuned his eye to any variation of expression or gesture, sought with fastidious attention signs of a recurrence of that unique comprehending look. But it is safe to say that her gaze did not find him, however much he willed it to, during this period of their intercourse.

He gained small pieces of information about the young female. Though he had no command of language, he was able to pick up names. The name of this girl, at least he thought her name, was Miss Piles. Piles! he said to himself. What loveliness. He learned that she owned a gabardine coat. She often ate apples. On one occasion she was holding a dog. He learned something of her social circle. She was always in the company of the same group of girls. Their constant presence troubled the boy, for he feared that they would make her too much like the rest of the human population, that she would become silly and frivolous like them and lose whatever it was that had enabled her to notice him.

But the large questions remained unanswered, the chief of these being the precise nature of her feelings towards him. It was very likely she had left the path and approached his window out of mere curiosity, and had no other thoughts about him. But something about that look she had given him seemed to indicate something more, that a connexion existed between them. It seemed to suggest—in contravention of all common sense—that there was something about him worthy of drawing from other people an interest that was not chiefly medical. And he began to wonder, as any physically hideous person does after an intimation of romance, if there was not something else at play, some fate or destiny designed to prevent human beings from being alone.

There was no indication yet, of course, that she was actually interested in him. But he asked himself if such a thing was conceivable. Could it not be, then, that Miss Piles's type of ideal lover comprised small, square, hard, hairless, featureless boys? Was this asking too much of the universe? Could it be that she had some fault in her eyes, or a mental problem, an illness of some kind, that caused her to become attracted to him?

Such were the wonderings, at once self-loathing and narcissistic, with which he whiled away the hours. He did not acknowledge that each sighting of Miss Piles represented the extinguishment of a thousand wishes he had not dared to articulate to himself, and the igniting of a thousand more, nor did he realize that his mind was becoming, in this fatuous process, like a grate of dim overworked ashes.

13

It took a while for the boy to recover from the shocking incident of being looked at by a girl. But life went on around him, and the doctors continued in their charge to develop the prosthesis. Dr Oppenheimer, true to his word, released Dr Teller from his prior duties and appointed him as a special theoretical advisor. He gave the calculations which Dr Teller had refused to do to the young Dr Fuchs, and the Theoretical Division began to operate more smoothly.

Hiccups soon arose, however, in the work of the Los Alamos doctors. By late spring it became gradually clear to them that they would have to design not one but two prostheses—that the physical demands of each of the boys were to be quite different. They spent longer and longer hours in the Technical Area, debating into the night. The boy, ignorant as ever, watched them working and scarcely noticed the disruption.

General Groves was summoned from Washington, but his arrival was somewhat delayed. His wife had inconvenienced him by having one of her nervous episodes. The general picked her up from the U.S.O. center, where she had very nearly made an embarrassment of herself, and drove her home. She sat beside him in the car, gazing at him as he drove with great dark eyes ringed with liquidated mascara.

'Deano,' she said. 'Oh, Deano.'

Deano was another of his nicknames.

'That's enough,' he said.

Ten minutes passed. They were driving through wisteria trees.

'I'm worried about Gwendolyn,' said Mrs Groves. Her voice, in moments of this kind, had a tendency to go very high, and then to fall away, within a few words, into a whisper. 'I don't think we'll have enough money to—to send her to college.'

'Don't worry,' said the general. 'I have put away stocks, and I will sell them.'

He said this to appease her. It was not true. A patter of rain was heard on the windshield. He turned on the wipers.

This was the last thing he needed. He feared he was losing his grip on the boys. The war was going badly too. And now his ridiculous wife had to stick her nose in. It was the fault of the family, he thought. She had a mad sister who had married a Chinaman. Trashy sort of people. She ought to forget all about them and get on with things. Financial matters were not for her to trouble herself with. There were some tasks he left to his wife—the decisions about hairdos, for instance—but for the most part he had a handle on things. She had no idea of the great significance of the boy. She did not even know the boy existed.

'Perhaps, my dear, it's your work at the U.S.O.' he said, tenderly. 'It's getting to you. Tiring you. I think you ought to give up the singing for a while.'

'The singing—' said Mrs Groves.

He knew what she was thinking. What would she be without her singing? Hour after hour, doing her arpeggios, with no regard for his need of peace and repose. He thought obscurely of his long walks in the zoo with Gwendolyn in the pram, when he was still a First Lieutenant. All your twenties crammed with toil, as the poets say. Who said that, he wondered, Longfellow?

Mrs Groves did not argue. She knew his word was final. The rain had not ceased. He hoped it was not as bad as this in New Mexico. Nothing is worse, he thought, than the hard rain they get in New Mexico. He had always hated storms. He glanced at her again, at the mop of thinned wavy hair, at the weak, black, shimmering eyes. She held a scrunched tissue, a Kleenex, in her left hand, palm upward, as though it was an infant bird.

'I'll get a job at Garfinckel's,' she said.

'Garfinckel's,' he said, in a tone of disdain.

'Mm-hm,' she said, taking up the tissue in her right hand and dabbing at her nose. Then, after a pause, went on, 'We are so different in some ways, Deano. As different as you could imagine two people to be, in some ways. I know it's such a great burden for you, and your work.'

What was he supposed to say to this? She knew nothing of his work. Was she being sarcastic? Women's trouble, he thought. The eyeliner trickled. He thought of all the doctors in Los Alamos, waiting for him. He imagined them saying, Where is General Groves? Where is Groves at this crucial juncture? He saw them all before him, bent upon the precise hour of his arrival. In a way, it was how he wanted it to be. Drawn tight—plucked right. That is how one makes the finest music. He would arrive like the sun on a well-ordered orchard. He thought of the regiments encamped in the deserts of North Africa, and in the jungles of the Pacific.

There was an image in General Groves's head of a perfect boy, an orderly boy, utterly perfectly made. He knew they would not attain this. He had done the same thing with the large five-pointed building he had recently constructed for the War Department. What mattered was not the attainment of the idea, no—but that the men believed in it. They would hold to this ideal and thus attain the closest thing to it that their combined energies could generate. A project like this would be measured in gracefully executed compromises. Plans were not worth a plumb nickel, at the end of the day. To clench one's teeth, to be realistic, but not to compromise, to press on, in spite of the absolute weariness of the million inevitable failures of any great task—that is discipline. General Groves knew this. And he almost considered explaining it to his wife. But he decided against it.

'I'm sorry,' she said. 'I'm sorry, Deano.'

It was two o'clock. Time for the Joe Penner Hour, with the celebrated 'Wanna buy a duck?' routine, which the general did not like to miss. He switched on the radio.

'This ought to cheer you up,' he said. 'Listen. The duck's name is Goo-Goo.'

That evening he was in Los Alamos. He and Dr Oppenheimer stood outside one of the storehouses, where some old failed prototypes lay on the ground, and discussed the recent problems. The air was still—crystal. There was a scent of piñon. Behind them, in the west, the ranges of the Jemez seemed to loom extremely close.

'Forty-nine is proving difficult,' said Dr Oppenheimer. 'Temperamental.'

Forty-nine was the code-name of the other boy. The director paced relentlessly on the crunching gravel and smoked as he talked. General Groves had some chocolate turtles in his pocket, which he dipped into continually.

'How much does this slow us down?' he said.

'We'll be lucky to have one boy ready within a year. The trouble is we really ought to have more than one. It's no good having just one, if the Germans have two or three.'

'Think the Germans could be having the same problems as us?'

'Don't know.'

Dr Oppenheimer bowed his head. His face was eclipsed by the wide flat brim of his hat. He flicked, with a long white finger, a piece of ash from his necktie.

'We'll get it done,' he said. 'I'm sure of that. My concern is that they could still beat us to it.'

The general took the opportunity to raise the delicate matter of espionage. According to Intelligence, he said, there were almost certainly attempts being made, by Germans, or even Russians, to spy on their operation. He said that the name of anyone associated with Communists must be reported to Intelligence.

This caused Dr Oppenheimer to think of his letters—the letters on his mantelpiece—from the woman in California. His old flame. The problem with this woman was not merely that she was not his wife. She also happened to be a communist. He could not help but wonder what the general would think, if he knew of this woman.

'Compartmentalization,' General Groves was saying. 'That's the way to do it. To every man his own little piece of the job—and nothing more.'

He chewed on one of his turtles and watched the sun lowering over the Jemez mountains. They heard the sound of a canyon wren—a shrill ecstatic plummeting cry.

'In life too,' the general said, 'compartmentalization is very useful. Especially for a soldier. I remember when I was a young man, when I was in France. I said to myself, Groves, you must decide what your lot is. Are you going to be somebody who spends his days bowling with his buddies, who goes and plays craps at the Monte-Carlo, who fornicates with French prostitutes? Or are you going to be somebody who—who devotes himself to his country, and his God? I made up my mind.'

This idea was quite alien to the director. He could scarcely imagine what it would be like—to be one man only, one self, to have three or four women, for all the six hundred thousand hours of your life. Dr Oppenheimer wanted to be everything at once. He watched the sky congealing, turning red, the Rayleigh scattering. In places it was as though the ground had turned to glass.

'I partially agree,' he said, 'but no scientific inquiry can succeed without some degree of openness.'

'Hmm,' said the general.

They walked back inside and discussed the few logistical changes that needed to be made and other specifics of their course of action. Then the general took leave of the doctors and returned to Washington.

PART III

1

Towards the end of the summer Dr Oppenheimer went to Berkeley and met with Dr Lawrence, who had an office there. Dr Lawrence was enormously optimistic about the future of the treatments, and assured Dr Oppenheimer that he would have several more patients ready to send to Los Alamos over the next few months.

An hour after his meeting in Berkeley was concluded, Dr Oppenheimer took a train across the bay, to San Francisco. It was a warm humid evening, the sky was clear, the water was still.

He sat smoking, his hat and valise on the seat beside him, his eyes fixed vacantly on the window. The train rattled across the Bay Bridge. Dr Oppenheimer seemed to pay no attention to anyone around him, and stared, hardly blinking, with an intense concentration, at the girders passing in the fading light.

When the train stopped, he rose to his feet at once.

'Your hat,' said a gentleman in a gabardine coat.

'Thank you,' said Dr Oppenheimer. 'What can I have been thinking?'

He gathered up his things, put on his hat, and left the carriage. For some time he wandered through the crowd in the Transbay Terminal, round the steps and rails, looking about him.

At length, something arrested his attention. It was a woman, dark-haired and pale, leaning alone upon a rail, her head bowed, her hands clasped, one leg crossed in front of the other. Dr Oppenheimer approached this woman, he removed his hat, he kissed her, and they passed together out of the terminal, talking in low voices.

The imprudence of this course of action was evident, even to the director himself. Undoubtedly the sensible thing for him to do after his meeting would have been to go to a hotel, take a room, fall asleep, and leave early in the morning for Los Alamos and the boys. But that is not what Dr Oppenheimer did. Rather, in contravention of all rational considerations, and in a clear divergence from what he had told the Army, and his wife, he had yielded to the importunities of the woman from his past—Jean Tatlock was her name—and had agreed to meet her.

He was not guided in this by any overpowering emotional investment in Jean Tatlock, nor, it is important to note, by any significant dissatisfaction with his marriage. It was a decision that he took lightly, and indeed it gave him great joy, after working so long and so intensely on the difficult questions of the boy's treatment, to take a decision lightly, to commit himself, without having to care about anything, into something resembling a life.

To Dr Oppenheimer, it was as simple as this—the woman had been feeling depressed, and she had asked him to come, so he had come. But to say he did not also sense the strange intoxication of infidelity, to say he did not also crave, in some small way, to be again among strange bedclothes, as in his younger days, to feel again the clutch of strange hands, and the hairs of strange heads, to wake again in a single woman's apartment, to be shaken by uncommon emotions, to feel raw and dubious and to be utterly uncertain again, and on the precipice of great incidents of the heart—to say he did not also want all this would not be entirely accurate either.

For the most part, Dr Oppenheimer opted not to probe his own judgment. Now that he was here, inconceivably, in the presence of Jean Tatlock, he felt the tingling sense that accompanies spontaneous decisions. He felt the blood flowing freely from his nervous heart into his extremities, as though the universe itself was conspiring with him and compelling him to action. And as he passed out of the terminal, with his hand in his pocket, and her hand in his hand, in his pocket, it seemed the most natural thing in the world, and he pitied all those people around him who were not committing adultery.

All this will come to no good, he said to himself. Nothing will be as you expect. It is impossible to predict just how it will all turn out. Your life is uncertain and strange again. It is the old strangeness—you had almost forgotten this. This feeling. Do not speculate.

They sat in a small bar on Broadway. He listened to the faint Mexican music—was it Mariachi music?—and he looked at her sweet familiar miserable face. She had green eyes, a wild tangle of black hair, a low Hellenic jaw, marble skin, a deadpan stare. He loved this—he almost loved her for her deadpan stare. She was a doctor, a pediatric psychiatrist—twenty-nine years old, four years younger than his wife. Conversation came naturally, as though no time had passed. They talked briefly about the war, the millions of murders. Dr Tatlock was stunned that he had actually come. It was wild, she said—*wild*, that was the word she used. She had an excellent speaking voice, a contralto.

'Why won't you tell me what you're working on?' she said.

Dr Oppenheimer said nothing.

'It must be some kind of war work.'

She leaned her head against the window, a cigarette in her hand. He took a drink of tequila, put down his glass, and, smiling, moved it carefully across the tabletop, following it with his eyes. She watched it too. They were not alone, but the bar was quiet—a small Monday night crowd. The dance floor was empty.

'Tell me about your situation,' he said.

'You know my situation. I've told you everything in my letters. I've made mincemeat of my life.'

She laughed an unhappy laugh.

'You exaggerate,' said Dr Oppenheimer.

'I don't know where to begin.'

'Begin in medias res.'

'Well, I have a new shrink.'

'What's he like?'

'Not all bad, I suppose. He's very—how do I describe it?—he has a very skeptical animus. And I still go to party meetings. I mean, I still believe in it all. I suppose I do. I just wouldn't want to go on living if I didn't believe that in Russia everything is better. I don't know. The war has confused things, you know? It's awful.' She stabbed out her cigarette. 'And there's of course the other—well, other dull things I'd rather not go into.'

'You don't have to.'

'Ah, but I want to tell you, Robert. That's the difficulty. There's no one I can explain things to like you. I can't put my finger on the problem. It may even be that the problem doesn't exist, at least not in the way I think it exists. It's like there are two incompatible states in my head.'

'Which are?'

'Well, it doesn't matter what they are. Never mind what they are.'

She sighed, and for an instant her face broke into a helpless kind of smile.

'I'm boring you,' she said. 'I know it's stupid but I can't help but take the whole thing absolutely, tremendously seriously. I suppose you think I'm a terrific mess.'

He hesitated—long enough to create an uncertainty—and said, 'Nothing about you bores me.'

This caused a small change in Dr Tatlock, which was not lost on the observant Dr Oppenheimer. A light went into her eyes, a faint glistening glow, like dew on a damask rose, and though she dropped her gaze to the table, and went on talking in a casual tone, he saw that she was flustered, and knew she was as enamored as ever. Her defenses were broken.

He felt a thrill in his blood. He had almost forgotten what it was to make an advance with a woman. He wanted to leap towards her and throw his arms about her and recite to her all the old foolish poems he had committed to memory in his long, almost interminable adolescence. All the other people in the bar, and all the people walking past outside in the neon haze in their hats and coats, could just as well have been citizens of ancient Rome, he felt at that moment so distinct from them. He feared none of them and he took none of them seriously. He was far from the boy, far from the institution. He had stepped off the hill and out of the war. How unreal it all seemed!

'We should go,' he said, 'before long.'

'Sure.'

'You—er—you have some place I can stay?'

'I'm still in the old apartment.'

'With the balcony?'

She sucked on her cigarette, nodding.

'Le balcon,' she said.

For a moment they did not speak, but eyed each other. It was like the old days. On the sidewalk, in the trains, at the parties, at the party meetings, in the bed, at the bus stop, in the lobby, in the car, on the balcony, in the mornings, in the evenings—always tethered at the pupils. The old days.

'Thank you for coming,' she said.

He got them another drink. When he came back he put his arm around her, and he smelled her—rose and patchouli. Very unlike his wife. She slipped a pale hand into his coat pocket, and withdrew an object, which she held up before her face and scrutinized with a charming, puzzled, cross-eyed look.

'What's this?' she said.

It was a lithium battery.

'Stay out of my pockets,' he said.

He sat down. She smiled, lifted her rounded chin and

swept the black hair back from her face. The headlights of Broadway danced around her neck. He knew he should not be doing this. He now wanted more than ever to go with her, to feel her hands, her soft, slim refined hands, and her cold soft skin.

But she kept talking, analyzing herself, as was her custom. Dr Jean Tatlock was a great lover of self-analysis. And even more than analyzing herself she loved analyzing her analysis of herself. Evidently she wanted to get to the bottom of whatever was eating her. So she went on, describing to him her days, which consisted, she said, of seeing her young patients in the morning and coming home in the afternoon and lying on her bed in various postures among the silk and the satin and the tulle and the pillows, and there were certain days, she said, certain inescapable days, when it would take her all day to boil an egg, or to change the bed, or to bring herself to appear before the cashier at the grocery store, or the bus-driver, or any other so-called human being, and when she would just have to lie there like a piece of tenderized meat, and wonder if the heart had finally fallen out of everything and if everything was finally seared, smeared, bleared, singed, tinged, tainted, trodden, and so on, beyond repair—all this she analyzed, re-analyzed, examined and weighed before him, each item in its turn.

Dr Oppenheimer made a few remarks, when called upon. He offered no hollow words of comfort or flattery. He said nothing predictable. When he spoke, it was to subject her problems to his rigorous scientific and moral reasoning, which he knew was exactly what she wanted. She did not want to be pitied. He quoted from Spinoza's Ethics and the Nitishatakam of Bhartṛhari. He spoke of eternal truths. This impressed her greatly, and probably even helped her. A few such phrases was all it took—careful, restrained, balanced phrases—to give her the impression that he understood her as nobody else did, and that he could articulate parts of her soul with which she herself had been previously unacquainted.

Their few hours in the bar seemed to pass quickly. The time slipped away without effort or thought. Soon they were back in Dr Tatlock's green Plymouth and were talking of other things, and she was trying to remember the poem about the trinity—'Batter my heart, three-person'd God...'—trying to get it out from beginning to end. He had always preferred the one that began, 'Since I am coming to that holy room...' And before they could remember either of them, they had begun to kiss one another. Then they were in the apartment, remarking, between long wordless (almost wordless) periods, on the night's clarity, and how all of San Francisco could be seen from the balcony, for there was no fog, for the first time in the history of San Francisco it was a night without fog. All could be seen— the black slab of the sea, the sky, and the pale houses spread out in rows, like tombstones, and every lighted window, and the thousand little lives, shifting like grass. They were side by side, almost asleep, and she was holding him against her, knowing he would soon be going again, and talking to him half-asleep with closed eyes, so as not to lose a minute of his conversation, and holding onto him, as though it were a question of physical parting, with all her strength.

2

The next morning, Dr Oppenheimer felt a sense of misgiving. He knew he must return to Los Alamos. He must go at once, he thought, to the airport, and buy a plane ticket, and fly back. He said all this to himself while he was dressing. It was the third time they had dressed that morning and finally they were doing it in earnest. He was putting the buttons through the button-holes of his white shirt, looking out over the bay, when something shifted, in his stomach, and he felt suddenly as though he had ingested a large quantity of sand. He felt it distinctly—the settling of a cold, dense, small weight.

Now that it was virtually over, the foolishness and the danger of his action was clear to him. What the devil was he doing? To meet with a card-carrying Communist, when his every move was sure to be scrutinized, was absurd. And what an unkind thing to do to his wife. She would murder him. And if the Army found out—he would lose everything. All he had worked for, this great opportunity would be lost, they would take it away from him and give it to somebody like Dr Lawrence.

'I must be off, Jean,' he said.

She was silent for a few minutes, though she had been talking previously.

'Won't you tell me where you're going?' she said.

Dr Oppenheimer did not look at her, but kept his eyes fastened on the balcony, the water gleaming grayish-blue, and the tall red bridge.

'No,' he said.

He sat down and put on his shoes. He gazed about her cluttered apartment, which looked just as it had always looked, full of old books chosen for their antique appearance, long dead roses—she considered them more beautiful than living ones—draperies, scent-bottles, pill-bottles, paintings, small marble busts and figurines, jewelry, perfumes, makeup, clothing scattered in sumptuous folds. Dr Tatlock was standing before the mirror in a black dress. He watched her pushing her earrings through the holes in her ear-lobes, putting on her lipstick, frowning, peering, holding her head at different angles. And it saddened him that all this beauty was bleeding away, and real life was returning.

They left the apartment and went down to her car. She insisted on driving him to the airport. He could see she was upset and wanted him to stay longer. She kept looking at him—gazing at him adoringly, with long, submissive, melo-dramatic looks, farewelling him with her eyes, admiring him for the last time. She began to speak wistfully about their parting.

'It was so short,' she said. 'And now, when will I see you? Just as I convince myself you actually showed up, I have to convince myself that you're gone again—'

She had become all skittish, like a deer. She kept lingering back, hesitating, deliberately walking slowly, not wanting it to end. It was plain to see some effort was required to prevent herself from weeping.

Dr Oppenheimer was rational about things.

'It's reality,' he said as they drove down the Bayshore Highway. 'We always knew it would come to—er—something of this nature. Sure, things are unpleasant now, but it's reality. It's the world. Happiness is not so important. Man is not meant to walk around in a state of perpetual euphoria. That would be awful. A sort of priapism. Unhappiness is—noise, you know. You can make a machine with no specification but that it must run noiselessly, but what matters is what it does—what does the machine do, that is what you must determine. You see?'

She did not reply. He felt that his genius was not working. It was a sun-drenched day—wide glittering pale gray California concrete, sunny cars, sea-blue sky.

Now that he had begun to panic a little, the charm of her melancholy was wearing off. If he was not careful she would cause a scene at the airport, and draw attention to him, and he had begun to imagine what calamities would ensue if somebody should happen to recognize him. His mind was now full of the boy and the Army and the terrible trouble he may be in. He even sensed some duplicity in her asking him here. What could she possibly have expected? She had asked him to come. He had helped her.

She could not ask for more than he was capable of.

They arrived at the airport.

'Do you want me to come inside with you?' said Dr Tatlock, as they got out of the car.

'No, no.'

'Oh.'

Dr Oppenheimer drew breath.

'You must try not to rely on anybody,' he said. Then he added, 'And you must stop the letters too, for a while.'

She looked at him tragically. Dr Oppenheimer felt bad about this, to an extent, but he also knew that because of this merciless remark, at some future time, some future tenderness let fall, supposedly by accident, from his lips, would seem all the more genuine, to Dr Tatlock. Its long-term impact, then, upon her affections, was still to be in his favor. In time she would appreciate his honesty.

'You know,' he said, 'I am always straight with you. Aren't I?'

He tried to console her.

'Things will be alright,' he said. 'Really. I know you'll be alright.'

He took her hand, as before, and held it tightly. He looked at her, with feeling. He meant it. He wanted her to be happy.

She walked him to the terminal. Her mood seemed to improve.

She didn't want to fight, she said. Finally they reached the door and could go no further.

'It was wonderful to see you,' he said.

They kissed.

'Good luck with whatever it is you're doing,' she said.

For a moment she stood before him in all her nacreous

misery, and he saw that her cheeks were flushed and suffused with blotches of the palest lavender and rose. He felt terribly sorry for her, and wondered if it was genuine. So little time had passed, it seemed, from getting off the train until now, that he felt he had hardly seen her at all. He almost wished he could stay and cease from all his work with the boys. He pushed his hat back from his head, straightened his tie, and turned from her. He felt a terrible weariness. He knew he would go and she would stand there and watch him go and he would not turn back because he abhorred such sentimentality and did not want to give her the wrong idea.

'See you again,' she said.

He murmured something, something clever, as he went, but it was lost in the din of the airplanes, swooping and roaring high above them. And she did not ask him to repeat himself, as far as he knew.

Some time later, as he sat in the airplane, observing in the window his own tired reflection, his cheek poised gracefully on two thin fingers, Dr Oppenheimer regretted his bluntness towards Dr Tatlock, and thought he should probably have been a little nicer. But it is better, he thought, to part with honesty and objectivity, than on false terms.

He now had to address the rather prickly questions of what to tell his wife, and what to tell the U.S. Army. It was strange to him how rarely he had thought of Mrs Oppenheimer during his trip, and beforehand. It was as though the whole thing had had nothing to do with her, until this moment. There was a good chance she would not suspect anything. She had known he was going to California, and he had not told her what time he would be back. His work often detained him, and he could not have been expected to telephone her, because of the secrecy of the work. In fact, regulations required him to conceal from his wife what he was doing or thinking at any time. She would probably not even ask him about it. And if she did, it was easily explained.

But some sense of virtue made him doubt that this was the right course of action. He worried also about the Army. Would General Groves notice that he had made no call, sent no telegram, told nobody, sent no message? Could Intelligence find out where he had been?

The plane landed in Albuquerque and Dr Oppenheimer arranged for a car to take him up to the mesa. Usually logistical arrangements vexed him, but today he executed them with ease. He did it all as though by instinct, his eyes watching everything with a strange, detached alertness, as though observing somebody else. The last twenty-four hours had changed him in a way, had made him unafraid of life and its challenges. He felt light and alert. He felt like a physical part of the physical universe. He felt like John Wayne. I am John Wayne, he said to himself, and I do not wave a white flag at life. An energy that was not his own compelled him onwards, a humid wind blew him on, Flaubert's vent tiède, with the extraordinary ease that is found in dreams. His body went on taking care of its own affairs and he was free to remain in his mind. It was still better, he thought, to be troubled with women, than to be alone.

He arrived in Los Alamos. No cataclysm accompanied his return. No Military Police arrested him at the gates. The same uniformed guards were there as always, and they greeted him in their usual bored fashion. There was no congregation of crazed wives waiting in the street. All was normal and at peace.

He had decided he must do the honorable thing and tell Mrs Oppenheimer the truth. Just as Genji, on his return from exile, did not hesitate to inform Murasaki about his escapades, so Dr Oppenheimer would proceed with a frank and factual account of his time in California, withholding nothing. She was depressed, he would say, and I had to go. He even briefly considered the possibility of mentioning the thing casually, as though in a modern and liberal marriage such as theirs there was nothing unusual in spending a night with another woman—but he soon discounted this. He would need to apologize. An apology was unavoidable. He had committed an indiscretion and he must take responsibility.

He got out of the car and walked up the road towards his house, his valise in his hand. How strange it was that this simple object had been with him all along. He had hardly noticed it, yet here it was, in his hand. The sun had sunk below the plateau and the land was dark. The sky seemed enormous. There was a sense one always got when returning to Los Alamos after being in a city, a sense of being up on top of the earth, in a strange nowhere, floating above civilization. He saw lights in the offices of the Technical Area where doctors were still working on the boys and their prostheses. All his work was there, and all the uncertainties and the unsolved questions of the boys. He felt a deep unease.

He was just as confused as he had predicted he would be, but in a way that was not as he had predicted, as he had also predicted. None of this was any consolation. His lips still had the distended feeling from his time with Dr

Tatlock. He stood a moment beneath the huge black sky perforated with stars, wanting to laugh and to cry aloud, wondering if his wife would be asleep and if he should wake her, or tell her in the morning, and how he should tell her. He gazed down along the stretch of his front lawn, towards the knotted garden and the pines. Then he went into the house.

She was sitting at the table with a glass in her hands. She was very still. Her eyes, fixed upon the table, were ice-cold. He looked at her, and as the moment swiftly passed in which he could have made an immediate confession, he decided that it would be simpler to say nothing to her about Dr Tatlock.

'Well, I'm home,' he said.

And he talked to her briefly about Dr Lawrence, and Berkeley, and the beautiful mountains and the mist and the sea. She received him cordially, asked him a few vague questions, but said very little and hardly looked at him. At length he told her he was awfully tired, from the journey, and retired to bed.

'I'll come with you,' she said.

But in a most uncharacteristic act, she did not go at once, as she had said she would. She remained a little longer at her place, at the table, staring down before her, without moving.

3

Mrs Oppenheimer's unusual quietness, which persisted for some weeks after his return, convinced Dr Oppenheimer that she knew of his indiscretion.

He was not sure how she knew—whether she had found the letters, or arrived at the conclusion by some other method of deduction. She was cold with him for several weeks. She spoke to him less, paid more attention to gardening and other solitary activities, and devoted more time to their son. But she did not raise the matter of Dr Tatlock. After a few weeks, her mood seemed to ease without any apparent reason, and she began speaking to him as before. They started fighting again, which convinced him they were still in love. The subject of his trip, however, was not alluded to.

Dr Oppenheimer felt the usual regret that follows affairs of this kind, and for a time he could not look at an Army officer or a person from Intelligence without feeling the return of that weight in his stomach. But nobody said anything, and soon the complexities of the prosthetic designs fully occupied his mental energies. The war was not going well—the number of American casualties had risen rapidly, the fighting was savage everywhere. The doctors were pressing ahead, and with his mind full of mathematics, he had no time to stew about anything.

In time the Oppenheimers acquired a kind of unspoken understanding. They became like two entangled subsystems—he knew how things stood between them, without knowing precisely how she felt towards him, or even how he felt towards her. He still expected that a resolution would occur at some future time—but he did not know how, or when. There would be plenty of time for serious arguments after the war. For now the matter seemed to have disappeared out of sight.

He did not hear from Dr Tatlock, and this gave him great relief.

4

That summer the doctors decided, with the general's approval, that they must have a test—a complete trial of the workings of the prosthetic system.

Tests are an unfortunate fact of life for little boys. One cannot hope to attain a place in the world without being exposed to rigorous examination. The institution at Los Alamos, in spite of its experimental approach, was not immune to this axiom. The boy had no idea of this plan. He was largely left alone at this period, for the doctors were focusing on the problems of the other boy. The boy felt some curiosity.

Occasionally he saw prosthetic parts being carried past him—metal pipes, tin boxes, steel plates and panels, rods, plugs of various shapes and sizes, antennas and various other anatomical components. But he paid them little attention.

The girl continued to infest his thoughts. He had been ignored before. He had spent his entire life being ignored—but not like this, not like this.

Ridiculous notions now filled hours of his days. It was love—there was no other name for it. He was in love. Excessively in love. He tried in vain to gain an insight into Miss Piles's schedule. If he saw her on a Wednesday he said to himself, She must come to the Technical Area on Wednesdays. The very day of Wednesday would acquire instantly in his mind a romantic hue. And he waited, going so far even as to count down the days. And if he saw her on a Thursday, he thought, Maybe Thursday visits will be a regular occurrence. But the following week he was always disappointed. She never came with regularity.

He placed great stock in his sightings, and continued to stare at her, whenever he saw her, with all his might. These brief identical exchanges, occurring days or even weeks apart, were to him like chapters of a lengthy chivalric romance. His catalogue of observances was extensive— Miss Piles bounding down the steps of Building C in her green blazer. Miss Piles at the gate, in silhouette, her thin dark-haired shape, with the sun behind her. Miss Piles attempting to pick, with a stick, from her white tennis-shoe, a piece of chewing gum. Miss Piles with her friends, in the courtyard, in her shorts, in the rain. Miss Piles lingering by the window, inserting a curler into her hair, inspecting herself in a hand mirror. Miss Piles coming down the path in the pines, with an S.E.D. man, deep in conversation. Miss Piles dropping her bag and reaching down to fetch something from it, disclosing as she did so a rarely-seen segment of her pale upper thigh. Miss Piles trying on one of the S.E.D. men's glasses. Miss Piles doing her imitation of Dr Teller, with a heavy stoop. A girl, possibly Miss Piles, shouting about bugs or worms. Several possible Miss Pileses in a crowd, bobbing along, mid-flight, multi-armed, blur-bodied, raven-headed. Miss Piles, in lilac, laughing, blushing, covering her face with her hands.

The boy would train his eyes upon her and stare and stare until she became a blur of colors, draining her image for all it was worth. One advantage of having no eyelids was that no move or gesture could escape his attention. He could monitor her constantly. Sometimes he was almost sure that she saw him and returned his look, and that by some non-verbal, non-gestural mechanism, meaning had been conveyed. Then he felt it most keenly—the tragedy of two people of identical feeling who were condemned by mere circumstances to live separate lives.

It was a tiring business. He felt the weariness of longing. He did not think of giving up on Miss Piles—he was too eager and credulous and, in spite of everything, optimistic, to give up so easily.

5

Summer was gone from Los Alamos. All through the fall it rained. The leaves fell from the cottonwoods. In the high Jemez, the wildflowers wilted in unison. Soon the thick black smoke of Army-issue coal burners hung over the town, and the streams froze in the canyons. Snow came down on the alien land, on the mountains, catching in the pines and gleaming on the barbs of the high fences and on the roofs of the watchtowers. It lay thick upon the desert, broken by the green bushes, and on the slopes of the mesas, a strange gray-blue bordering the earth-colored cliffs. Day and night the snow came down that winter, in a slow, silent bombardment, barely felt. The insects gradually went quiet. In the sky was heard a faint howling, and in the air the stirring of the trees, not only in the twigs but deep in the boughs, as though they were longing to break asunder. Heartening news arrived from Europe. The Allies had won, at great cost, the Battle of the Bulge. Though in the Pacific things were less encouraging. As 1944 crawled towards its end, the doctors began to itch for new forms of recreation.

One day a group of eminent professors drove a few miles from the town, into the mountains. At a place called Sawyer's Hill there was a steep slope, dotted with pine trees. They arrived in a big Army tractor with some heavy ropes. One of the doctors—Kistiakowsky was his name—had taken from his workshop a very long string with lumps of whitish clay strung along it, like a chain of Christmas lights. He kneeled at the base of a pine tree and carefully encircled the trunk with his string. Then he went to another pine tree and did the same, and then to another, until a great many of the trees of the hill were encircled, in this way, at the base of their trunks. Then he walked a long way back away from the trees, uncoiling his string as he went, letting it lie in the snow. The other doctors, dressed in their heavy coats, stood waiting, watching, in the brittle silence. At a length of several hundred yards, Dr Kistiakowsky pushed a little button at the end of the string. There was a great bang, the birds scattered, the trees threw themselves all at once face down into the snow. This was how Dr Kistiakowsky created a ski run for the doctors. And in time, when the area was cleared, the ski run became very popular among the doctors and their families, and on many a snowy day Dr Bethe or Dr Fermi could be seen, winding and weaving down the mountain, with smiles on their faces.

One who was not seen very often that winter was Dr Teller, who was applying himself enthusiastically to his Advanced Design. It was difficult work. In Dr Teller's design, through a complex interplay of components—controlling and channeling, at super-speed, the release of energy within the machine—the mental impulse could be enlarged, magnified, made five or ten times more powerful. For the design of each of these interrelated stages, meticulous and time-consuming calculations were required.

He had met a few times with Dr Oppenheimer. Though the director was clearly focused on the more rudimentary prosthetic designs, he seemed to agree with Dr Teller that the enemy was probably far ahead, and this required serious attention.

The war affected Dr Teller greatly. In his office he pinned a map of Eastern Europe to the wall above his desk, upon which he kept a record of the advance of the Soviet Army. He became totally absorbed in his work. He worked sometimes at home and sometimes in his office, pacing about with his eyes to the floor, sketching bodies and bodily components late into the night.

He stopped speaking to almost everybody but his wife, who remained a patient listener to his theories. It was as though the entire outcome of the war, the future of the boy and of all the other similar cases, rested on his shoulders, depended on his ability to complete this work. It was a matter of time before he completed his calculations and presented a viable model of his design. Then there would be no option for the doctors but to reorient the whole course of treatment according to his recommendations.

When he entered, from time to time, the part of the Technical Area where the boy was kept, he made a point of glancing into the boy's room, making sure all was secure and everything was in its proper place, even putting on the black gloves from time to time and picking him up. He felt something of that rush of anxious excitement he had felt when Dr Szilard first came to see him in Washington. To the boy, plunged as he was in his fantasies of the girl, the sight of this greasy-haired Hungarian, with his bulbous nose and his tired eyes, was thoroughly uninteresting.

6

In the last week of 1944, the director's wife received a visit at home from Captain de Silva.

'Awfully sorry to bother you,' he said. 'This will not take long.'

She ordered him to wipe the snow from his shoes before he came inside.

'This is a Navajo rug,' she said. 'Have you seen it? Marvelous, isn't it?'

He looked about him at the house. He seemed fascinated by it. She showed him the living room, and some of the paintings they owned. She offered him a drink, he declined, and before long she was poised on an armchair, her legs tucked beneath her, a crystal ashtray on the chair beside her, and he was sitting stiffly across the room, talking about the trout streams around Los Alamos, and the hunting of deer, and asking if her husband ever went trout-fishing.

'I don't believe so,' she said. 'Are you going to take off your hat?'

'Oh, terribly sorry.'

'It's quite alright.

She waited, smoking, until he had taken off his hat.

'Why, Captain, I would never have taken you for a bald man,' she said. 'Now what is this all about?'

'There's something you may be able to assist us with,' said Captain de Silva, placing his hat on his knees. 'You see, Intelligence has been trying to put a few things together. There was a trip your husband made in June. To California. We just can't account for what he was doing there.'

'I suppose you ought to ask him,' said Mrs Oppenheimer.

'You know what men are like with these things. That's the reason I'm asking you. Do you happen to remember the trip I'm referring to?'

She looked him dauntlessly in the eye.

'No,' she said.

There was a pause.

'You don't?'

'Don't remember,' she said.

Mrs Oppenheimer took a sip from her drink and set it down. She held her cigarette over the ashtray and tapped it lightly. Then, passing a pale hand upwards to her pale neck, adjusted absentmindedly the collar of her shirt. She felt him watching her as she did this.

'He travels around so much, Captain,' she added. 'Really so much. I can't keep track of it.'

'We try to keep track of everything, you see.'

'I should think you do.'

They eyed one another for a moment longer. The faint sound of a blast echoed through the cold, crisp air.

Mrs Oppenheimer had still not raised with her husband the subject of his idiotic escapade, and did not intend to. As far as she was concerned the entire business was behind them. And what could she have done, in any case—pack up her son, secure her fourth divorce? It was nonsense. Stupid even to think about it.

The captain made another attempt.

'It was the fourteenth of June. Flag Day. Do you observe Flag Day in your home?'

'No. Do you have a match? Thank you.'

'You're absolutely sure he didn't mention anything to you?'

'He doesn't mention anything to me,' said Mrs Oppenheimer. 'He takes security very seriously. Now Captain, I really must get back to—'

'You know, Kitty—may I call you Kitty?'

'If you like.'

She was beginning to feel the insult in the captain's words, and though she was not the type to be made to feel ashamed of any aspect of her life, she resented the assumption that he could come into her house and euphemize as he pleased. She would not say a word against Robert. She had forgiven him. Why is it, she thought, that the impulse to forgive is always so closely analyzed? Besides, all she was saying was more or less true. He did not talk to her about his work, at least not in detail. He never had. It was one of his inaccessibilities— one of his charms—that he never discussed his work.

'Intelligence has to check everybody's associates, you understand. And our research indicates that some of the people that you and your husband were friendly with, back in California—well, some of their political views raise questions for us.'

'I really do not like to talk politics,' she said.

'You don't go in for it, huh?'

'It bores me into the earth,' she said.

'Never joined any political organization?'

'I am sure your research has answered that for you already,' she said. 'I was in the Party. Very briefly.'

A fly landed on Captain de Silva's sleeve. They both noticed it, though neither commented on it.

'That's right,' he said.

'My second husband fought in the Spanish War. Shall I go through all my husbands for you?'

'Oh no, no, I don't think that will be necessary.'

He smiled at Mrs Oppenheimer. Then he looked down once more at the fly, now moving along the armrest of his seat, smacked it with the flat of his hand and studied it a moment. From the ruin of its body, wrinkled like a raisin, the yellow bubble of the omentum inflated, popped—pus flowed. The wings were like crumpled cellophane.

'But don't you think that's a significant detail?' he said, flicking the tiny corpse from the armrest onto the floor, 'I mean your knowing Communists, and having been a Communist.'

'I wouldn't say I ever was really a Communist.'

'Oh? What would you say you were?'

'I wouldn't say I was anything.'

The question of what she was was not a question Mrs Oppenheimer felt qualified to answer.

'You went to meetings, didn't you? You paid dues? Isn't that what they call them—dues?'

'Ten cents a week, I think. But I gave it up.'

'Would you say you became disillusioned with the Communist cause?'

'Sure.'

'Do you think you have been completely disillusioned? Or are you still—fuzzy?'

Mrs Oppenheimer thought about this.

'I have been disillusioned for a long time,' she said.

A trace of a dark smear remained on the edge of the armrest. The captain's finger was massaging it idly, erasing it bit by bit. Mrs Oppenheimer observed this with revulsion. She thought of the black innards mingling with the oils of his fingers.

What were the thoughts that passed through the mind of a fly, she thought, at the moment of its squashing? She tried to imagine it—the terror, the nausea, the confusion, the thoughts, or half-thoughts, or quarter-thoughts, the dim notion of the weight of the hand beginning to be felt upon its exoskeleton, of the hand beginning to push. And she tried to imagine what tiny desperate movements the fly would make in that last moment, what minuscule flailings of its little limbs, what fractions of hairsbreadths of efforts to keep the great mysterious thing away, before its entire body was crushed flat, its entire functioning system entirely overwhelmed by the weight of the hand, before every rigid thing in its body shattered and was reduced to a paste, what desperate stirrings and scramblings—But she could not imagine it, sufficiently. There was a limit to what she could imagine.

'You don't think that's significant?' said Captain de

Silva. 'To the army I mean, to the question of national defense?'

'To the war?'

'To America,' he said. 'America itself. And the cultivation of its interests. Has anyone ever approached you about passing information to the Soviets?'

'Of course not,' she said.

'Anyone ever inquired about your husband's work? Ever seemed a little too curious about things?'

She smiled at him. 'Never,' she said.

'They have all sorts of tricks, you know,' he said, turning his head at various angles to examine the home, as though it suddenly interested him far more than Mrs Oppenheimer, or the topic of their conversation.

'If anybody came to me with that kind of junk, I would spot them a mile off.'

She wondered if he was trying to get her to mention the boy.

'Not that I would have anything to tell them anyway,' she said. 'Because I don't know a thing about what Robert does all day. Anyway, it's ancient history as far as I'm concerned. I haven't had anything to do with the Reds for years. Robert was never even in the party. And he adores this country. Wouldn't be here if he didn't. Surely I don't have to tell you that.'

He said nothing to this, merely nodded, then went on combing the room with his eyes.

Mrs Oppenheimer sipped her drink. They ought to talk to Mrs Bethe, she thought. Mrs Bethe would be sure to vouch for her right-wing credentials. Fool that she was, she had made the mistake of telling Mrs Bethe she was distantly related to Wilhelm Keitel. Now half the town despised her.

For a few minutes more, Captain de Silva listed the names of various Communists and fellow travelers, most of whom she hardly remembered, many she had never heard of. She saw herself, ten years younger, in a boarding house in Ohio—on street corner, in her dungarees, selling the Daily Worker. It was not the sort of thing she could easily explain to somebody like Captain de Silva. The issue was complex. She had been in love. She had gone to a meeting and written her name down and paid a few cents and attended a meeting or two—did that make her a different sort of person to the sort of person Captain de Silva was? Was she, had she ever been, a Communist? The truth was that Mrs Oppenheimer had never had the time, never had a moment in her life, when she had felt it necessary to give a damn about what she was. It was actions that interested her. Deeds. What is a fire if it is not burning? The one thing she could not stand was doing nothing.

Finally the captain concluded his questioning, thanked her kindly for her time, and departed, with a few final glances at the walls and the window frames. Her attitude to the entire exercise was by now one of exasperated amusement. It was at least an interesting way to spend one's day, she supposed—better than sitting on the windowsill and filing her nails. She watched him go, wandering down the street past the houses of the senior staff, beneath the stony sky. Things were growing pale. The mountains were completely white.

She thought of her husband and what a fool he had been to go and see a woman like that. It was so plainly and childishly stupid that it did not bother her at all. He could not have done anything more idiotic if he had tried. In fact it amused her. She wondered if she should tell him about the captain's visit. He would want to know. She had better, she thought—but then again, why raise it? She stood there a little longer, looking through the open doorway, telling herself how thoroughly amused she was, about the whole thing.

When the maid came into the living room, Mrs Oppenheimer was pouring herself a small glass of scotch. The maid had been cleaning the bedrooms, knowing not to disturb the discussion. She was a dark woman with jet black hair, parted in the center. Mrs Oppenheimer brightened instantly at the sight of her.

'Rosa!' she cried. 'Quieres algo de beber?'

'No, thank you,' said the maid.

7

It was New Year's Eve. All were gathered in the Lodge, the venerable meeting hall of the original boys school. It was a rustic building of pine and aspen—like a log cabin on a grand scale. It had been handsomely decorated. There was red, white and blue bunting everywhere. There were streamers of crepe paper around the log posts, and on the enormous elk's head, and on the wrought-iron chandeliers. Over the old stone fireplace, somebody had formed *1945* out of tin-foil. The hall was filled with tables and with people, sitting and standing. A piano was playing.

Mrs Oppenheimer sat with the children. She wore a simple Ceil Chapman sort of dress in dark blue silk, with a belt, her hair in its usual elegant disarray, and her hand, with its cigarette, upraised by her face. She observed the crowd, turning from time to time to the children's card game when called upon.

'My goodness,' she said wearily. 'You're all so good at this.'

'I have two jacks,' said one of the children.

'Oh? Oh yes, dear.'

A little cough escaped her lips.

'Excuse me,' she said. 'Now, look at you, Paul, you were close. All you needed was a six or a three.'

The young Paul Teller studied his hand.

The cheerful murmur of voices swelled through the hall. It was cold outside. The windows were dark. It was like being in a ship. She put out her cigarette, drained her third glass of brandy and soda and lit another cigarette. At some distance, in the crush of the crowd, the long slender shape of her husband passed. He wore his dark suit. Fawners flocked about him. His pale head, hatless, received its praise, made its unintelligible replies.

It had been just a few days since her visit from the captain, and since they were in the habit of not mentioning things to one another, she had not mentioned it. In a way, she was enjoying it—knowing something he did not. But in a way, also, she did not want to have to mention his infidelity. She preferred to go on pretending it had not happened. For the truth was, Mrs Oppenheimer could not help but feel a tremendous and inexplicable attraction to her husband. He was, in spite of all, somehow less tedious than the rest of the human population.

The revelers passed the table in a constant recirculation. They were, in their formal dress, like week-old flowers—cymbidiums and cattleyas, faded and browned and limp at the extremities. There was Dr Teller with his terrible posture. There was the dome of the head of

Dr Bethe, squinting, chewing on his bottom lip, his wife beside him. And there was Mrs Parsons being a marvelous hostess, and there Dr Serber, one of the sycophants from Berkeley, buck-toothed, wiping his nose, his eyes flitting left and right.

The trouble with people, thought Mrs Oppenheimer, is that they all run out after a certain point. You find out what they like and what pleases them and displeases them and that is that. Everybody was just sort of—exhaustible. But she was inexhaustible. And her husband, though he could be a genuine pig, was inexhaustible too.

'What did I need this time?' said her son, Peter, laying his cards flat on the table before him. 'I have a ten. Ten is the biggest.'

'I have the most cards, though,' said the young Henry Bethe.

'You both lose,' said Mrs Oppenheimer. And she tried to explain it to them. 'See, you needed a four—oh, forget it.'

After a few minutes more of this tedium, Mrs Oppenheimer rose to her feet and decided she would go, by way of the bar, to her husband, and spring the thing on him at last. The children chirped and squawked at her, but she ignored them.

The tables were arranged rather inconveniently, and she had to sidle through them, stumbling a little, past little crowds of people who all turned to look at her for no reason other than that she was the director's wife. At one table somebody was proposing a toast to the men in the Pacific. A cheer went up, a swell of strained tracheae. At another table a few drunken soldiers were smoking cigars. People were waving sparklers.

'Pardon me,' she said imperiously.

At the far end of the room, at the piano, Dr Teller was addressing Dr Fuchs in his unfailingly loud voice.

'Heisenberg showed me this in Germany!' he roared. 'You substitute the two-handed mezzo forte for a one-handed forte. It sounds even better, don't you think?'

A flurry of notes followed.

'Oh yes,' said Dr Fuchs, shyly tapping his finger along with the beat of the music. 'Very good, yes.'

Near them stood Mrs Teller, her black eyes staring out vaguely at the partygoers.

The director's wife was not halfway through her transit of the hall when Mrs Teller noticed her—the smart brisk gait, the elevated chin, the cigarette. Their eyes met across that smoky expanse and Mrs Teller raised her hand in a kind of awkward wave. Mrs Oppenheimer, however, did not return the greeting. She made no reaction at all. She allowed her eyes to move past Mrs Teller, as though she had not seen her, and she continued walking until she was swallowed once more in the crowd.

Why did she do this? Arriving at the bar, Mrs Oppenheimer considered this question. She did not know. She thought how confused Mrs Teller must have been. She thought of her expectant hand shrinking away, as though stung. It was an awfully unkind thing to do—not in the scale of suffering it caused, but in its simple arbitrariness. Its willfulness. What was it, she wondered, in this small act of sadism, that had suddenly so appealed to her?

There are great cruelties, she thought, and there are small cruelties. And does anyone ever go through life without committing a few small cruelties? She ordered her drink and stood listening to the music. It was no longer Bach, but something else. The Beer Barrel Polka? Gretchen am Spinnrade? She thought of her mother, a domineering woman of the old Hanseatic sort, who had thrown herself into the Atlantic Ocean several years prior, suicide by ocean liner having been popular at the time. Something in the tinkling music called her mind back towards Europe, to the Germany of her girlhood summers. The high hedges, the heavy curtain tassels, the porcelain and the silverware, the beautifully cut liqueur glasses, the expensive tutors whom she had beguiled. She asked a passing S.E.D. man for the time.

'Twenty minutes to midnight,' he said.

The wreck of a year was finally crawling to its conclusion. She wished it would get itself over with. She was not upset, of course. She was an unflappable person—rarely upset about anything. She could not find any part of her that was affected by her husband's actions. She asked herself how she felt about it and received from herself no answer. It was though it was something that had happened in somebody else's marriage, in the marriage of two people she had never met nor ever had anything to do with. She heard him again—his deep, meticulously-shaped, orderly sentences. Smoldering away. Her caro sposo—her dear old thin white stranger. She must tell him about Intelligence, she thought. She would tell him. She would get a rise out of him, then they could be done with the whole sordid business.

8

Dr Teller had not easily given up his place at the piano. He had espoused to all who were interested, and many who were not, his philosophy of music.

The only person he felt had understood him was Dr Oppenheimer. The director, bowing his head, coughing, smoking, knuckling his eye, had made several erudite remarks. Mrs Bethe had declared that she did not care for music. Music had never been a part of her life.

Now the crowd had rearranged itself. Dr Fermi was talking about Italy and the partisans. Dr Teller's wife was fretting about their son somewhere and the Oppenheimers were nowhere to be seen.

The talk of the war was making Dr Teller think of Hungary, as he often did. Budapest was under siege, being torn and stretched out of shape by two equally repugnant monsters. The last he had heard of his family they were alright, but one could not be sure. It was strange. In peacetime, if any member of his family had found themselves in such a position of danger and uncertainty, he would immediately suspend all his work. He would be on the telephone with the embassy, or with the police, he would assemble a search party for those unaccounted for, he would not be able even to think of his medical work until the emergency had been resolved. But since the war was on, and everybody was in the same situation, his routine was barely affected. He could go to his office, he could go to lunch, even go out to social functions, as he was now, as though nothing at all was the matter. It was strange, he thought. But it was the war.

The crowd had begun to talk about Mussolini and the inevitable comparisons were being made.

'He's a frustrated journalist. That's what Mussolini is,' said Mrs Fermi. 'The man has obviously never had an original idea in his life.'

'And what is Hitler?' said Dr Teller. 'A frustrated something, I'm sure.'

'You can't compare anybody with Hitler,' said Dr Wilson. 'The man's uniquely evil, isn't he?'

'Not at all,' said Mrs Bacher. 'Every hundred years one of these maniacs seems to pop up. Who was the fellow who used to build pyramids out of human skulls?'

'Genghis Khan.'

'No, no. Not him. But you see—they are as common as Coca-Cola.'

'And always men,' remarked Mrs Fermi. 'Have you noticed?'

'In my opinion,' said Dr Teller, 'It's not our enemies we need to worry about.'

'How do you mean?'

'Stalin is the one to watch,' he said. 'His ideas are more widely accepted than any of the others, and just as dangerous.'

'It's not the ideas so much that are the problem, I don't think,' said Dr Wilson.

'It is,' said Dr Teller, in a tone of polite correction. 'Look at what happened in Hungary. The Communists were perhaps one tenth of a percent of the population. Yet they were able to overturn every aspect of society. And the economy. My father lost his position because supposedly lawyers didn't have any value to the Communists.'

'Edward,' said Dr Fermi, with his impish grin. 'I detect an element of personal bias.'

'Not so!' said Dr Teller. 'After four months we got the fascists, who were no better. The Jews were blamed for everything the Communists had done. We have seen both sides of it, in Hungary, and suffered both.'

'They're all as bad as each other,' said Mrs Bacher. 'Out to destroy everything—the whole earth. Every living cell.'

'This is a frightful subject,' said Mrs Bethe, adjusting her stole.

But once Dr Teller was started on a theme, it was always difficult to turn him from it. And soon he was enlightening everybody on the problems with the Soviet mentality.

'Communists everywhere think the same way,' he said. 'They think that in order to be free you have to step on someone's neck. I shall give you an example: Lev Landau'—he shook his finger in front of Dr Fermi's face—'You remember Dr Landau. Russian fellow. I knew him very well in the twenties when we were studying the—well, neurological matters. He used to play tennis with my wife. The same age as me, exceedingly knowledgeable, a very sensible man, and a believer in Communism. Landau was sent to jail in 1939, because he wrote a pamphlet. A little pamphlet against Stalin. For which they locked him up.'

'It was terrible what they did to Landau,' said Dr Fermi.

'An abomination,' said Dr Teller.

'Still, they are giving Hitler a run for his money,' said Dr Serber.

'With our help.' said Dr Wilson.

'And I suppose it's not such a bad thing from our point of view,' said Dr Serber, 'If all their good doctors happen to be in jail.'

Dr Teller turned to him furiously. 'Look at Trotsky,' he said. 'An ice-pick in his head. Bukharin—we used to see him always in the medical institute. You were not there. Shot dead. Ryokov. Zinoviev. Shot. Look at them in Moscow, lining up for food, no running water. Tisza! Did any of you meet Tisza? An excellent doctor—'

'Alright,' said Dr Wilson, raising a large strong hand and placing it on Dr Teller's shoulder. 'I understand your point.'

Dr Teller squirmed out of his grip.

'I know about these things,' he said. 'In Hungary we have seen these things happen. And if you don't want to end up in a prison camp—you have to be ready. Just because you have a little freedom now does not mean you will have it always. Each day you must wake up and ask yourself if you still have it. Don't wait until the disaster comes. Ask now. There can be no compromise. No dealing with people like this. Russia is not your friend. They are thinking always, How do I snuff this fellow out? That's what they are thinking.'

He had worked himself up into quite a state. This was evidently a point in which he felt strongly. His face was flushed, his dark eyes looked even darker than usual.

'Anyway,' said Dr Wilson, 'I'm not defending them, I have no reason to.'

'Ten minutes till the New Year,' said Mrs Bacher.

This at last euthanized the conversation, and the group broke off into various divisions. Dr Teller went outside with some of the Europeans, who began to talk mathematics, steering clear of anything that related to the boy. Dr Wilson and Dr Serber proceeded to the bar. Mrs Bethe went off with a group of her subordinates to reminisce about the pears and apricots of Stuttgart.

In the chill outside the Lodge, Dr Teller sat on the edge of one of the wooden deck chairs. The doctors were talking about the obscure connection between infinity and negative one-twelfth—the sort of topic that usually interested him—though he hardly spoke to them. There were plenty of partygoers outside. Some were dancing about like lunatics. All this fuss, he thought, over the old circumstellar journey, while the world was in flames. For an instant his thoughts went out to all space, to the sprawling silence, the rare celestial bodies, the bright-clouded Earth rolling in its black limbo. He blew a cloud of cold condensation over his plump hands, and watched it dissipate.

He thought of his old colleague Dr Landau. The soldiers marching down Váci Street. Rows and rows of ordinary faces. He thought of something Dr Fermi had said to him in New York, in the early days of working on the boy, when it had just been him and Dr Szilard and Dr Bethe.

'I hope it doesn't work,' Dr Fermi had said. 'I hope sincerely that we fail.'

He could see what he meant. He felt the same way. But then—if it did work, they must have a plan. If it did work, then they must be sure that they were ahead.

When Dr Teller was a boy, in Budapest, he had seen bodies dangling on the trees in the public square, and on the light poles—bloated bodies, plastered all over with little splats of human spit and mingled mucus, their throats garroted with rope or wire, the heads crooked from their necks. He remembered the swollen, filthy bodies, the genitals, the narrow legs, the leg hairs, the ankles, and from the black curled toes, the drip, drip, like candle wax, of the black blood. He thought of the boy. The boys. The Advanced Design. The urgency of their work.

There was a fear within Dr Edward Teller. He had always been a fearful person—deathly afraid of the dark until the age of seven. It had never really gone away. Chronic terror. There had not been a moment in the last several years, he realized, when it had not been there, within him. It was indescribable. It was like being high in the branches of a tree, or in a vacuum chamber, with the air slowly thinning. He longed to be back in his office, so that he could work on his calculations.

9

The front of the Lodge was a colonnade of logs that opened upon a darkened expanse of lawn and leafless trees. It was here that the guests had now began to spill. Bodies moved in the dark. In the meagre shelter of a green ash, muffled by the hoarse singing of a group of metallurgists, the Oppenheimers had at last found an opportunity to speak in private.

'Darling,' said Mrs Oppenheimer, turning to him, mid-step, with some formality, 'I have been meaning to tell you something. De Silva came to speak to me the other day.'

'Oh yes,' he said, watching the people move among the logs. 'Still probing us, is he?'

'Pertinaciously.'

'All about your mother's second-cousins twice removed, I suppose.'

She laughed.

'He was more interested in you, in fact. Frightfully interested in you.'

'Uh huh.'

'He wanted to know what detained you in California.'

There was a pause.

'When?' said Dr Oppenheimer.

'On the fourteenth of June.'

He looked down into his drink, then studied her for a moment with his electric eyes. She knew this look as that which came over him when he was considering options, calculating, pondering—the Frege–Russell look, the look of the logical atomist. When he spoke again his voice was quieter than before.

'And what did you tell him?' he said.

On account of the cold, Mrs Oppenheimer was wearing a man's military blazer, which she had taken from a chair in the Lodge. She looked absurd and beautiful in her cocktail dress and the green square-shouldered coat.

'Surely you don't think I'd go telling people what I thought about anything,' she said, 'especially not some perfect hog of a G-2 man.'

For a while longer he was at a loss, and she added politely:

'You have nothing to worry about. I thought you ought to know he was asking, that's all.'

He nodded slowly, looked at her and saw the cruel look of satisfaction in her eyes.

Suddenly Dr Oppenheimer was aware of an inconvenient fact—the fact that others may know of his infidelity, and that they may assume, based on that knowledge, that he was a cruel person. This distressed him. For he knew, fundamentally, that he was not a bad person. Anyone who thought this would be making an error. His actions may have been indiscrete, perhaps even harmful, but there was context. The context needed to be explained. And it had nothing at all to do with his fundamental character. He was Robert Oppenheimer, for heaven's sake. He was not a cruel person. He had read ethical philosophy from the East and the West. He had read and appreciated and even memorized passages from the novels of Marcel Proust. He believed in the equality of women, and he knew the difference between right and wrong. Now people were going to misunderstand everything and draw all sorts of conclusions about him. He needed to explain things—first to his wife, then to Intelligence. With sufficient context he could put it right. And in the execution of this resolution he began: 'Kitty—'

But he was interrupted by the arrival of Mrs Parsons and her husband, the admiral, informing them that the children were coming outside, that everybody was gathering, and that they must hurry, or they were going to miss it.

The crowd had begun to move with purpose. People were rushing from the doors onto the lawn, jostling and giggling in the dark. They were sucked in, and for a moment he lost sight of his wife completely, swallowed in a blur of khaki, as the soldiers clamored around them. There was a confusion of voices. He realized he was walking beside Admiral Parsons. Some people were still dancing, drunk, attempting to dance. The countdown began.

'Ten, nine, eight...'

Shadows moved upon the lawn, crowds of figures, watchers, rising and slipping away. His wife stood unmoving in the throng. How truly terrifying it is to have only a few people who love you, he thought. Each man his paltry few. And without them, the indifferent silence of the millions. How precarious it is—how close to loneliness we are at all times without realizing it. He felt like he was losing his footing.

The burst of a blast echoed through the Lodge, shaking the logs. A volley of Roman candles howled skyward— he felt their deep percussions—the firecrackers cracked, tadpoling and rattlesnaking through the night in writhing froths of sparks. All observed their tiny meteoric flights— the hiss of vapour, the high white crack in the night— the flash, boom—and the shattered meteoric shells.

The dancers swooned, lips kissed, children ducked, covered their heads, Mrs Bethe yawned, a soldier fell, striking his skull, smashing his glasses. 'Heavens, are you alright?'—another purplish cloud came boiling and swirling upward, the people swayed— 'I'm fine, thank you'—Children were being ushered through the throng, 'Look up!' said Mrs Wilson. 'Look Henry, look! Up!' Up he looked, up, it was hypnotic, spiraling lights. On the deck-chairs, in the trees, people froze and stared. The lights glowed red on their faces.

Some of the younger revelers—the S.E.D. men, and the soldiers—had fanned out from the Lodge, into the streets of the town. Earlier, in the evening, they had raided the laboratories for grain alcohol and now they were quite drunk. Some of the soldiers lifted up some of the WACs and slung them over their shoulders—the girls shrieked with joyful shrieks. Their faces were flushed. Dogs had begun to bark all over the town. Some of the S.E.D. men sang Auld Lang Syne. They strayed, green bodies, through the streets and out onto the trails. The candles cracked and burst in stars of sparks above. They wandered down the slopes into the canyons, sliding and stumbling. The dirt clouded over them and stained their clothes. Their hair was messy, their frocks were ruined. They chased one another. They whooped and hollered carelessly into the night. It was 1945, they cried. 1945!

In his room in the Technical Area the boy lay stockstill on a table. He watched the window. It was dark. He saw nothing, only himself. He heard the shrieking laughter and the bursts and the sighs of the last candles, fading across the mesas. Somebody was happy, he thought. He looked at himself. Gray, square, small. He wanted to forget himself for a while. He wanted to be asleep, and then he wanted to wake, and to be in that moment, that brief moment, after waking, before you remember who you are.

10

In late January the doctors started the boy on a new course of treatment. It was high time something was done with him, for he had spent too long in the dark storeroom, obsessing about Miss Piles.

The treatment involved a steel frame, twenty feet tall, similar in appearance to an oil derrick. It reminded the boy of the headframe in the Congo. There was a pulley system at the top of this apparatus, and a cable that dangled down the middle. Near the bottom, a few feet from the floor, there was a platform with a square hole cut in the middle, through which the cable passed. This square hole fit the boy's dimensions precisely.

Dr Fermi secured the boy to this cable by means of a special clamp. The boy was hoisted up slowly to the very top and held there for a while, dangling. The doctors would then take some gray bricks from a box and arrange them carefully on the platform so that they surrounded the square hole. Then they would all stand back, some would cover their faces, Dr Fermi would press a switch, and the boy would drop from the top of the apparatus, plummeting directly downward at great speed, and passing through the square hole. Before he could hit the floor, a brake would be applied and the boy would come screeching to a stop.

The boy found the whole process terrifying. He did not like being so high up and plummeting down from 20 feet in the air. Each time they dropped him, he felt a terrible throb of fear inside him, fear and anger and confusion all combined into one. Even after the first few drops, when he knew he would not hit the ground, it still frightened him to be dropped. For there are some fears that are deeper than reason and thought, and the fear of falling from a great height is one of them.

But the boy of course had no way to indicate to the doctors that he was afraid, and suffered through his plummets in silence, dangling and dropping, like a cow in abattoir, with no alteration in his facial expression.

It was on seventh or eighth drop that the boy began to notice how hot the room was getting. The air itself had grown stifling. As he paid more attention to this, he became more certain that he was not imagining things. It definitely was getting hotter with each of his drops. Something was happening—something quite strange. It was almost as though *he* had done something.

The doctors continued to bustle about. There were a great many doctors in the room, at least twenty of them, all dressed in dirty white coats. They crowded around the apparatus, climbed ladders to reach its upper parts, hastened around it with boxes and ticking instruments and slide-rules, and fumbled at dials and panels on the machines that surrounded it. Dr Fermi had rolled up his sleeves and loosed his collar. Now and then doctors called out to each other across the room about cross-sections or multiplication constants, rates of descent, and other matters which the boy could not understand. The ticking machines, so familiar to him now that he hardly noticed them, filled the air with their ticking and their faint red blinking lights.

In a chair at the back of the room sat Dr Oppenheimer, silently smoking, watching the boy.

11

Dr Oppenheimer was satisfied with the boy's progress. Though the boy did not know it, the purpose of the apparatus was to bring certain stimulated tissues into momentary proximity with one another. By giving the neurons an opportunity—a very brief opportunity—to communicate with one another, the doctors could measure just how much brain material would be required to make a prosthesis work.

He returned one afternoon to his office, after a very busy morning, with the intention of preparing some papers for Dr Lawrence, who was soon to make a visit to Los Alamos. The big test loomed. He had some blueprints on his desk that had arrived from Wendover Airfield—sketches of the prostheses in silhouette, outlines of various fishlike bodies. Some were squat, some slender, long, fat, round, squarish—all were bilaterally symmetrical, though none of them were particularly human. There were lines of measurement and weight specifications. The great difficulty was getting the bodies light enough. For the airmen wanted them light, as light as possible.

That morning it had rained, on and off. The director had begun the day by walking his son to the daycare center, his wife having had a fall. He had spent some time watching the boy on the apparatus and talking to Dr Fermi. Then it was down to Admiral Parsons, whose team was in a canyon, testing some body parts, to talk about the test.

At eleven o'clock he had one of his weekly meetings with Dr Teller, who had begun by updating him on the Advanced Design, but had entered on a long tempestuous digression about the war—the Soviets had been arresting Hungarian citizens, he said, and deporting them to labour camps. He worked himself into a great stink about this, and Dr Oppenheimer agreed with him emphatically, in terms even more acerbic and far more eloquent, which seemed to please him. After that Dr Oppenheimer returned to the Technical Area and spoke to Dr Wilson and some of his men, one of whom complained of having lost some of the hair of his head. Then he discussed the test with Dr Fuchs and Dr Bethe, and finally returned to his office. Such was Dr Oppenheimer's crowded morning. He had just sat down, taken out his pencil and paper, and turned his attention to the blueprints, when there was a knock at the door.

'Come in,' he said.

It was Captain de Silva, who had come to ask him if he had heard that Jean Tatlock had committed suicide.

Dr Oppenheimer was at that moment putting his

pencil into a cup. He missed the cup and sat for a moment with the pencil in his fingers, looking at it. Incapable of confronting immediately the series of questions that came into his mind, he applied himself to the more manageable and pressing problem of how to remove Captain de Silva with a minimum of conversation. He replied quickly that yes, he had heard. But he was not sure what to say after this, and he sat, with the pencil still in his hand, looking at the Captain, who was leaning against the doorframe and gazing up into the lintel, blinking his eyes.

'There's just no explaining events like this,' the Captain said philosophically.

There was a pause.

'How did you—'

'How did I what? How did I know? Intelligence keeps an eye on things, as I'm sure you're aware. Associates. Ordinarily of course it's not our procedure to tell a person about any aspect of their file. But these'—he cleared his throat in a way that seemed almost consolatory—'these are unique circumstances.'

A cold sweat had formed on Dr Oppenheimer's brow.

'Thank you,' he managed to say.

'Do you want to talk about it?' said Captain de Silva, resting his eyes upon the director in an exceedingly friendly manner. 'I am sure there are very few people who you would be able to talk to about this. It's a terrible thing. We always knew she was unstable, of course. But still. Just thirty years old.'

Dr Oppenheimer looked at Captain de Silva.

'I'm alright,' said Dr Oppenheimer. 'Thank you.'

When Captain de Silva had gone Dr Oppenheimer did not return to his work. He telephoned California, trying frantically to remember the names and numbers of other people who had known Dr Tatlock. When he attempted to speak to the operator, his voice would not leave his throat without a great effort. Finally he got through to a woman, a mutual friend. She confirmed a few details. Barbiturates—a pile of cushions—a bathtub, partly filled. This was quite enough. The woman was weeping. On the telephone her voice sounded like a buzzsaw.

'Poor Jean,' she said. 'She seemed to take the war personally. We can't believe it. None of us can believe it.'

It made him sick. He thanked the woman. He put down the telephone receiver and told himself to be practical. He thought about Captain de Silva. He felt suddenly, more than perhaps ever before in his life, that he was being observed. He picked up the telephone receiver again and gazed at it at length. He attempted to unscrew the mouthpiece, without success. Then he got up and turned to a picture, an original Dürer, that was hanging on the wall. He had brought it with him from Berkeley. He removed it from the wall, examined its back, set it down, then went to the bookcase and began removing the books, one by one. For some time he continued in this manner, examining the bases of his pueblo pottery, lifting up and checking behind and studying every surface of his office. He felt about under his desk, in the dust and spiderwebs. He started opening the drawers. Then he stopped.

What was he doing?

Dead, he thought. He tried to imagine it. It was not possible. She could not actually have done it. He felt the chill shadow of death in the ends of his fingers, and on the nape of his neck. It was true—it was done, irreversibly. He had a strange sense that the thoughts, the sense of shock, now coursing through him, were the mere final emission of something that had long since taken place. He could not go back, he could not visit her. He could not talk to her. He could never talk to her again. There was nothing he could do. Though it was not an illogical outcome, nor an unpredictable outcome—it struck him as impossible. How could it be possible that such a thing had happened, and he had not been able to prevent it?

He sat in his chair and smoked. Outside it was darkening. His blue eyes glowed in the glass. His long narrow figure seemed to occupy a much smaller space than it had previously. He had not realized just how isolated he was here in Los Alamos. With those few phone calls to California, those few words with people he had known before the war, the real world had come flooding in. Into the sealed and spotless room of his skull it had flowed in a cold murk, upsetting all the furniture. He realized how little reality there was in his view of things, with regards to Dr Tatlock. He had not taken her seriously, somehow he had not thought of her as a complete person. He realized he had been conducting himself as in a dream. There was no aspect of his trip—not Dr Tatlock, not the train journey, not the bar, not the car, not his wife, not even the city of San Francisco—that had seemed real to him. It was just scenery, pictures, empty buildings, something for him to inscribe his uniquely important life on. Nothing had seemed genuine or real to him unless it confirmed some thought or some assumption within his mind, some little piece of the pitiful story he had been telling himself, about himself.

Now she was gone, and his whole outlook seemed

small, crude, callous and monstrous in its ignorance. She was gone—this was irrefutable. He comprehended at once the great terror and complexity of the truth he had not faced, for whatever reason of stupidity or arrogance or fear. The sense that he had made an error, a terrible, fundamental error, hung over him. Well, he said to himself. Well. You have gone a little insane, Robert. You have lost your wits a little. You have lost your way a little. You have not thought things through. You, who always think things through so well, have not paid due attention to what was going on around you, to the concerns of those around you. Yes, he had gone a little insane. Spellbound in the mountains, he had strayed from his reason, sabotaged a little of his own life... But it was not irrecoverable. Not quite. Because now he knew about it.

He rose, crossed the room and stared, at length, into the waste-paper basket. He tried to determine at what point he had begun to stray from his reason. He tried to recall the way he had been, the way he had seen things, before the war, and to recall his feelings and his principles then. Surely those principles must have been good. He had always thought of himself as a good man—a factual, reasonable, principled, judicious man. He had thought a great deal before coming to work on the boy. He was a man who thought things through.

He walked back and forth in his office and smoked and looked at the blueprints and asked himself if he was utterly certain that he was still, at this moment, a reasonable man, if all his actions and decisions were reasonable, and if he really had considered all possibilities. But it sounded like a childish question, the answer to which should have been obvious. Surely he was overthinking. Trying to blame himself. This was normal. It was to be expected. He knew that he was not actually responsible in any way. She had been depressed long before he came along, and long after. But still—

He sat a while longer in his office with his misgivings, clutching, holding together with both hands the little torn balloon of his head, waiting for the discomfort, the sense of error, to subside. His day, which had been so full, was suddenly empty. Evening fell. He looked out the window. He watched, as though to see if the world would keep going as before. Crows moved in twos and threes through the quiet air, landing on the drab buildings of the Technical Area, and on the powerlines. He heard voices faintly through the walls. Calm numerical talk. Everybody was still bustling away quietly at their own affairs. Dr Lawrence was still going to arrive that week. The blueprints still needed his confirmation. He still had to read the reports on the other boy. Though he could not see the grass, beyond the pines, he could hear its breathing, its soft swell and fall. He looked through the window at the trees and at the edge of the pond, which was just visible, and counted six ducks, in the gathering dark.

12

Mrs Oppenheimer was in the garden with her son when Dr Oppenheimer returned home that evening. Dark clouds, miles long, surged in the tempestuous sky. She wore blue jeans and brown boots and a broad hat, and carried a spade. Though the weather was cool, her sleeves were rolled up above her elbows. She threw herself methodically into the flower beds, wasting no time, hacking at the dirt, uprooting weeds and tossing them over her shoulder.

'Peter, dear, bring me that pail,' she said. 'We'll have a nice lot of daffodils soon by the look of it. Hurry up now.'

As she watched her husband's car pull into the driveway, Peter tottered towards her with the pail and dropped it at her feet. 'Find me a weed,' she said. 'Can you see a weed?'

The child stared blankly at the garden. He was dressed all in yellow, with a new red ribbon. He wandered around and flapped his arms. Finally he began to cry for some reason. It was evident he had no interest in flowers. He cried and cried, irrepressible, in a trembling soprano.

'For God's sake, Peter,' she said, lighting a cigarette.

She sat and watched him. He continued to cry. What the hell could one do, she thought. She waited until his voice became fainter. Then she put out her cigarette and lit another. He wiped his nose with his hand. Infants were impossible to speak to, thought Mrs Oppenheimer. But who is it possible really to speak to?

She felt it was time for her to get away from Los Alamos, for a little while, to prevent herself from going insane. There is only so much gardening a woman can do, before she has to take somebody's head off. The other wives had jobs, terrible little brain-eating jobs as typists or computers, or secretaries, or librarians, or schoolteachers. She had tried to work in the town hospital for a time, filing the blood samples and blood counts, but she simply could not stand being told what to do, like a common WAC. She had no interest in the blood counts. And why did the blood always need to be tested anyway? It was better for somebody else to do it, somebody who was good at being told what to do. There was no shortage of these people, these *patriots* as they were called, there were hundreds of enthusiastic *patriots* everywhere, bursting with pep. Yes, she said to herself, I must go to Santa Fe.

Dr Oppenheimer came into the garden. He walked slowly, his hands in his pockets. His face was pale, his eyes had not lost the fixed, feverish look they had worn since his conversation with Captain de Silva. He coughed as he approached, and then he coughed again—a sharp, familiar sound. Neither he nor his wife even noticed it any more, this cough had so long been a part of their lives. Perhaps if he suddenly ceased to cough, if one day for a period of a few hours he neglected to cough, perhaps then they would notice it. But as he came into the garden they did not.

'You look tired,' said his wife, drifting towards him.

He replied that he was. She was delighted to see him home. It was rare that he tore himself away so early from his prostheses. But then, perhaps it was a little later than she had thought. The time did get away. They talked briefly of tedious matters. He told her Dr Lawrence was coming, then, with a newfound sense of anxiety, wondered if he was permitted to tell her this, if Intelligence was recording somehow. She proposed a martini.

'We're out of vermouth,' he said.

'It's the thought of vermouth that counts.'

'I have to sleep. Busy morning tomorrow. War's not going to win itself.'

'Suit yourself,' she said.

But he did not go at once. He lingered. All about them the shadows were growing heavier. Deepening into pits. Fathoms deep. There were no longer any sounds, no wind, no voices, no automobile motors. Finally he told her about Jean Tatlock. That is, he told her that she was dead. Suicide. That she had been greatly depressed. He did not go into any other details. For an instant they looked at one another. There was a silence. At last Mrs Oppenheimer said the only thing one could say, under the circumstances, that it was a horrible and sad thing.

'And what's more,' she added, 'it's an awful waste.'

Then, as though to make clear this was all she had to

say on the matter, she called for Peter to drop a stick that he had picked up.

'It's only a stick,' said Dr Oppenheimer.

'Did you hear about Tokyo? They have some sort of new aircraft. Seems they've taken out the whole city almost.'

'I am very tired,' he said. 'And do not want to talk about Tokyo.'

She continued to move about in her sprightly fashion, waving away the insects of the evening. She had moved on from the weeding to the pruning. Crouched before a mountain mahogany, the secateurs in her hand, she told her husband to take Peter inside, or he would catch a cold. And when they had gone in she reflected for a moment on the situation. She felt no personal grief of course, never having met the girl. But it was curious—somebody comes interfering in your life and then goes and drops dead— really, what a thing to have happened! Something in the universe was set on making a spectacle of her life. But she would not be made a spectacle of.

Night fell and Mrs Oppenheimer continued gardening. It was really too late for gardening. The clouds were poised for rain and it was to be a marvelous shower. It was that perfectly leaden stillness that precedes rain. She thought of the great eruptions, millions of years ago. She tried to imagine it—the sky volcanic black. The flames for miles. What could one do? If it were to happen right now? Can't call a fireman, she thought. The firemen are all on fire. Try to crawl your way out of it? It gave her the shivers. She felt as agile as a rabbit, hastening between the flower beds with all the earth so still and gray and dark around her. So pervasive was the tranquility that she wondered if all the town's citizens were now asleep, if by some coincidence the improbable event had occurred that all were simultaneously unconscious within the municipal limits, all with the exception of herself. A thousand people idle in their bodies, in their beds. And her mind leapt from this thought, for some reason, to her husband's work, and the boys. Mrs Oppenheimer knew her husband was destined for great things. She went on working, digging and scraping and pruning, until her toil was finally suspended, by the falling rain.

The next day, rising late as always, leaving the children with the maid, Mrs Oppenheimer drove to Santa Fe. The rain had stopped, so she could put the top down on the Cadillac. In Woolworth's she bought some crystal glasses, a tablecloth and a huge white stuffed bear that she decided she must give to the baby. She ordered an ice cream sundae.

'This is vile,' she said to the waitress. 'And I would like my money back.'

Then she wandered a while in the Plaza, in her big sunglasses, the bear slumped over her shoulder, carrying her shopping bags, waiting for a bar to open. Birds were pecking pleasantly on the lawns. There were old women in shawls and men on the park benches reading newspapers. She watched the people in cowboy hats moving slowly across the porches and tried to pick out the spooks. She knew that somebody was watching her but she did not know who. After what she called a few drinks in the hotel, she decided Santa Fe had bored her to death. But it was not yet time to go back. She felt she must drive somewhere. So she threw the bear into the trunk, as though it were a corpse, with her other shopping bags, and drove to Chimayo, a detour of only a few miles, to look at the famous church.

As she was driving out of Santa Fe she saw a strange thing, in the rear vision mirror. She had just driven over a bridge. It was a man, under the bridge, in an evening suit, with a briefcase in his hand. Christ, she thought, she had finally gone coo-coo.

In Chimayo, in the high dry hills, it was quiet and peaceful. Tedious beyond expression. Mrs Oppenheimer watched the shadows of the vigas grow longer and longer on the yellow adobe walls. And she watched the sunlight shrinking from the crucifixes and the holy candles, and the thin ceramic statues, and the bees floating around the graveflowers and the carefully trimmed junipers. A group of plump pilgrims was scrambling at a little hole that contained sacred dirt, stuffing the dirt into bags and rubbing it over their hands and faces. Mrs Oppenheimer wavered through the cold chapel, past the altar and down the aisle. She saw herself in the reflection of a pane of glass—fine posture, narrow as a whip, a light sunburn, the sunglasses up on top of the head, in the blur of the slight frizz. A local woman stood in the nave and watched her without expression. Against a wall were the abandoned crutches and canes of cripples. Prostheses. She stood in the doorway and smoked a cigarette. The local woman walked towards her as though she was going to speak to her, but Mrs Oppenheimer turned away, strode back to the car in her quick, straight, stiff manner, and drove off.

It no longer excited Mrs Oppenheimer to drive on these precarious highways in the wild canyons. She thought about the first time Dr Oppenheimer had brought her out here, just after they met. He had been so charming. Contemptuous of everything, like herself. Sitting on a bed together, passing a bottle of wine. Desert light. Trying to hold onto one another, to feel one another, completely. The insufficient hands. He had seemed to have unlimited curiosity in her.

But one discovers limits. Always. Everything its special limit. Every little light has its time of going out. Bad decisions are made. The tongue runs riot. Everything uglifies. You start to doubt. Maybe it was never quite like that, you say. Maybe ours was never that holy romance. And in fact, you say, maybe he merely liked me because my anatomy rotated and bounced in a way that corresponded with something he had seen or dreamt or extrapolated from a billboard or a book or a magazine or a Hollywood picture in his youth. Then the heartlessness creeps in, the terrible insouciance—the disregard. As though you are worthless. An old maid. How does it happen? she wondered as she drove along the winding desert roads, winding higher and higher. You put your entire life in someone's hands without realizing it. How does such a thing happen, to an intelligent being?

The wind was getting in Mrs Oppenheimer's eyes and she began to wish that she had not put the top down. The car thundered eastward through the wide flatness, past San Ildefonso, across the Rio Grande and up towards Los Alamos at great speed. Even when sober Mrs Oppenheimer always drove fast, though she was not quite sober, on this occasion. She gazed out through her sunglasses at the white buildings within the high fences, and she thought once more of that man under the bridge, and his briefcase.

PART IV

1

Dr Leo Szilard, fast asleep in his train carriage, his cheek against the window pane, was awakened by the cry of a whistle. He saw, as he awoke, a wooden sign with white lettering—Spartanburg, South Carolina. He rose abruptly, took up his bag and his trench coat, hastened down the aisle and hopped lightly from the train. Two men in gabardine coats dismounted after him.

In the pocket of his trench coat, Dr Szilard had the name and address of a man. He stopped and rifled through his papers. Where was it? He withdrew the paper. James Byrnes. This was the man to see. There was always a man. With Roosevelt the man had been Alexander Sachs. With Truman it was James Byrnes, of Converse Heights, Spartanburg, South Carolina.

Spartanburg was a quiet, handsome, tidy town. The doctor hastened through the leafy streets. The men in the gabardine coats hung behind him, never less than a block away. When he stopped, they stopped. The house of Mr Byrnes was of red brick—southern colonial, antebellum, with white window-shutters and a large porch with a gleaming colonnade. A black maid answered the door, took the doctor's trench coat and bag, and led him into the parlor, where he waited for some time among vases of dahlias and oil paintings of men with heavy moustaches. Floral odors assailed him—odors of dahlias, and camelias, and dogwoods, and various others. All was quiet. There was a grandfather clock, but it seemed to have stopped. Flies circled, landed, and crept across the doilies.

After some time Dr Szilard was called into the study, where he was received with all the appearance of civility and kindness. Mr Byrnes was a short man of about sixty, with a face that seemed to be melting on either side, sliding down the lateral slopes of his skull. He wore a three-piece suit. He knew all about the boys, he said— he had heard it all from General Groves.

'Now what's this all about then? Can I offer you something? A cigar? I have a little chewing tobacco here, if you're partial to that. This is not a backwoods establishment; I have plenty of spittoons.'

The study was spacious and very empty, with huge, heavy, spotless mahogany furnishings. Dr Szilard seated himself and, making his best attempt at brevity, conveyed his arguments to Mr Byrnes.

He told Mr Byrnes, in short, that the boys must not go to war. Not only was it unconscionable, it was strategically unpropitious. The boys were of such an unusual nature—their prostheses were so potentially powerful—that their appearance in battle could not but inspire mimicry in the Russians. The result, he explained, would be an escalation of competitiveness between the two nations, to the great detriment of the infirm infants. Helpless boys would be raised in military institutions for years to come. It would send the whole international medical community down the wrong path—the path of exploitation, and irresponsibility, and undeniable danger.

Mr Byrnes patiently allowed these points to be elucidated, listening with a faint smile to the rapid Hungarian-inflected voice. He took up a few papers and rearranged them on his neat desk. Then he clasped his hands together, the fingers interlaced, and raised them to his heart.

'General Groves says there are no boys like this in Russia,' he said.

'They could acquire them,' returned Dr Szilard instantly.

'But we've already got them, you see. We've got quite a few. And, it makes sense, while we are at war, to use them.'

'We will win the war,' said Dr Szilard dismissively. 'That is clear now, with or without the boys.'

Mr Byrnes nodded.

'I see what you're saying. But I have to think about these things as a politician. With Russian troops in places like Rumania and Hungary—', this he accompanied with a significant glance, '—We have to show them we're not going to just let them do what they please. These boys, as you say, are going to be fairly effective soldiers. That's what Groves tells me, and I believe him. Don't you think the Russians might be a little more manageable once they see what we are capable of?'

'No,' Dr Szilard shook his head. 'No. This is very

dangerous. You will start a competition here, a really disgusting kind of competition, that neither we nor the Russians are prepared for.'

'What would you have us do, then? Stop working on the boys? Sit on our hands, wait for somebody else to do it?'

'Of course not. We should keep working. But I am saying that our focus now should not be on sending our patients to war. It should be on getting them out of war. Getting them as far away from war as we can possibly get them. We have a unique opportunity to create some kind of standard—some regulations—'

Mr Byrnes could not resist scoffing at this suggestion. Then, righting himself, he put to Dr Szilard an idea that had been floated recently among the leadership.

'Have you ever considered, Dr Salad, the possibility that these boys—that their utility in battle—may actually change the conduct of war itself?'

'I have, sir, yes.'

'What I mean is, doctor, that someday in future, we could have a situation in which there would be no way to go to war without getting these boys involved. That any future war may in fact primarily, if not exclusively, involve children.'

'Yes, that is exactly what I am telling you.'

'But you see, no rational leader would ever start a war in which the combatants were primarily children. Dr Szilard, no leader wants to start a bloodbath of little boys. It would be very unpopular among voters. You see what I'm saying, Szilard? The certainty that one could never go to war, without bringing the boys into it, would make everybody think a hell of a lot harder about going to war in the first place.'

'Mr Byrnes, I—'

'All we have to do is maintain a balance with the Russians.

Make sure they don't get ahead of us. We'd all end up better off, in fact. That's a hell of an idea, isn't it? But it doesn't happen if we don't show the world what these boys can do.'

Dr Szilard looked about him, as though for assistance— he saw the emptiness of the office, the golf-putting mat in the corner, the polished trophies, the photographs which all contained Mr Byrnes—and he thought of the Peloponnesian War.

'Your mistake,' he said, after a long pause, 'is that you impute rationality to the leaders of men. Maybe you are right that Stalin would have enough sense not to start a war with these boys. Maybe. But what about the man who comes after Stalin? Will he have enough sense? And what about the man who comes after him? Or what if someday we elect a senseless madman as our own President? And what about the future, Mr Byrnes, when the whole world knows about these boys, and when there are boys in England, when there are boys in Africa, when we have armies of child soldiers sequestered in the fields and meadows of Siberia, and in the slopes of the Himalayas, and in Germany, and in Iran, and in China, and in Palestine, and in Turkey, and in Brazil, and in Japan, and everywhere, hidden in the gorges, and in the forests, and in the tundras, and in the deserts, and in secret places everywhere— I guarantee you, Mr Byrnes, that someday, somewhere, somebody will be mad enough.'

'Well, you ought to speak to that silly fellow, and not to me.'

'Mr Byrnes. We have the opportunity not to go down this road. I was in Germany in 1933. Do you know what they said about Hitler? It will never happen, they said. I tried to tell them. No no, they said, maybe to some other nation of unfortunates, they said, but never to sophisticated people like us! Well, I assure you, sir, it does happen. It will happen.'

My Byrnes laughed affably.

'I don't know what to tell you, Mr Salad. This is the way we're playing it as far as I'm concerned. Maybe you can find somebody else who agrees with you. But I won't. I just don't think you're speaking practically. We're ahead, we need to stay ahead.'

Outside, the trees shifted in the Southern sun. Dr Szilard began again:

'I'd like to discuss the matter with President Truman. Or at least with his cabinet. I could make a short presentation.'

Mr Byrnes smiled. 'Now listen, Salad. That's enough. We can't go on here all day. You talk to me as though I don't know who you are. Well, I know who you are. You're the fellow that got this whole thing started. When it was the Nazis you were fine. Now it's the Japs, and you just happen to get cold feet. I realize the Japanese never did anything to your people. But they did something to us alright. They murdered two thousand of our guys in cold blood, without any warning.'

'My people?'

Mr Byrnes rearranged the papers on his desk once more, though there was no need for him to do so.

'The boy is being provided for,' he said. 'He has his rights. His Second Amendment rights, among others. You know there's a twelve-year-old kid serving on the U.S.S. South Dakota as we speak? Nobody forced him to be there, he's there because he damn well loves this country.'

'If that is true, sir, it is an outrage.'

'To fight for his country? Wouldn't you do the same for Hungary?'

Dr Szilard looked at this man before him, at his smart suit and his melted ice cream face. If he had seen this man in the street, or on the train that morning, he would have thought nothing of him. They would have passed one another with utter tranquility—yet here they were, speaking in raised voices, execrating one another, as though they were brothers.

'Mr Byrnes,' said Dr Szilard, rising from his chair. 'You offend my sense of proportion. I am not thinking about Hungary right now. I am thinking about human decency.'

They looked at each other. Each man thought there was a terrible error in the other's thinking.

Dr Szilard removed from his pocket a letter addressed to the President. He placed it on Mr Byrnes's enormous desk and asked him to pass it on. As he uttered these words the hopelessness of this meeting was clear to him. He thanked Mr Byrnes for his time and turned to go. At that moment the maid came in with some sweet tea. But he was already on his way, moving his legs in spite of a sudden locomotive difficulty that made him that caused him to walk, or to feel that he was walking, like a wind-up toy.

Dr Szilard refused to be cowed by this foolish man, and in his heart he did not take him seriously. He would press on, he said to himself, as he passed out the house, putting on his trench coat. The gabardine men detached themselves slyly from their place in a distant street. He would find another avenue. He would press on.

2

A fortunate thing had occurred. The boy had been placed
by a window—not face down, not upside down, not on
his back, not on the floor, not under a heap of papers,
not behind an oscilloscope or a calculating machine, but
right up against the window, his face almost touching the
glass—and he could see Miss Piles in the courtyard.

It was not for any particular purpose that the boy was
placed here and afforded this enviable view. The doctors
were having a meeting and she was there before him, in
the midst of a great stream of people leaving the Technical
Area for their lunch hour. It was early May. The sun shone
down on the motley heads, on the gravel, and through the
window, onto the boy, suffusing his few features with a
tender glow. All through the courtyard and on the porches

people walked, talked, smoked cigarettes, flapped their limbs at one another, and so on. A few cars made their way through the swarm, and the faint brass cries of horns could be heard, muffled by the glass.

In the boy's room an important conference was in progress. For some time the doctors had been discussing the test, sitting in creaking wooden chairs, crossing their legs, getting up and going to the blackboard. Dr Lawrence and General Groves were there. They had all been discussing the other boy. The boy had not seen the other boy in weeks.

Miss Piles was among the stragglers outside. She appeared, vanished, reappeared. Carefully he followed her with his eyes—that is to say, with his attention, for his eyes remained granite still. She wore a khaki dress. She moved listlessly, light-footed. She opened her mouth now and then and he strove to hear if she was speaking—he heard a faded sound, a peal of girl-babble, shrill and shattering. Was that her cry? How graceful she was. She seemed out of place in the midst of all these coarse, fat, reddening bodies. She was of a different order of being, a different creature entirely. She came to a stop in a small group near the porch of the opposite building and began talking to some people there.

He could see her well—her bowed legs, her head slightly inclined in profile, her black hair tied in a ponytail, her gesticulating arms, and even the movements, subtle and fine, through the back of her bodice, of the curves of her shoulder blades. Any minute now she was going to turn her head. This was what he was waiting for. A turn of the head, then she would see him and remember. He had been so long without a glance from Miss Piles, and so exhausted of late by his drops on the apparatus, that he felt almost due for some moment of affection, or at least recognition, from the young lady.

'Gentlemen,' said General Groves. 'Let's talk about the test site. Where are the men from X-2 Group?'

The boy heard the shuffling and the unrolling of papers. Somebody else, Dr Wilson perhaps, began to speak.

'This is where our test will take place. Just a few hours away. Can you see, Dr Fermi? Is my hand in the way of the—'

'Stand here, doctor.'

The doctors in the room began to shift and move. And the little group on the opposite porch moved too. They began to go their separate ways. The girls bent forward, passed perfunctorily their lips across each other's cheeks. The blurred colors of their garments shifted. Their small hands clasped and unclasped, embraced, brushed against girlish shoulders. What were they doing? They withdrew in a slow ebb—strewn colors, a flood of flowers.

'Pardon me.'

'I beg your pardon, Mrs O'Leary.'

'Here is the site. The base camp, here. You can see it marked out here. We'll have three shelters. A north shelter here, a south shelter—Here is Tularosa, by the way. The Oscura Mountains here. This is Alamogordo. Our test site.'

The faint tapping of a wooden pointer accompanied these words.

'I understand we have an air base in this area,' said the general.

'Yes, sir. This whole area is the, uh—what was the name of this, Oppie?'

'The Jornada del Muerto,' said the voice of Dr Oppenheimer, in flawless Spanish.

'How far away is the nearest town?' said the general.

'Thirty miles or so, isn't it, Serber?'

'Something of that nature,' sniveled Dr Serber.

'Will that be far enough?' said the general.

'Oh, certainly.'

As the group on the far porch dwindled, Miss Piles remained, conducting a kind of oration—so it seemed—to another girl and an S.E.D. man who were sitting on the steps. Quite a change had come over Miss Piles since their first meeting. She had seemed timid and withdrawn then. But here she was, talking with confidence. She seemed hardly the same girl.

The boy tried to prepare himself for the moment of her look. He felt a little nervous. She began to rotate. Now? Not yet. She turned her head. Now! There! He tried to stare at her as meaningfully as he possibly could. Had she seen? It was difficult to say. There was no immediate signal. She was still talking. No matter. She would glance again.

The boy looked at the S.E.D. man to whom Miss Piles was talking. He was sitting on the porch steps with a cigarette behind his ear and she was wandering idly around him, leaping down off the porch, and up again, and down again. There was nothing special about this S.E.D. man. He was tall—yes, but everybody was tall, compared to the boy. His clothing was dull. He wore shorts, ridiculous shorts that accentuated his fat, bristly legs. His hair was blond. He was unlike the boy in a hundred different ways.

'What about the boy's yield?' said Dr Lawrence.

'The yield is a fascinating problem,' said Dr Fermi. 'And a very difficult one. I suppose it depends on which division you're talking to. We are by no means in agreement here.'

'Five or ten kilotons,' said Dr Bethe, in a quiet voice.

'Yes,' said Dr Fermi. 'Perhaps. What we can do is create

an estimate of volume displacement, assuming a spherical wave of energy. Simple dimensional analysis. But this is very rough. Do not forget we have also the different energies, the thermal, the chemical, the, uh, ionizing—do we have time to go into this?'

'We can brief you later on our methods of calculating the yield,' said Dr Wilson.

The boy understood none of this talk. And he did not listen to it. For he was entirely occupied with studying the girl in the courtyard, examining afar her ambiguous face. Still she did not turn to him. She did not express anything. She did not cease her infernal hopping. And finally, after several minutes of fruitless watching, in which their eyes refused to meet, she did something that was entirely unexpected and made no sense to him at all—she sprang lightly backwards, widened her hands, and dropped, in mock exhaustion, in a clownish curtsy, onto the S.E.D. man's knee. The boy saw it all—the S.E.D. man looking up, her hands parting, the approach of the slender body, the thin green fabric of her dress sliding and rumpling and growing tight in places as she pressed her weight, what little weight she had, upon his knee. For a minute or two she remained there, talking to the others and sometimes turning to face the S.E.D. man. She laughed, stopped laughing, bowed her head, raised her head. Then, and only then, did she look at the boy.

A painful feeling went through him.

Miss Piles rose to her feet and straightened the hem of her dress. She glanced again at the boy. There could be no doubt. It was revolting. Vulgar. He felt strangely numb. She turned and said something to the S.E.D. man. The S.E.D. man laughed. He seemed entirely indifferent to the whole affair.

'Then we are decided,' said Dr Oppenheimer. 'The test will be on July 16th.'

'I'm satisfied with that,' said Dr Lawrence.

'That gives us a little over a month,' said General Groves. 'Everybody on board with that? Dr Fermi?'

'Yes sir.'

'Dr Wilson?'

'Yeah, I guess so.'

'I don't want there to be any delay. I want to remind all of you that your work here is very valuable. We are all doing our utmost here to speed this war to a victorious end. Not just here in Los Alamos. But in all our sites. At all levels—'

The general made a short speech. After a few minutes Miss Piles had gone away. Her group had dispersed. The S.E.D. man was gone too. The courtyard was much emptier than before. A few stray soldiers remained. The boy did not focus on the porch anymore, but on the empty expanse of the road. In great displeasure he watched the crows strutting and pecking on the gravel.

Dr Teller was now talking about his Advanced Design, but few were responding to him. The boy tried to follow what Dr Teller was saying but he could not. He could think only of that vulgar, stupid thing. It was an insignificant thing, he knew it was insignificant, but it bothered him. It stung him. The meeting began to wind down. The doctors were ready for their lunch. The general quietly got the attention of Dr Oppenheimer, and they lingered back from the others.

'Yes?' said Dr Oppenheimer.

'I want to talk to you,' said the general.

The boy heard the faint cough and hiss of a match.

'Of course,' said Dr Oppenheimer, his voice faltering slightly. 'Let's talk.'

3

The director and the general took their lunch in the Lodge. With its magnificent view over the mountains, the Truchas peak and the valley of the Rio Grande, it was a favorite dining spot for the senior staff. But the two gentlemen sat deep within it, by the huge empty fireplace, under the elk's head, where little could be seen of the living.

Dr Oppenheimer looked weary and unsettled. His skin was pale. Lately he had fallen prey to a profound unease. Misgivings plagued him. He kept repeating to himself a line from Proust. L'indifférence aux souffrances qu'on cause est la forme terrible et permanente de la cruauté.

'Tomorrow we'll talk to Parsons and straighten out the plans for the deployment,' General Groves was saying.

'Yes.'

'The weather requirements and the geography and so forth.'

'Yes.'

They were eating roast beef, potatoes and green beans. The general cut his beef into long, thin pieces.

'Then we'll need you in Washington. First of June we have our committee with the Secretary of War. All the military leadership will be there. Mr Byrnes—you know Byrnes—Mr Bush, from the Carnegie Institution. I suppose we ought to have Lawrence there too.'

'Lawrence would be valuable, I agree,'—Dr Oppenheiemer coughed—'Fermi would also be good to have.'

These were important logistical matters. High-level meetings. Matters of the greatest significance, in the lives of the boys. But Dr Oppenheimer was not quite able to focus. He felt he had to keep reminding himself of the justness of the war, and the philosophical necessity of the treatment, and so on, and he could not deny that there was something about the boys, something about the way they were doing it, that inspired in him a great sense of revulsion and of wrong.

'It's no use deploying these boys out in a damn field somewhere,' said the general. 'No sense in that. No matter what our objective is, it needs to be in a built-up area. Somewhere settled. Waiter!' He raised his hand. A soldier in uniform came to the table with a jug. 'Give me some more water. I don't want any ice in there. Good. Good, that's enough. Take this away, would you?'

He passed the soldier his empty plate.

The general had been ravenous. He spent a long time wiping his mouth with a napkin. He made sure to scrape at the corners of his mouth three or four times, checking the napkin to make sure there was no more food. Then he spent a long time folding the napkin. Dr Oppenheimer lifted, on the end of his fork, a cold, limp piece of meat, and put it into his mouth.

'I meant to ask you,' said the general, leaning his fat body forward, nudging with his girth the edge of the table. 'Did anyone ever—approach you? I mean, in a way that may be of interest to Intelligence?'

There was a pause. A creaking was heard in the rafters and the logs of the Lodge.

'How do you mean?' said Dr Oppenheimer.

The general remained relaxed.

'We have known for a while that several people are transmitting information about this institution to the Soviet Government,' he said. 'And I'll tell you the truth, doctor. Intelligence says they have reason to believe that you yourself were felt out—I don't say asked, mind you—but felt out. Felt out.'

'Is that so?'

Dr Oppenheimer chewed slowly his pulp of beef. His heart beat in the cavern of his chest. The general sat still before him, regarding him with his long flabby face, his second chin hanging trembling over his khaki shirt and khaki tie, the stars gleaming on his well-pressed collar, his shoulders rounded, his plump hands flat upon his folded napkin.

'I'm curious how you feel about that,' said the general. 'The idea of it. Passing a little information to the Party.'

'I feel it would be treason,' said Dr Oppenheimer without hesitation.

The general nodded, a dewlap-shaking nod, his placid expression unchanging.

'Of course,' he said. 'Of course. You're right there.'

The creaking continued.

The general went on, 'The fact that you may not have reported this at the time—well, that's understandable. I'm sure, at that time, you may not have even thought of this kind of medical work being—sensitive. You probably thought it was unimportant. That's fair enough. Or maybe it was unclear—maybe they didn't ask you outright, so you gave them the benefit of the doubt. No one would hold it against you for not reporting it back then. I wouldn't worry about that, of course.'

Dr Oppenheimer put down his fork. Evidently some kind of confession was expected. He wondered if they expected him to implicate Dr Tatlock. It would be absurd—she had done nothing. But perhaps it was not the truth they were after. Perhaps they wanted some hollow display of loyalty. He did not want to indulge them. It was distasteful.

'I would be hesitant to report it even now,' he said, in a voice so nonchalant he surprised even himself. 'Only because I don't want to implicate anybody unduly. I mean, I don't think we ought to go around impugning the loyalty of every man we meet. There may be people who are only marginally associated with that sort of business and who are in reality quite innocent...'

As he spoke he watched the general's face for an indication of how his words were being received. But the general gave nothing away, and interrupted him gently, without a trace of anger or accusation, as though all too happy to engage in this intellectual exercise:

'Ah, but you see, your assumption there is that you are a better judge of men than Intelligence.'

'Not necessarily. I just don't want to waste Intelligence's time.'

'Naturally, but—'

'To be frank, General, I don't think Intelligence is immune to—how shall I shay—misconceived ideas. It may even have a tendency towards paranoia, in some matters.'

He wanted a cigarette. But he had not finished his meal. And it seemed altogether too complicated and somehow incriminating to put his plate aside and to reach into his coat for his cigarettes and matches.

'Don't you think it's their job to be paranoid?' said the General.

'Paranoid? No. I don't think so. That kind of personal—er—speculation can be a dangerous thing. It can slow us down, I mean. We can lose time.'

'Maybe so,' said the General, tilting his water-glass carefully to one side, 'But if you don't tell me, you know, Intelligence would expect that I order you to tell me. Don't you think that would be a reasonable expectation, from their point of view?'

The water rose to the lip of the glass, rose and subsided. In its marbled shadow lances of reflected light rocked and trembled. Dr Oppenheimer thought he heard music—faintly, as from a neighboring building, plucked strings. The general's gray eyes rested upon him. They wanted his confession, they wanted something, a cock-and-bull story, they did not care. It was a ceremony of initiation.

He heard the click of a clock. Spools of tape turned behind the logs. The waiters lurked attentively. He understood suddenly that they had been watching him all along. The men in the train, the men in the bar, the cars in the night, the ears in the walls. He had no secrets. His every deed, his every word had been recorded, and it had all accumulated into a character that was now being used against him. A long chronicle of missteps. Even this conversation—yes, even the very dialogue through which he was presently squirming—that too he had misjudged, miscalculated, and though he had said nothing during this conversation that was in any way consistent with himself, with the self he believed himself to be, it was all now part of his file.

How could any man be confined to a file? For most of his life a man is made of errors and half-thoughts, ill-formed. Now and then, years or decades apart, he utters a true statement, worthy of recording. Surely a man could not be held responsible for every single thing he did, or he would end up dragging his former selves along behind him, as though chained to them, through all the mud and mire of his days.

And yet he realized, as he sat there with his roast beef and with the general leering at him as steadily as a sniper, that it was a game he must play. He must give in to the general. They had cornered him. He had no other option but to go on with his little charade.

'Well,' he said, with a guffawing sort of laugh that was not at all like his actual laugh, 'I wouldn't expect things to get that far. I mean, early on, yes, there was a bit of talk among some doctors...'

He proceeded, disgusted by his own feeble coyness, to mention a few names—old hard-liners, Communists he had known before the project, men who would never have been allowed to work on the boys in the first place. He even embellished a few things, made a few clever insinuations, just to please the general. He did not mention Dr Tatlock.

'I never considered any of it particularly threatening,' he said. 'I mean I can't imagine that anybody here would dream of passing information to a foreign government.'

The General listened carefully. He asked him to repeat the names of the men and the approximate dates he had last spoken to them.

'You're sure those are the only incidents?' he said.

'Yes.'

General Groves made no notes. There was, of course, no need for written notes. The director had merely to speak clearly. At length the general smiled—a wry, lopsided, Vaudevillian smile.

'Good man,' he said simply. 'I'm sure it's all probably nothing, as you say. But better to have it out in the open.'

They went back to their discussion of the meetings, the committees, the deployment, the things to be prepared for his trip to Washington. He gave his assurance that he would keep the general updated on the theoretical work and the developments relating to the test, all that occurred in the institution, and the general replied cheerfully that he too would be watching things closely, over the coming weeks.

They parted for the afternoon. General Groves went to watch the S.E.D. men walking around sternly in a yard for forty-five minutes, and to preside over some other affairs of a strictly military nature, while Dr Oppenheimer returned to his office, with his misgivings.

4

In the meeting room, now silent but for the usual coming and going of doctors, the boy was brooding. Had he the advantage of arms and legs, he would have torn the room to pieces, he was so greatly frustrated. An hour of logical reflection had transformed his obscure sense of humiliation into real anger, and the more he thought about Miss Piles's behavior, the more clearly it struck him as a deliberate insult.

He was sure she had done it all on purpose to mock him, and he wished every evil upon her in retaliation. He longed to be able to speak, so that he could insult her in some way. He wanted to condemn her publicly, to take her into the town and make insulting remarks about her bowed legs, to find whatever it was she hated about herself and expose it and make her feel—he did not know. He wanted to be very unkind. He cursed her for ever having invaded his thoughts, declared in the secret of his soul that he wished she had never been born to torment him, and thought himself more deeply in love than anybody had ever been.

Deep down it was not the girl, nor the loss of any potential love-affair, that so aggravated the boy. It was the fact that by sitting on the knee of the S.E.D. man Miss Piles had touched, with a cold finger, the very substance of his dreams. And in that moment the thousand hypothetical lives which he considered to be his had all collapsed at once before him. Her action had simply reminded him of what he was—a lonely person. And so he had become cruel, in his bitterness. For lonely people have cruel thoughts. He declared to himself, as he sat stewing in the meeting room, that this moment—the moment that the girl had sat on the S.E.D. man's knee—would be remembered as a momentous moment in his life, and vowed that he would never forget it.

Later that afternoon the war in Europe ended.

In Los Alamos, the news was received with a mixture of joy and unease. America was still at war with Japan. Their work was continuing, the boys were still in development, their orders remained the same. But it was impossible now to deny that their objectives had changed. The Nazis were defeated, and the original impetus for their work was now gone.

It became gradually clear that a rift had emerged, between those doctors who thought the prosthetic work should continue exactly as before, and those doctors who questioned whether it was still necessary. Dr Wilson fell into the latter category, and he called a secret meeting to debate the question with others in the senior staff. Dr Lawrence was a firm supporter of the idea that they should continue to work on the prosthesis. Dr von Neumann agreed with him. And Dr Serber added that if they did not complete their test, they would never know if it was even possible to make a prosthesis.

At first Dr Oppenheimer, wary of the eyes of Intelligence, stayed out of these events—but as the director, it was inevitable that the other doctors should seek his views. He said finally that he tended to agree with Dr Bethe, who thought the work must continue until the end of the war, but that after the war, the design should be placed under some kind of international control. The doctors disputed these matters intensely, and most discreetly, without reaching an agreement. But they all continued to work on the boys.

One day Dr Oppenheimer and Dr Bethe were walking back to their homes from the Technical Area, when they passed Mrs Teller on the road. They were on the opposite sidewalk to Mrs Teller, and were talking in lowered voices, and did not notice her.

'Of course we will have to tell the Russians about the boys,' Dr Bethe was saying. 'It's ludicrous, I don't know what these people are thinking.'

'It's impossible to talk about this with the Army,' said Dr Oppenheimer.

'The issue is—'

'The issue is that the whole thing is in American hands, and it needs to be put in international hands.'

'After the war, you mean.'

'Of course, yes.'

'Which may be any day now. It may be all over tomorrow.'

'I doubt it, but here's hoping.'

They passed out of earshot, still speaking frantically.

Mrs Teller was surprised to hear this. She stopped on the road, with two bags of groceries in her arms. Since the early days of the war she had not discussed the boy with anyone other than her husband. She stood there for a while, gazing out along the road, towards the canyon edge. A sheer drop. A fog was hanging about the plateau. She had been up early to telephone the Red Cross. For several weeks now she had been calling them, asking every day about her family, her friends, and anybody who might know where they were—without result. Perhaps better than anybody in Los Alamos, Mrs Teller had cause to celebrate the defeat of the Nazis. But not for one second would she trust the Russians. How fragile it all was, she thought, as she watched the fog move across the tops of the pines. The supposed peace. How easily it could all break apart again, once America lost its lead. She put the doctors' conversation out of her mind and walked on, though it occurred to her a few times over the following days. She thought about it while folding the laundry, and once while pushing the lawnmower over her lawn. It concerned her.

That weekend there was a square dance at Admiral Parsons's house and Mrs Teller was in attendance. They had cleared out all the furniture from the living room, and a little man with an accordion stood at the front of the room, crying out:

'All join hands as you circle the ring, singing, O Johnny, O Johnny, O—'

Mrs Teller watched the dancers twirling, reaching and fumbling at one another in their threadbare suits and dresses. Western music was playing from a Victrola. The man with the accordion was short in stature, with a tiny head. She wondered if he was a dwarf.

'Promenade!' he cried. 'Yes, promenade! Now take that corner girl and promenade! Everybody having a good time?'

She stood a while by a large table where there was a punch bowl and a few dozen bottles of beer, neatly arranged, on napkins. Everything was precisely organized. It was like a high school prom. Admiral Parsons's wife was an excellent host. There were people all against the walls, lined up against the walls, in the halogen light.

Mrs Teller was determined not to talk about the war with anybody. She scanned the crowd. There was Mrs O'Leary, there was General Groves, there was her husband, gesturing furiously. She wondered where Mrs Oppenheimer was.

At last she had the good fortune to catch sight of Dr Fuchs, whom one could rely on never to talk about anything of substance. She went towards him and, turning her head at the last minute, as though happening to notice him, said:

'Why Dr Fuchs—there you are.'

'Good evening, Mrs Teller,' he said quietly, 'Everywhere I go, there I am.'

The accordion was quite loud and it was difficult to hear his low lisping voice.

'Do you like the punch?' said Mrs Teller.

'Yes, it's nice.'

This was just the sort of painless exchange she was after. They stood a while watching the dancing and listening to the music. Then the man with the shrunken head announced that the next dance was to begin. A new square was being arranged. He cried:

'Take your partners—step right up here.'

'Shall we dance?' said Dr Fuchs.

'Oh. Yes, alright.'

She took his arm and they joined the dance. Dr Fuchs was what the world called charming, that is to say he was tall and kept his mouth shut. There was nothing particularly appealing about him. He was colorless, like a moth. She was grateful to him for having taken on the responsibility of Dr Teller's calculations, and thus given her husband the freedom to focus on his Advanced Design. But since she was not allowed to know this, she had no means of thanking him.

He was a good dancer. This could not be disputed. She felt his limp hand clasping and unclasping her hand, brushing limply against her waist, and she looked, with some amusement, at his boyish face with his round spectacles, staring resolutely at his feet, following the steps with precision.

It was a joy for Mrs Teller to dance, to caper in the blur of dresses, to spin, focusing on their hands and feet, and the squares, the all-important squares. She did not have to think about her family or the war. Quick and frantic, her dark hair fanning about her, she gasped, O! caught her breath—her cheeks flushed. Dr Fuchs led, then Dr Fuchs followed. The music bounced along at a constant pace.

But after a few minutes, abruptly, Dr Fuchs looked up at something over Mrs Teller's shoulder and went very pale. He turned and, hastily excusing himself, plunged awkwardly into one of the other groups of dancers, which drunkenly absorbed him. Mrs Teller, somewhat affronted, looked around to see what had startled the young doctor, and saw nothing of interest, only the crowd of the same old faces, Dr Oppenheimer standing in the doorway, Dr von Neumann drinking directly from a bottle of champagne, Dr Serber spilling his drink and sanctimoniously quoting Apollinaire: 'Saison rapide, saison qui chante. Les avions pondent des œufs...'

Dr Fuchs made his way through the crowd. The mixture of the music and the voices was suddenly jarring to his ears, and the arms and legs of the dancers, knitted together, flailing and flapping, seemed to him like the tendrils or feeding tubes of a vast organism composed of interconnected torsos and heads. Everywhere he turned— a churning swell of gleeful faces, viciously laughing. He tried heading for the door—no, couldn't go that way— shrank back, tried another route. An elbow nudged him. He apologized. The dance went on, thrashing and rotating. Now the arms went up again, every right arm up, hoisted up. The feet thumped. Manic laughter. Dr Fuchs veered to the right. Mrs Teller sighted him again. 'Klaus!' she said.

He ignored her. He needed to get out. The thought of all these squirming, well-dressed bodies crammed in between him and the exit suddenly revolted Dr Fuchs, and he bowed his head and made a wild plunge towards the doorway. Mrs Teller wondered what on earth had come over him. Was he angry with her?

In fact, it was not Mrs Teller that he was avoiding, but Dr Oppenheimer, and he had been doing so for several days. It was not rational of Dr Fuchs to do this, but he did it nevertheless, propelled by a wild fear, like a child's fear of monsters. The most important thing for Dr Fuchs was that the director should not see his face. For if he saw his face, he would recognize him, that something would click, that the director would remember.

Of course, the polite thing to do (and Dr Fuchs was known to be unfailingly polite) would be to explain the situation to Mrs Teller, to explain what exactly had happened in Santa Fe. But Dr Fuchs did not speak to anybody about such things. His activities in Santa Fe were a part of himself that he kept very carefully concealed—compartmentalized, in fact, from every other aspect of his life. He had been delivering a briefcase full of technical drawings, drawings of the boys, to a man who was waiting for him below the Castillo Street Bridge. He had met this man before and had passed on his communications without incident. But such was his luck, on this occasion, such was the thoroughness of the sadism of the cosmos, which apparently insisted on imbuing every instant of his life with awkwardness and clumsiness, that just at the moment he was about to make the drop off, with briefcase in hand, just as he was walking towards the meeting point, at the very nanosecond of his arrival, the director's Cadillac had passed across the bridge.

Dr Fuchs stumbled out into the cool blue dusk of the garden, sweating, skinny, straightening his glasses, quite sure in his heart that he would be garroted from behind at any moment. He looked up and saw, absurdly, the little suburban garden party spread before him—housewives babbling away in civilized conversation, American flags fluttering on the fences. A fat woman came wobbling across the lawn in a flowing mantle, crying out in a high voice, 'Gentlemen! Gentlemen! We are having a game of charades!'

'No, thank you,' said Dr Fuchs.

He walked aimlessly over the uneven grass. The roar of motors could be heard—of cars loaded with giggling WACs and soldiers, heading back to the dormitories. They blew their horns in celebration of the surrender, and their voices sang, 'Over there! Over there! Send the word, send the word, over there...'

5

Dr Lawrence did not dance. He sat on the porch by himself, looking out at the roofs and fences of the Technical Area and the trees and the darkened masses of the Jemez mountains.

Though a sociable person by nature, he had grown weary of the conversation at Los Alamos, particularly the foolish philosophical debates about the boys. He looked forward to getting back to Oak Ridge, where there was not so much empty space and empty talk and handwringing. He could not understand why doctors wanted to meddle in things that had nothing to do with them. What on earth could make them think that way?

A heavy presence, lowering itself into a chair beside him, stirred Dr Lawrence from his reverie.

'Terrible stuff, this negro music,' said General Groves.

Dr Lawrence listened—somebody had put a radio on, or a Victrola. A voice sang, half-drowned, through the scratching and scraping, 'Where are you? Where have you gone without me?'

'Awful,' he said.

'You grow up with your mom and dad shaking and jiving to this stuff, it's no wonder you get the delinquency,' said the general.

'That is if the father is in the picture,' said Dr Lawrence. 'Very often he isn't.'

General Groves nodded solemnly.

'Many of them in Berkeley?'

'Oh no,' said Lawrence. 'Berkeley is really quite a respectable place. Even moreso, I think, with the war on.'

'Interesting,' said General Groves. 'Fairly red, though, from what I've heard.'

'Oh, yes. It's as red as carbolic soap up there. But what can you do?'

They sat, listening to the music. The General began to tap his foot.

They talked of their early lives. Dr Lawrence, who had had a few beers, told the general about the beginnings of his career, his first machines, about his struggles for funding, about his struggles to be taken seriously by the medical establishment, about the great changes that had occurred in the field—even about his mother's abdominal cancer, and how he had driven her to the laboratory in Berkeley in the early thirties, and how he had said to her, 'Lay down, Mother,' and fired the beam into her uterus, and how he had helped her down out of the machine and walked her back to the car, and driven her home, and held her handbag while she vomited into the rhododendrons, and all the terrible months thereafter, and the doubts and trials, and how in the end it had worked, and how today she was as fit as a fiddle, all thanks to the machine. And they sat for a moment, Dr Lawrence and the general, in the midst of the quiet music, thinking of the boy, smooth and tumorless, in his room, and Dr Lawrence considered explaining to the general some of his ideas for after the war—testing centers all over the country, all in competition with one another, each with one or two hundred human subjects. They could use boys, or they could use prisoners, or if the military stayed involved they could even use soldiers. All they needed was neurological tissue. There were sure to be a few losses, but that was nothing compared with the enormous advantage it would provide to civilization. He wanted very much to put these ideas to the general and to secure his opinion on their feasibility. But he knew what the regulations were.

They listened to the rabble withdrawing from the house, the doctors with their foreign accents, and the soldiers, all disheveled from the dancing. It was curious what men would do, the general thought, under the spell of mammal attraction. Dr Oppenheimer was merely one example. That foolish business with Jean Tatlock. You cannot blame a man, he thought magnanimously. But then—it was weakness. Weakness. Staring out into that high crisp quiet night, away from the tobacco smoke and drink and insubordination, General Groves felt total confidence that they would succeed. He gazed up at the moon that had stalked him all his life, since he was a blushing pink babe in a nainsook gown. He thought of the great evil the Allies had almost purged from the earth, and he felt a great faith in the boys.

'Do you think they'll call us all sons of bitches after the war?' said Dr Lawrence.

'Not if we win.'

After a silence, the General spoke again.

'As long as they say, "That son of a bitch was right," then it's OK with me.'

Dr Lawrence laughed.

The general then related to Dr Lawrence a dream he had had several nights earlier. He had been seated at a bar, wearing a pinstriped suit. The bartender, who was the motion picture actress Greta Garbo, had offered him a glass of champagne. General Groves was a great moviegoer, he told Dr Lawrence, though he could not name a Greta Garbo picture if you asked him to. He preferred comedies—Laurel and Hardy, the Marx brothers, Duck Soup, and so on. Those were fine pictures, he said. In any case, there was something immensely calming and comfortable, the general said, in the way Greta Garbo offered him the glass of champagne, the fact that in spite of her celebrity she was so casual and kind. She offered it to him, he said, the way a friend would offer you a drink when you were tired after a hard day at work. He was not sure if there was even any discussion of payment. He did not remember paying. She had then asked him what he was going to do about the creature.

'The creature?' said Dr Lawrence.

Greta Garbo had said something about how terrible the creature was, and it had seemed obvious to the general, in the dream, that he needed to find the creature at once, in order to destroy it.

'You are acting like a man with a brick in his pocket,' she had said.

And he had looked towards the doorway of the bar, with the expectation that the creature would come through the door at any second. That was all he remembered.

6

Preparations for the test consumed the energies of the
doctors over the next few weeks. On the first of June the
director went to Washington for the meeting with the high
command. No sooner had he arrived and taken his small
office on the fifth floor of the New War Building, than he
was informed that somebody had come to see him. When
the name of this man was given, Dr Oppenheimer felt a
sense of mingled irritation and curiosity.

'Send him in,' he said.

Down the corridor with pompous tread came Dr Leo
Szilard—fat, short and shabby as he had always been,
turning his head to look at the doors and into the offices
as he passed them. He hammered on Dr Oppenheimer's
door, paused a moment to withdraw from his pocket

a white handkerchief and wipe it across his face, then entered, in a great fluster, forgetting to take off his trench coat, and pouring a mound of papers onto the desk.

Dr Oppenheimer rose with his usual grace and economy of movement, welcomed his guest, towered over him, indicated a chair for him, took out a cigarette, reseated himself, smiled. They made conversation.

'You were involved in the early work, weren't you?' said Dr Oppenheimer.

Dr Szilard nodded deeply.

'I was, yes.'

'With Teller and Fermi.'

'Yes. Those were very different times. I have fallen out of favor, you see.'

'I see,' said Dr Oppenheimer, with one of his uniquely comprehending sidelong glances. 'It's not something I have complete control over, unfortunately. Some very restrictive decisions have been made.'

With this Dr Szilard expressed emphatic agreement.

'I must be honest with you, Dr Oppenheimer,' he said. 'I am very worried. I think our time is running out to express these things that, frankly, nobody is considering.'

He proceeded to lay out his arguments—the same arguments he had related to Mr Byrnes, though they were all the more urgent now, because time had passed. Dr Szilard had gone over these words and concepts so frequently in his head that he was incapable of distinguishing what he was saying from a stream of nonsense. But he tried to trust himself to retch out the thing, the one thing, though he had no idea what it was, that was necessary to say.

Dr Oppenheimer listened in his usual way, cigarette in hand, his blue eyes locked on his visitor. Then, when Dr

Szilard had concluded, he turned his face to the window, and the summer's day, and considered the matter carefully, smoking. Finally he said something that Dr Szilard had not at all been expecting.

'The boy is shit,' he said.

There was a pause.

'I beg your pardon?'

Dr Oppenheimer was silent a moment longer.

'The boy can have no military significance. He'll be something to look at, that's for sure. But he won't be useful in war. He could never be an effective soldier. He's a child, after all. For now we have to leave these decisions in the hands of the military.'

Dr Szilard regarded the director for a moment—the high, proud, small head, the electric eyes, the short black unruly hair—and wondered if he was serious.

'But Dr Oppenheimer, from a moral standpoint, if the boys are indeed—er—as you say, then that is all the more reason we must not make this grave error of sending them out there. The Japanese, you see—' He reached for his papers and began going through them. 'It is quite clear to me the Japanese are going to surrender. The Russians will invade Manchuria. That will force a surrender. And they may give up before that time anyway.'

He rifled through his papers. Somewhere he had maps, newspaper clippings, carbon copies of all his recent letters.

Dr Oppenheimer put his cigarette out in an ashtray and glanced at the papers. 'The Russians, huh?' he said, with a cold glance.

'We can—ah! Here is another thing, Dr Oppenheimer, this is something nobody talks about—We can do a demonstration. We do a kind of test, you see, test the prosthesis, and we invite some observers from Japan. Such a demonstration would show what these boys are capable of. If they still refuse to surrender, then fine. Do what you like. Send the boys.'

'Who would we invite to such a demonstration?' said Dr Oppenheimer. 'Hirohito? You think the Japanese would come? And if they did, you think they'd believe what they saw?'

In Dr Oppenheimer's voice there was a distinct note of contempt. And indeed, he was annoyed with Dr Szilard, without knowing precisely why.

'We must not forget our role, Dr Szilard,' he said. 'We are not statesmen.'

'But we are the only ones who understand. If the statesmen do not understand, it is up to us to understand for them.'

Dr Oppenheimer coughed. Dr Szilard went on talking. Dr Oppenheimer began to shake his head.

'No... No...'

The Hungarian would not be silenced. He went on talking and Dr Oppenheimer went on listening, though it irritated him more and more to do so. His points, Dr Oppenheimer knew, were reasonable points. But they were not new. They were all points that Dr Oppenheimer had considered long ago, before even beginning to work on the boys. And there was much that Dr Szilard was not taking into consideration—the saving of American lives, or even of Japanese lives, the possible prevention of war, the international situation. It seemed foolish to sit here now and discuss these points as though he had not already considered them.

'Dr Szilard,' he said, in a somewhat more forceful tone. 'I must ask you. Who are you to talk about the psychology of the Japanese? And to accuse our leaders of not understanding what they're doing? These are wise men. They know all the facts. They know more than we know. It is their job to send our sons to die. Who are you to accuse them of not taking their decisions lightly?'

Some color had come into the director's cheeks. He heard the ticking of the spools. Ghosts in the walls. He thought of Dr Tatlock. He put a cigarette in his mouth and went to strike a match but the match broke in his fingers. He put the cigarette on the desk.

'I don't disagree with you,' he went on, somewhat confusedly. 'I mean, I don't think it's all right either. I think the whole thing is hell. What do we do? Wait for surrender? What if it doesn't come? We all know we are caught up in something terrible. You think we don't know? You really think we are unaware? Do you really think, Dr Szilard, that when we look around us, we do not see all of the—the unpleasantness of it all—'

Dr Oppenheimer knew he was expressing himself poorly, was not sure even that he agreed with himself, but he went on:

'It was our lousy luck to be born, I mean to be alive, at this time. We didn't start the goddamn thing. We just happen to be in it. Look at Tokyo. That was eighty thousand people. Dresden. Twenty-five thousand. Hamburg. The Blitz. What the hell is different about this? You can't just look at one or two boys and say—You can't—You know what your problem is? You want heaven and earth too, Dr Szilard. You say, Well, if we all behaved in a nice way we would have no trouble. Sure, I agree with you there. But that is not ethics. That is not ethics.'

Dr Oppenheimer was looking straight at Dr Szilard, straight into him.

The Hungarian paused.

'My feeling,' said Dr Szilard at length, 'is that the boys are different. They are essentially different. And our leaders fail to see that. I merely want to express these concerns to you in the hope that you will please make use of your influence.'

'I have no influence,' said Dr Oppenheimer. 'I give scientific advice. I tell them mathematical facts. I make recommendations on the design of the device. I have no influence on anything.'

'You have quite a bit more influence than I do.'

'Dr Szilard, I'm afraid we're out of time.'

'Please think about this,' said Dr Szilard. 'If we do this—'

'If we don't do it, somebody else does it. It can be done. It's not our fault it can be done.'

'But it's our fault if we do it.'

'It's the fault of the Japanese, who refuse to end the war.'

'They are boys.'

'They are,' said Dr Oppenheimer. 'Yes. They are.'

Dr Oppenheimer stood up. If Intelligence was recording him he must make sure he was firm with this man—firm, diplomatic, calm.

'I wish we could meet under less trying circumstances. Thank you for coming here. You have made your concerns known to me. I will tell them all I can. All that is in my capacity to say, I will say. You have my word on that.'

The director was not unfamiliar with Dr Szilard's arguments. They had been known to him from the very beginning. They were natural concerns. They had always been present in his mind, always. And lately, of course, he had felt it all the more strongly—the sense of wrong, the crude and simple sense, which no vulgarity or humor or overstatement could quite extinguish, that he was doing the wrong thing. It was that little voice awakened by Dr Tatlock's death, the voice of his misgivings, always telling him that he was on the wrong side of things, coaxing him towards the inescapable conclusion that who he was and what he stood for was contrary to human happiness. It was a feeling that was always there, waiting to utter itself. Unfathomable folly. It was an excruciating feeling. Like razor-footed scarabs crawling over his heart. Every way before him was wrong, crowded with wrongs, every path concealed a morass.

Still, he knew that going ahead with the prosthesis was the least worst option. They were now at war with the war itself. They must do whatever it took to end it. There was no way to dispel the feeling of error, other than to persuade oneself to ignore it. It was like a surgeon who puts on a pair of new white gloves, and slices, for the first time, with a sterile and shining scalpel, into a human body. It will always feel unnatural, even though it is necessary. So it must be with the boys, he thought. Clean and decisive. He wondered, as Dr Szilard left the office, how many boys it would really take, before the Japanese finally gave up. Ten? Twenty?

Dr Szilard came out of the building with his papers bundled in his arms. He set off southwards down the street, and the wind began to pluck the papers from his arms, causing him to tighten his embrace. But he did not turn back to pick them up. He allowed them simply to float behind him— pearl-white, tumbling, spinning, sailing in arcs, chased and borne by the whirling air.

He decided that if the director was going to be complacent, he must mobilize the doctors himself. He would write a petition. He would begin by circulating it among his own small team, then get it somehow to Los Alamos. If they could not immediately halt the prosthetic work, they could at least ensure a demonstration of the boys' abilities before an international audience. With such schemes brewing in his head he reached the National Mall, and proceeded at full speed onto the grass, through the middle of a frisbee match, deep in thought and entirely oblivious to the two young American sportsmen who had begun to execrate him with all their might.

The next day, at the meeting with the military high command, the general's suit was freshly pressed and his stars were polished to a mirror finish. Beside him sat the Secretary of War, and beside him Mr Byrnes (representing President Truman), and a group of long-faced men from the Carnegie Institute, and beside them various other men from the government. Dr Oppenheimer, Dr Lawrence and Dr Fermi represented the scientists.

One by one the men gave their opinions on the deployment of the boys. It was evident that none of them understood, on a practical level, just how the prosthesis was supposed to work, but this was immaterial, for their statements almost entirely concerned the Japanese, and the very low likelihood of their surrender. The time came for Dr Oppenheimer to speak on behalf of the doctors, and he felt their eyes settle upon him, a crawling sensation, and with a voice that seemed to come from the ceiling, rather than from himself, he made the following address.

'The opinions of our scientific colleagues,' he said, 'are not unanimous. They range from the proposal of a purely technical demonstration of the prosthesis, to that of the military application best designed to induce a surrender by the Japanese. Others emphasize the opportunity of saving American lives by immediate military deployment. I think'—he coughed—'I think I speak for the three of us here today when I say that we find ourselves closer to these latter views. We can propose no technical demonstration likely to bring an end to the war. We see no acceptable alternative to direct military deployment.'

It flowed out of him in a single continuous exhalation, and when he finished speaking the heads and the eyes if the military men and the government men remained iron still, as though everything he had said was quite reasonable and even obvious—and perhaps it was—and then somebody spoke, and somebody else spoke, and the conference went on as before.

At the conclusion of the meeting the men were in agreement. They rose, leaning over to grasp each other by the hands, their neckties sweeping the tabletop. Pieces of paper were stacked and sorted. Chairs were pulled out and put in with scraping sounds. Dr Fermi wiped the sweat from his forehead, then he coughed heavily into the palms of both of his hands, a hideous, loud, retching cough, full of phlegm and mucus. The chief point of agreement of all the gentlemen present was that the boys must go to war as soon as they were able to do so. As soon as their prostheses could be proven to work they must be deployed immediately to Japan, without any prior warning. This business being finalized, the doctors went back to work.

7

A glorious summer was taking shape over the plateau, but Mrs Oppenheimer had shrunk away, and was rarely seen. Among the ever-observant wives of the senior staff, her disappearance from social life was seen as the confirmation of a long-standing hypothesis—that she was a woman of deciduous charms, and perhaps even a Nazi sympathizer.

Just what it was that occupied Mrs Oppenheimer, during this period of personal decline, cannot easily be described. She herself did not know quite how her days were extinguished so rapidly and with so little incident. For she did not have a routine, but rather a limited range of activities and obligations from which she chose, according to her indisposition. There was her son, of course. This occupied a considerable part of her time.

From the hour of waking to the hour of breakfast, when the weather was fine, it was her habit to lie on a deckchair in the yard with her white sunglasses on. After breakfast she played solitaire. Afternoons were generally for cooking, cleaning, laundry, gardening and looking after her son. She had a maid to manage things when her energies were lacking, which was now at least five days a week. Sometimes she simply sat in the kitchen, smoked packs of cigarettes and listened to the blasting in the canyons. She found the days too slow and the months too fast. Sometimes she went riding, but not often, not often.

Every few weeks she had occasion to fall down the garden steps. She would go tumbling, arms and legs flailing, sometimes crying out, sometimes in perfect silence. Then moments later she was to be observed leaning nonchalantly on the picket fence. All the neighboring wives would somehow hear of these unfortunate precipitations. She received visitors. Mrs Bacher was particularly scrupulous in her inquiries after her health, and could be relied upon to keep a more or less public record of the details of her home and condition.

Though she did not care much for such gestures of generosity, Mrs Oppenheimer continued, at least during the early part of that period, to convene gatherings of her own. Avoiding her officious well-wishers, she would seek out younger, more malleable, more readily exchangeable companions. Springing upon them at the commissary or at the day-care center she would declare that they must, absolutely must, get to know each other. Then she would propose an hour or two of cocktails, followed by a long walk across the mesas or the caldera or along the trails of tuff or through the volcanic plains.

These expeditions rarely eventuated, though the cocktails proceeded without fail. Having assembled the women in the garden or before the fire, she brought them trays of martinis and observed, with quiet enjoyment, the disintegration of their conversations.

Sometimes they listened to the war on the radio.

'How many million now? Fifty-six?'

'Yes. Fifty-six million now.'

'Shall we have another?'

'Oh, Kitty, I couldn't possibly.'

'Nonsense!'

Nobody but Mrs Oppenheimer enjoyed these gatherings, and after a time she too grew tired of them, and they ceased. She became too tied up—this was how she put it, too tied up—even for them. And as the summer drew on, the combination of her cocktail hours (now solitary affairs), her apéritifs, digestifs, nightcaps, liquid lunches and various other avocations caused Mrs Oppenheimer to begin to struggle with even the simple verbal transactions of polite society.

When Mrs Parsons, for instance, came craning her neck over the picket fence of an afternoon, her eyes boggling, an enormous smile fixed upon her face, saying things like 'It's steak night at the Lodge,' or, 'It's a nice day,' or, 'I heard you had an accident last week,' or, 'Have you thought about secretarial work?' or even that insoluble question, 'How are you?'—then Mrs Oppenheimer would feel strange sensations washing over her, as though she was standing before a crumbling edifice, or in a room filled with inexplicable objects, or in the midst of a river violently coursing, and she would feel something she was quite certain was her own big heart, roaring like a bull at its gates, and there before her, all the while, in spite of all these thoughts, would be that monstrous gleaming rictus, those cheeks smeared with blush, the Victory rolls, the blue day dress, the skirt apron, the picket fence and the drooping heads of the red carnations, and flowing out of all of it that flood of meaningless words—lodge, steak night, nice, secretarial, accident, how, you, and so on. It may as well have been a dog barking at her from across the fence. And occasionally, unfortunately, in her collapsing state, Mrs Oppenheimer would respond in regrettable terms.

One day in late June she put her head in the washing machine.

'Come on,' said Dr Oppenheimer. 'Up.'

It appeared she had dozed off. Her cheek was pressed comfortably against the back of her left hand. A pool of saliva had formed. She did not want to get up.

'Get your hands off me,' she said. 'You rattlesnake.'

Dr Oppenheimer had just got back from the office. On the floor was a basket of clothes and a glass bottle.

'You really ought to let Rosa do it,' he said.

She had extracted her head and was sitting up.

'When Rosa does it everything ends up—spotted. You know, spotted. I have to do it. I can get anything out.'

'Come on now. One, two.'

'Damn you.'

He heaved her up. She fumbled for a long time with her shoes, white pumps, trying to secure them to her feet. Then she gave up. A lock of dark red hair hung down over her face. She cast a troubled look at the clothes half-spilled from the machine, the wet clothes, limp and clinging to one another. She saw the bottle.

'I am going—to—the bathroom.'

'Careful now.'

'Please. I'm quite capable.'

She opened the door, stepped into the soggy foam of the hallway floor, felt the entire western side of the house tilt, lean against her forehead, knocking with a dull thud. The wall. Her left arm upraised for navigation, she sprawled her way down the spinning corridor until she found, with her forearm and her left cheek and her lips, the cold wood of the bathroom door. Now came the intricate problem of the handle. But to her shock it yielded almost immediately—they understood one another—it swung wide its mouth. They gasped, she and the door. Something smashed. She wondered, falling, if she was at a point of crisis. She felt her diaphragm leap, upheave, she began to scramble, claw, her hair—never mind. The floor was hard, cold—she was a long time in the bathroom.

The director seated himself at his small desk in the master bedroom and attempted to complete some work. Before him was a sheet of paper with a schedule for the day of the test. The test was drawing near. On each side of the page were the boys' code-names: twenty-five and forty-nine, and under these headings a list of the things that needed to be done with them on the 16th of July.

He knew he ought to find out what was the matter with his wife. He knew he ought to attempt to help her. But his options were limited. To elicit a moment's sincerity from Mrs Oppenheimer was no easy matter. He had as much chance of having a heart to heart conversation with a king cobra. And besides, the test was consuming most of his mental energies.

He heard the sound of fumbling at the door handle and prepared himself for whatever dose of venom he was about to receive.

She leaned in at him. There was silence. Her hair was in a frizz.

'Thank you,' she said.

'Not at all,' said Dr Oppenheimer.

She looked at him a little longer. Then she came forward and leaned against the edge of the desk, bolt upright, and said:

'Did you put Peter to bed?'

'Yes.'

She reached for a half-smoked cigarette in the ashtray.

'Tomorrow I'll be alright,' she said faintly. 'Up in the morning, early. I want to be up at dawn. That's what I need.'

She wandered into the center of the room with fragile steps. Part of her wanted to lie down, but she could not. The room was swimming slightly, left and right. Few know as well as drunken people this sensation of waiting for one's body—the swimming world, the mind a tethered bubble, wanting to sleep, and the whole vestibular system overcome with inexplicable antagonism. With care she prepared to dismount—to hunch, sidle, bend, denude herself, dispose of her day's carcass in the creases of the bed—she looked with longing and disgust at the crumpled sheets.

Then she drifted back to the director.

'Do you know what your problem is?' she said. 'Let me look at you.'

She put her hand below his chin and he complied, angling his head upwards. He saw his pale face stretched and duplicated upon her irises.

'You're petrified,' she said.

'Huh,' he said.

He looked down again. He put one of his hands on her waist and pulled her closer to him. Her dress was of a thin material. It had little gardenias, red and white.

'No use sitting around trembling about it,' she said. 'You have to look at it full in the face, whatever it is, and say, Well, I'll show you, you big ass. That's what I think.'

He laughed and coughed simultaneously.

'Yes, well. Thank you for the advice.'

He wanted to tell her about the boys. To unfold it all to her. He thought of turning on the radio, of turning it up to full volume and telling her, but he did not do it. He did not want to draw suspicion. After a while, Mrs Oppenheimer turned away from him with a sweeping gesture—a formal, gracious, elegant one-armed gesture of refusal—wavered over to the window and peered through it.

'There they are,' she said. She paused. 'Watching us again. No home to go to, evidently. Nothing better to do than observe our tedious lives. Aren't you bored stiff, watcher? Do something else. Get up, go. It's not difficult. Look at this silly fool.'

'Who?'

'Spooks,' she said.

The street was still. For a moment she stood studying it. Dr Oppenheimer arrived at her side and they peered out together, two skull-white faces. Then Mrs Oppenheimer brought her fists together and the curtain hissed along its rail.

8

That same evening Dr Teller returned home from the Technical Area somewhat earlier than usual. He lay down on the sofa, not removing his jacket, but undoing his shirt collar, and speaking, at high volume, as usual, to his wife, who was doing something in the kitchen.

For that entire year, he said, he had worked on his Advanced Design, forming the best possible theory of how each of its components would work. But today his weekly meeting with Dr Oppenheimer had been postponed—and not for the first time. He had not even been allowed into the Theoretical Division meeting, because of regulations. This was probably Dr Bethe's doing. For though Dr Bethe was not his superior, he continued to take enormous pleasure, said Dr Teller, in drawing attention away from the Advanced

Design. Even Dr Oppenheimer, who he had long considered such a sensible administrator, seemed suddenly to have lost his interest in these important ideas, and to have developed tunnel vision, as the test drew closer.

The Advanced Design was the most important work now taking place at Los Alamos, Dr Teller said, waving in the air a single finger. Since there was no doubt, he said, that the prostheses would work, it was essential now to look ahead, into the long term, beyond the present juncture of the war. The Russians were in the best position now that they had ever been in. They were surely working on boys of their own. People were blind, he said—just as blind now as they had been in 1939.

Dr Teller drew breath.

And what was worse, said Dr Teller, was that they continued to give him these jobs, these little irrelevant tasks, things that could easily be handled by others who were not so laden with responsibility.

All this he explained to Mrs Teller, who was now doing something with their son, putting him into a chair before the kitchen table, arranging plates and bowls, drawing a knife across slices of bread.

'Are you listening to me?' he said.

'Yes,' replied Mrs Teller, who was, by a strange force of habit, listening intently to her husband.

He said he had his doubts about this. She said she did not care. She continued moving about the kitchen in her restless, efficient way, reaching into the lurid army-green cabinets, and attending to Paul.

'I think I must simply accept that there are people on this earth whom I was never meant to get through to,' Dr Teller said tragically. 'It would be much more comfortable to like everybody. Before I moved here I even managed to do this—at least approximately. Sometimes I think people are all really fundamentally the same. And sometimes I think they are miles apart.'

He went on speaking—for he never concealed any item of his thoughts from his wife—and she continued to listen to him, to glance from time to time at his heavy morose face, his hairy hands folded on his stomach, his false foot poised on the arm of the sofa. Physically he had changed during the last few years. War has a general tendency to shrink bodies, but it had fattened Dr Teller. His face was flabbier, and his slouch had worsened, so that his head hung forward, as dark and as greasy as ever.

Paul twisted round and drew up his legs and then stood up on the seat in his chair and began to shout, for some reason.

'Sit, Paul,' said Mrs Teller. 'It's dangerous.'

'I don't know what to think,' said Dr Teller, ignoring this brief commotion. 'Do they dislike me? Is that what it is? Or does Oppie genuinely not see the importance of this work?'

Mrs Teller subdued their son. She handed him a little toy car, and he began to play with it on the table, making noises with his mouth. She went back to the pot where the soup was cooking. There was no soup for Dr Teller, for he had declared, with some pathos, that he was not hungry.

'You know,' Mrs Teller said, 'I have always found Oppenheimer to be a bit of a poseur.'

'Well, of course. He is the director. You can't have the most intelligent people at the top. You must have the most charismatic. That is how it works in America. Much of what they call science is one man walking into a room and shaking hands with another man and walking out again.'

'Do you remember when we first met him in California?'

'Yes, and he made that terrible spicy food.'

'And you lost your voice.'

They laughed.

'I am sure he meant well,' said Dr Teller.

Mrs Teller shook her head.

'It's hard to tell,' she said. 'I have a sense for people. And Oppenheimer—I don't know. I find him dishonest. And not as bright as everybody thinks.'

Dr Teller nodded.

'You may be right,' he said. 'In fact you probably are right. There is something of that about him.'

'If you'd only heard the things he was saying the other day, about the Russians. He talks straight out of his mouth, I think. Everything straight out of his mouth. I'm sure he says a different thing to everybody. The man has no real principles. His wife too. Oh I don't hate her as much as everybody else, but I don't think either of them has any ideas about anything. No real ideas.'

Having got this off her chest, Mrs Teller paused briefly over her pot and emitted a short sigh.

'What did he say about the Russians?' said Dr Teller.

As she ladled some soup into a bowl for the child, Mrs Teller gave her best account of what she had heard Dr Oppenheimer saying on the road to Dr Bethe. Dr Teller did not reply, but got up from the sofa and paced for a few minutes, ruminating.

Years ago when Dr Teller was a student in the Gymnasium, he had known a boy named Forgács. He had a problem with his thyroid. Iodine trouble. He had a tiny, shrunken body, and a squint. He could not do the mathematical problems. They used to dance around Forgács in a circle, making faces and noises and wiggling their hands in their ears. Forgács would become upset, then frantic, then furious. The best the young Edward Teller could do was sit by and not participate. But he had always noticed the change that had come into the eyes of little Forgács, whenever they taunted him. A darkening—like a match dropped into a well.

Such was the look—the very same—that came into the eyes of Dr Teller, as he began to reflect on his last few meetings with the director.

He had asked him, during his last meeting, for more people on his team.

'Everybody is needed for test work,' Dr Oppenheimer had said.

'Give me Serber.'

'Can't do that.'

'Why? What is Dr Serber doing that is so important?'

'That's classified,' Dr Oppenheimer had said.

A furrow rose in the bristled brow of Dr Teller. He began to think of other things the director had said, remarks he had made, during their weekly meetings, small denigrations of the Advanced Design. He remembered an occasion when Dr Oppenheimer had made light of a simple mathematical error in his presentation. He remembered another phrase which Dr Oppenheimer had used, in one of their meetings—'Keep your shirt on,' he had said. 'We'll find time to do these things.' The phrase had stood out to him even then. Keep your shirt on.

As he stood there, by the sofa, looking towards the kitchen, his head bowed slightly, watching Paul poke with a spoon at his soup, and run his toy car absent-mindedly along the tabletop, the true nature of the whole situation dawned finally on Dr Teller. He comprehended at last the true nature of Dr Oppenheimer's intentions—he wanted to win the war, save the United States, receive a pat on the back, then hand the boys over to the Russians.

Turning from the kitchen, Dr Teller began to limp down the hall. He thought briefly of going to the Steinway, of sitting down for an hour of vigorous practice. He was tempted to do this, but he did not. He had to follow his thoughts, unpleasant though they were, to their conclusion. He went upstairs, his prosthesis thundering on the steps, compelled by an obscure desire to be alone, in his room. There he remained for a time, thinking about Dr Oppenheimer, who did not care about the Advanced Design, had never cared about the Advanced Design. All was suddenly clear to him. That conversation at the party last year. His promotion. With an excruciating twisting of the entire mental apparatus, his own stupidity became immediately evident. He had been played. It had never been a promotion at all. Dr Oppenheimer had merely removed him, had taken away any power he might have had. By removing him from Dr Bethe's division he had limited the amount of access he had to classified information, and put him right where he wanted him.

All those months of recommendations had gone no further than Dr Oppenheimer's desk. All his projections, all his designs and redesigns, all those things on which he had spent so much time, seemed now to be useless. Everyone had been deceiving him. He saw before him the little narrow corridor of his life, running as a trench or groove through the universe. He saw his dark-eyed, earnest, studious self, unaware of greatness, ignorant of the true beauties of the earth. He saw himself fat and grave in his suit and tie, in his high buckled trousers, with his big metallic foot, scratching at his little pages while people like the director drank martinis and played poker and tennis and drove carelessly about in handsome blue convertible cars. And then he saw again, like a coming storm, the Russians. Up over the crown of the hill, he saw the Russian army coming, a million soldiers, small in stature, their mouths thrown wide in a rising song—a sudden blast of wind—fields of swooning swine—houses burst into confetti. He thought of his son, his wife, his family in Hungary. He paced some more in his room, uneven paces, his eyes on the floor.

It was a clever move. Yes, there was no denying that. Dr Oppenheimer had played him handsomely. But it was not a checkmate, not quite. There were ways out. Hungarians are men who know the ways out of tight spots. And Dr Teller was, as much as he was anything at all, a Hungarian. He stopped by his window and looked at it, at the glass, seeing nothing, and thought about the director with a sudden furious brooding hatred. Dr Oppenheimer had been indiscrete—he should have known better than to speak so freely with Dr Bethe. That was a misstep, Dr Teller thought. One indiscretion may be all it takes, Dr Teller thought, to bring the director undone. All that was needed, perhaps, was to apply a little pressure, sow a few seeds of doubt. The game was not yet over.

Mrs Teller continued to attend to the affairs of the evening. She sent Paul to his room and told him to dress for bed. Then she cleared his bowl and his plate of crusts from the kitchen table. She let the water run for a short time, for the water was always running out, and efficiently scrubbed the dishes and her hands. The telephone rang and she was, as ever, quick to answer it.

'Am I speaking to Mrs Teller?' said the voice.

'Yes.'

'I have some information about your family.'

In the room upstairs, Dr Teller heard a sound like a steam-whistle choked with soot. He hastened down the stairs.

'What was that?' cried Paul from within his room.

Dr Teller came quickly down the hallway, limping. He pulled Paul's door closed as though by instinct.

'Stay in your room,' he said.

He passed out of the hall and into the kitchen. The first thing he saw was the telephone, its receiver of red bakelite, swinging on its cord. Then he saw Mrs Teller. She was standing with her back to the sink, rigid, her hands drawn up to her face. Her hands were pale, sinewy, still a little damp. She looked at him with a hopeless look, like a ghost—she did not move.

'Mici,' he said.

Slowly she stretched out her arms. He went to her.

9

The final weeks of June slipped by. The doctors began to spend more and more time away from the Technical Area, at the test site. One day into the boy's room they brought the other boy, and he looked very different. He was perfectly round—a small smooth ball. The boy tried to meet his gaze, but he could not see his eyes. They carried him quickly through the room and he was gone. It was very unusual.

In the days before the big test, a wave of energy came over the doctors. Having long toiled under that practical pessimism customary to men of science, it began to dawn on them that the treatment may actually work. No matter how they felt about the deployment of the boys, all were possessed by this enchanting new feeling. They stayed later than ever at the Technical Area, talked louder and longer in their meetings, calculated long into the night, as though the war was going to end without them.

Finally the big day arrived. The 16th of July. In the morning a large contingent of doctors left the Technical Area. The boy heard the buses in the courtyard and the air sodden with the babble of men and their voices upraised in excitement, he heard briefly Dr Oppenheimer among them, saying, 'Yes, yes, yes...' then, in a churn of motors, their voices faded.

The boy was in a storage cupboard, facing the wall. All was quiet. It was as quiet as the nights, but it was day— a very strange thing, for the boy had always known Los Alamos as a busy place in the daytime. Around three o'clock the weather took a turn. Rain began to fall and make its tick tick on the windowpanes. Clouds grayened the earth. The voices of geese could be heard, scattered in deranged flight—struggling cries. It was a large storm, the slow-gathering kind, the kind that brings quiet before its fury, that looms miles high and makes the mountains look small, and sets the dogs barking and trembles in the ears of men.

Three men entered, all wearing spats.

'Ready to go, Cyril?' said one of the men.

The windows rattled. A low growl was heard, echoing from the heights of the Jemez mountains. The men placed the boy in a box. He felt some apprehension, and was quite sure that he was to be taken to Alamogordo, for the test. But not twenty minutes had passed and his box was opened, and he saw that he was still in the Technical Area. He was in an unfamiliar room. Against one wall there were several large metal boxes stacked on top of each other. On a table there were buckets and vessels of various sizes.

He could hear the rain, louder than before, crashing on the roof. And the men were standing over him, wearing masks— all wearing heavy masks with dark glass concealing their eyes, and long leather gloves on their hands. The wind was blowing very loudly now and the rain was falling heavily.

The boy had made an error in assuming that he was to be tested that day. For in reality, only the other boy was to go to Alamogordo, to the Jornada del Muerto, several miles from Los Alamos. The boy, on the other hand—the African boy—was scheduled for quite a different procedure.

His shape was to be altered.

One of the masked men picked him up carefully and placed him in a large white ceramic bowl. A lid was lowered over him. Inside it was cramped and dim. He felt this vessel being carried, rocking gently, then he felt it set down. He heard the closing of a door. The sound of the storm was muffled slightly, and he continued to try not to be afraid, for there was something about storms that had always made him afraid.

Then the heat began. The air grew stifling. The walls and the base of the bowl became so hot that it hurt to lie upon them, but he could not move. He waited for the heat to end. But it did not end.

Suddenly the furnace-room was full of light. Blinding searing-white sheets filled the sky above the mesas, and every canyon and ravine was illuminated. And then the noise came—the splintering impact of a great slow thunderclap, a vast soundwave spreading through space and time and shattering all that it encountered. And the rain poured on, and the wind blew, and the lightning flashed again in searing silence, and the thunder arrived for the second time.

In the furnace the heat had become excruciating. The boy's skin felt tight and constricted. A feeling like microscopic pinpricks, like tiny needles driven into him, spread across his surfaces. Acrid smoke came off him. He began, after a time, to glow with a weird red luminosity. Slowly, he softened. It was wrong—something was quite wrong. His thoughts were in confusion. There was nothing he could do. Agonizing minutes passed. Tongues of flame scraped, stinging, hiss-boiling, over his skin. He shook. He physically shook. He had gone all white—bluish white. He began to melt. And all that had once been his skin, skull, brain, lips, muscles, organs, bones—all melted, with extreme rapidity, into a raw clotted bubbling smoldering slime of flesh.

He wanted to cry out. It was like he was being punished. He had done nothing and he was being punished for it. Suddenly he was all wrong, anatomically. His molten crown was slipping down through his molten chin and his eyes, blinded by the sheer pain, were swelling up like bubbles in the glowing slag. For his whole life he had waited for the beginning of his life to come and it had not come. Suddenly he wanted to go back, crawl back into his paralytic childhood, back into his old drum, back into the warehouse, with his rats, where he was safe. He wanted to go back to when he was on his first train and he smelled the oranges in the orange groves. But that was all gone and never again to be met with. It was all gone—his rats, his drums, his old head, his old face, his old stumps. None of those things existed anymore as they had existed then, least of all himself. They had taken it all away and it was gone. For the first time the boy, who had no fear of death, became aware that he was not a thing of permanence. That some part of him, indeed many small parts of him, had already been lost, irretrievably. A great chunk of his life was gone and could not be got back again. A terrible thought seized him. He thought of himself as no longer being a boy, no longer dreaming as a boy, no longer being able to dream as big, of being too old and unable to go back, all his chances and opportunities squandered, and his whole youth wasted. He would no longer be a boy, he would be a different person entirely, the boy he was would be dead, and all his dreams would be dead, and nobody would care in the slightest. The furnace groaned. The roar went on, filled the vast gray gurgling sky, and roared over the cowering earth, tore its verdure, defaced and disfigured the pretty hills and valleys, and drowned the thousand birds of the trees. It went on—this was the worst of all, that it went on, refusing to cease, without the slightest cause or provocation.

The boy was heated to 1350 degrees Celsius. His flesh began to sputter and cough. It began to cry out in a little voice of its own, a voice he did not know it had. Little fires, darting, hastened and retreated across his surface, whereupon the doctors made the magnanimous decision to lower the temperature, to 1270 degrees Celsius, and to transfer him into a new receptacle, of peculiar shape, where he remained for another two hours. At last he slipped into a state of shock, in which the knowledge that he existed, and that he suffered, and that the suffering was not stopping, mercifully deserted him. But as luck would have it this was the very moment the furnace was opened.

They removed him from the furnace with tongs and left him to cool. Had he been able to look at himself he would have seen that he was now shaped like a ring, perfectly round—a hollow cylinder, six and a quarter inches in diameter with a four-inch bore, one and a quarter inches from top to bottom. When viewed from above, an annulus. Still gray in color. But he had no idea what he looked like, and did not care to inquire, at this juncture.

It became evident to the boy, as he slowly regained consciousness, that he could see only out of one eye. He was unsure what had happened to the other, whether it had been covered over, as with a cataract, or rolled inward, or been lost entirely. No, he still felt that it was there, just that it had gone out—extinguished, snuffed. Now he had but one. Its edges seemed frayed and bleary. His hearing was as good as ever. He heard the men continuing to work, opening and closing the furnace. He could still smell, as ever. There was a stench of burning. All was as before, all the same, with the exception of his eye, and his shape, and the numbness that covered every inch of his body and the knowledge that he would soon be in agony from his burns, but that it had not set in yet.

As his faculties returned to him, he realized at length that they had put him upside down on the table. He pondered this fact as the pain began to set in. They were breaking him down. This he could not deny. He was learning their ways. It was all part of his education. And would there be no end to his education?

Before him was a window. The storm had died down. Now and then there was a rumble of thunder. Night had fallen. He could not sleep. The pain was too great. He lay there for a long time gazing out through the glass. At one point, long after midnight, he thought he saw, far away in the south, the sun coming up. For an instant it was day, but not a minute had passed and it was night again. The boy lay motionless in the dark, until all that he heard was the gurgling, high above, of the black rain.

PART V

1

The next morning, Mr Juan María Montez woke up just after dawn, went out onto his porch, looked out at his cattle in the distance, and wondered what was the matter with them.

The sun shone down on the wide flat fields and on the blue-green slopes and folds of Chupadera Mesa, on its patches of red forest, and on its high escarpment. Through the far pastures his herd flowed, rippling, through the grass and the creosote bushes and the tarworts and the junipers, towards the edge of his land. Something about them, some miniscule detail, did not look right, to Mr Montez. He stood for a moment, a hand drawn up to his face to shield the sun, his back against the adobe wall of the ranch-house, looking.

As he ate his breakfast he considered the matter,

staring at the wooden table. His wife brought him coffee.

'Ire a revisar el ganado,' he said.

'Y a mi que me importa,' she said.

He drove out in his old truck through the dust and long grass. He stopped briefly to look at the water-troughs. Nothing seemed to be amiss. Then he drove on into the flatlands where the herd was standing. They were in a huddle, with heads bowed, not grazing, leering at the ground, as though scrutinizing it. Something was, indeed, quite wrong with them.

A few of them approached the truck. It was so quiet, so unusually quiet—for there were no crickets, and no birds, and no frogs—that when he turned off the engine he heard at once the breathing of his cows, the slow labored breathing, and their feeble steps along the grass. The cow that came nearest to the truck had a stretch of raw pink skin along its side. Another stood nearby with a great bald patch on its back—all the hair had fallen out and the bare skin shone pink as though sunburnt.

They had not been like this the day before. As he walked through the herd they lifted their heads and parted. They blinked at him with black impassive eyes, and their breathing surrounded him.

He noted that the ailment affected the entire herd. They all had hairless patches. On some it was on the left side, on some it was on the right side. Some had lost the hair on their rumps, others had lost the hair on their heads, and stared at him with weird, gaunt, leathery, raw-boned faces. There were trails of scabs and blisters on the exposed skin. Calves grovelled in the midst of the beasts, their knees trembling. The patches were not small, but huge swathes of bared skin. Stretching out his hand, he touched one of the cows in the middle of its forehead. It began to grunt, a hideous grunting, a retching, out of its four twisted stomachs. It grunted and groaned and its foul breath hit him in the face.

Mr Montez went back to his truck and drove north for a few miles, at first with a kind of desire to get away, but in time with the intention of surveying the entire property. He was not an excitable man, nor was he a superstitious man. His observance of the Roman Catholic religion came not from any particular personal conviction, but as a continuation of his ranch duties. It was necessary for him to maintain, like the fences and the windmills and the water wells, the feast days and the candles and the painted saints who had dwelled there since the days of Spanish rule. Nevertheless the state of his cattle had terrified him in a way he could not explain.

For some time Mr Montez drove around, seeing if anything else was amiss. He drove up into the high country in the west. There he saw, far beyond the boundary of his ranch, at a distance of several miles, a small group of figures moving across a playa. Thirty or forty human figures, all in white—from head to toe, with white hoods, masks on their faces, white gloves and white material covering their shoes. In perfect silence, desert apparitions, they moved across the empty flats, holding long objects in their hands.

When Mr Montez returned to the ranch-house there was a car and two men waiting for him.

'Hello,' said one of the men. 'We are from the U.S. Army. There was an accident last night. But it's nothing to be concerned about.'

2

Army buses and jeeps began to arrive in the courtyard in the Technical Area, back from the test site. Something had happened to the doctors in the Jornada del Muerto. Things were not the same. It was written on their faces. Their eyes were bloodshot, their cheeks sunken, their hair in a mess, their clothes dusty. They stared about them with blank besotted looks, they barely spoke.

Disembarking, they moved towards the buildings of the Technical Area. They had bags and boxes of data from their various recording devices. The other boy was nowhere to be seen. Dr Fermi held a rabbit in his arms. The rabbit was in a clear plastic bag. Its skin was hanging from its body and its jaw was missing.

One of the last doctors to step down from the bus was

Dr Teller. His shirtfront was streaked with dust from lying on the ground in Alamogordo. A pair of dark sunglasses was tucked into his breast pocket.

He intended to go and see General Groves, in the loading area. But he was in no hurry. In fact, he wished to take his time. On the bus he had had an interesting conversation with Dr Lawrence. He had not had much to do with Dr Lawrence before, and to his surprise had found him most receptive to the idea of the Advanced Design.

'We ought to be doing this now,' the American had said. 'Heck, we ought to be doing it last week!'

Unlike so many of the doctors, Dr Lawrence was not content to sit back and admire what had already been done. No, he was determined to outdo it. It was the sort of conversation Dr Teller had been hoping to have ever since he arrived at Los Alamos. They covered all sorts of potential occupations for boys. They talked of tanks, aircraft, balloons, zeppelins. They talked of redirecting rivers, changing the weather— things that would have seemed quite improbable, even insane, to anyone outside of the scientific community. The exigencies of the war, that is to say the present war, had quite left their consideration. Most encouraging of all was the firm concurrence of opinion he had found in Dr Lawrence regarding the Russians.

He gazed about him now at the green-painted buildings of the Technical Area, at the powerlines and the vehicles, and the unpaved roads between the buildings, and thought how small it all looked, after what he had seen in Alamogordo. He saw Dr Oppenheimer walking ahead of him with his hat on. He watched him stop in front of the porch, light a cigarette and smile his squint-eyed smile at the doctors gathering loosely about him.

Why was there such mania for Dr Oppenheimer anyway, Dr Teller wondered. He was not a great doctor. None of his ideas had ever been particularly original or groundbreaking. Was it all charisma? Because he could quote poetry? Dr Teller could recite the "Jabberwocky" from memory. Could Dr Oppenheimer do that?

For a moment Dr Teller joined the fringe of the group. Dr Serber was talking about the test, trying to describe what the other boy had done, trying to put it into words. Failing in this, he talked about what would happen next, and how the medical field would change, now that they knew it could be done.

Dr Oppenheimer had the same distant look that many of the others had. They all seemed dazed. Dr Bethe enquired of everybody where Dr Fermi had got to. They did not know.

He had gone, in fact, to Sigma Building, to saw through his rabbit, with a power saw.

'Well Oppie,' said Dr Serber. 'What's going to happen with this place? What do we do with it now the boy's heading off?'

Dr Oppenheimer squinted down at his cigarette and shrugged.

'Give it back to the Indians,' he said. 'Right now we still have work to do.'

Dr Teller heard this preposterous remark, though he held his tongue. At one time he would have spoken up and explained Dr Oppenheimer's error to everybody in no uncertain terms. But not today. No, today it was enough for Dr Teller to look on, in silence, with an enigmatic smile on his face. He was no longer so foolish as to believe that anything could be accomplished by speaking to Dr Oppenheimer.

He listened a little longer to the conversation, and soon slipped away from this crowd. He was going to see the general. He headed for the loading area where the boy was being made ready for his departure. He saw the figure of the general standing in the open doorway.

Dr Teller had determined precisely what he must say to the general. He would not say much. A few careful phrases. It must be done quietly, he had decided, and over time, and without the appearance of intention. He would first say to the general that he had seen Dr Oppenheimer on several occasions being *less than discrete*. It was probably nothing, he would say. He would pause and allow the general to process this information. Then he would add that he could not help but think that Dr Oppenheimer's actions were *exceedingly hard to understand*. This was the clincher. Exceedingly hard to understand.

3

In the loading area a large wooden crate was open on the concrete floor, and some soldiers were filling it with straw and body-parts. Through their swift hands pieces of machinery passed, gleaming—pieces of curved metal, green-painted, pipes, wires, small, intricate components enclosed in boxes. They moved about with urgency.

The boy was on a table, in a state of dejection. The pain had set in, and everything was an irritation to him—the sight of the unthinking faces of the soldiers, the sound of their heavy plodding steps. When a pair of soldiers, locked in their task, nearly collided, apologized and laughed in the fawning, simpering, mirthless way that people laugh when they nearly bump into one another, a feeling of violent contempt filled the boy's soul. He was angry at their stupidity, at the stupidity of those who controlled his life. What angered him was that none of them seemed to bother asking why they were doing what they were doing. Nothing they did had any discernible benefit to anybody. And yet it had all been arranged down to the smallest detail, and so they did it, without asking questions. Why put a boy into a furnace, or drop him from twenty-feet in the air, or fire him through a tube? What did they get out of this? Why did they choose this as their occupation?

He looked, with his remaining eye, at his new body, which he did not understand, passing in fragments into the crate. The crate was full of straw. On the side of the crate it said SPARE RADIO PARTS.

He felt that he had learned a lesson. It had taken him a long time, but now he understood. They were not there to help him. Not the doctors, not the soldiers, nobody. Nobody is ever there to help you, he thought. They are there to process you. They are not there to solve the world for you, but to solve you for the world. And they are not there to bring your dreams to fruition, but to grind them out of you, slowly, meticulously, so that you will crawl and grovel, without complaining, without a single complaint, perhaps even with a few murmurs of obsequious gratitude, into a life you did not ask for, and to remain there, without thought of your old aspirations, the futures you have discarded, the lives you let slip, your old crazed hopes—to put all these aside, and to remain content, content to be anything but an inconvenience, to the great process.

It was disheartening to comprehend that such a process was at work upon him and had been for some time, and with cold determination he told himself he would never yield to it.

In the doorway stood General Groves. He kept going in

and out to speak to the driver of a large black truck that was reversing into the loading area. From time to time he spoke to the soldiers, giving them orders, speaking in the easy manner of one for whom nothing had gone wrong, seriously wrong, in recent memory, and for whom nothing would ever seriously go wrong, due to the neat alignment between himself, his wishes, and his times.

'There'll be seven cars waiting in Santa Fe,' he was saying. 'Got it? Security must be paramount. Don't let him out of your sight. Do we have uniforms for the doctors? Quick now.'

'Yes sir.'

It was not the habit of General Groves to mingle with the ranks, unless he was making a point about something. But he had made an exception for the boy's departure. In order to ease the growing tension, he had made a point of taking off his tie, opening up his collar and rolling up his sleeves.

Admiral Parsons was walking back and forth in front of the crate, looking down into it. Now and then he reached down and adjusted something within it, or directed the soldiers to move something. The boy thought of the processing all these men must have undergone in their youths, and he pitied them—yes, he even pitied them—for the lives they might have had, the people they might have been, had they not yielded.

The admiral drew close to his table then went away, carrying a few of the boy's rings. There were fifteen rings in total, including himself. Nine large, including himself, and six small. The small rings were kept separate from the large rings, for reasons he did not understand.

The boy had realized by now that this was his departure from Los Alamos. He accepted this with equanimity. It had always been this way—a long stretch in which nothing happens, then someone at last arrives and takes a look at you, then a day later you are taken away. He observed the plump slouched figure of Dr Teller entering the doorway. He saw his heavy dark head sunk down among his shoulders and the heavy false foot swinging along as he walked, and the smile of a madman curling the corners of his lips. He saw him go to the general and he saw them put their heads together and begin to talk in low voices.

At last the time came to load the boy into the crate. One of the soldiers took him, stacked a few of his rings on top of him and lowered him down among the soft straw.

At the direction of Admiral Parsons the soldiers lifted a large flat board over the crate and all went dark. They nailed it down. He heard the hammering. A forklift arrived and the crate was lifted up onto the truck. The boy heard the quiet babble of doctors' voices, and the rumbling of the truck's engine. Then he felt the truck begin to move. Slowly it moved off from the loading area, and slowly up the dusty road, through the gates of the Technical Area, and on, through the gates of the outer fence. Thus, without fanfare, the boy passed out of Los Alamos for the last time.

A few of the doctors watched him go, stopping where they walked, or peering out through the windows of their offices. Some of the doctors refused to watch him, turned their faces as the truck passed, or looked down at the ground, or up at the sky, anywhere but where he was, as though wishing not to acknowledge his existence. And there were others yet who looked, but did not see him—among these Dr Bethe and Dr Wilson and Dr Fermi, and even Dr Oppenheimer—whose eyes remained glazed and impassive, and whose minds were still in Alamogordo.

4

The truck having departed, and the day's business having been completed, the director went home. He had not gone in to see the boy. He had looked briefly at the general standing in the doorway, stately and monochromatic with his people all about him, and had thought how the whole scene resembled, from that angle, and that distance, in the desert light, Picasso's *La famille des saltimbanques.*

He felt unsettled. It was something distinct from simple regret, something like madness, like his idea of himself and his actions were no longer things that occurred within the same plane of reality. He had been at home only a few minutes—enough time to pour himself a glass of scotch and drink it—when he had an idea. He went out into the garden and found his wife. He proposed that they go for a walk. She considered it for a moment.

'Alright,' she said.

She went in to put on a jacket and take an aspirin. He waited a few minutes, smoking.

'We could head out to White Rock,' he said. 'Or up towards Pajarito Mountain.'

'Fine—don't mind,' said Mrs Oppenheimer.

So they drove up into the mountains, passing through the town, past the rudimentary houses and the fourplexes and the barrackses, where people were still returning home. They drove through the security gate and up into the higher country and the pine trees.

'Oh, darn, I didn't tell Rosa I was going,' said Mrs Oppenheimer. 'I hope she saw us. Peter is still there in the living room. Well, he'll be alright, I'm sure.'

'She'll keep an eye on him,' Dr Oppenheimer murmured, as though talking to himself. 'We won't be awfully long.'

Mrs Oppenheimer ran a hand across her forehead. Her face looked rather pale—but still quite lovely, he thought, angular and noble. She scraped at the outer corners of her eyes with the fourth fingers of her hands. She had a particular manner of scraping the corners of her eyes, always with these same fingers, which he had observed in no other.

'You look tired,' she said to him. 'I suppose you didn't get a lot of sleep out there last night.'

'No,' he said. 'Not a great deal.'

'Didn't find the time to call me,' she said, with a brief half-smiling glance.

This was quite unnecessary, he thought, though perhaps not undeserved. She knew about the test and had made this insinuation for no reason other than to provoke him. He made no reply. He did not wish to say anything to her yet about the test. For Intelligence may be listening, even here, somehow—microphones in the car, he would not put it past them. He pulled off the road into a dirt clearing and stopped the car.

'Right!' said Mrs Oppenheimer, bounding out onto her feet. 'Which way are we going?'

They had parked under a cottonwood tree a few yards off the road. On one side it was all dry meadowland, grass and junipers, and on the other it fell away into the slopes and swales and valleys of the Jemez, crowded with forests of pine and spruce. He looked at the mountainside, at its trees minutely and variously stirring, and the light falling evenly and logically on its lineaments.

'Down this way,' he said.

They went down towards the pine-forest. The wind blew softly, stirring Mrs Oppenheimer's spotted dress and her loosely tied red hair. She pulled her jacket tight about her and straightened her shoulders. Now he could tell her. There was no way for Intelligence to hear them out here. The forest had been ravaged by the storm, and the skeletons of fallen ponderosas cracked under their feet. He must tell her. But he did not know how. She bent down and began fussing in the undergrowth. He stopped and said, 'What are you looking at?'

'Toadstools,' she said. 'Babies. These are the fruiting bodies.' She showed him. 'They come up in a kind of protective shell. The universal veil. There—'

She parted a crumbling log with two hands and he saw, in the midst of the dim decay, the small bowed head of a purplish fungus, covered with warts. And beside it he saw a few small protrusions peeping—strange shapes, like frosted tongues—out of the hollow.

For a while Dr Oppenheimer and his wife discussed the subject of mushrooms. She described to him the mycelium, the branching cotton-wool roots by which they hunker down and take a hold of the earth and cling to it, eager to remain alive, for some reason, clambering over the putrescence, disseminating their dust of spores, and dying immediately afterwards—a little peal of ordnance, and nothing more, a simple life. A day's life.

She walked on a few paces. But for a moment Dr Oppenheimer did not move. He was staring at the ground. He felt he could go no further. He could not speak. His eyes—wide, pale, luminous blue—were fastened on the ground before him, and the light was fading. He felt he could see through the earth, through matter itself. And for a moment he was remote from all men. He felt that he understood them, saw right into the core of what they were. And what he saw was an endless depravity, more terrible than anything history had yet known. He saw in the boy in his little room in Los Alamos, and the other boy, miles away in Alamogordo, on his scaffold.

'You have something to tell me, don't you?' said Mrs Oppenheimer.

At length, he looked up and informed her, in a low voice, of the outcome of the test, of what the other boy had done. She asked him how he felt, and if it had been as he expected, and she congratulated him, and reassured him, as best she could.

Then they headed back for the car. All about them, in the dark, things were stirring. Toxic bodies ascended from the earth on long graceful stems. Parasols of flesh. There was breathing in the pines, and flies flying out of the long grass, and lights on the mesa, and birds caroling in distant dales. Miles of living things, fragile things. Easily broken. And the war, he thought, was stirring too, in its way—a vast organism, swelling and receding, according to an obscure logic.

They came up out of the trees and reached the road-side, and in the faint haze of the lights from the town Dr Oppenheimer saw his wife, scarcely illuminated. She passed beneath the cottonwood tree and got into the car. She had a cigarette in her hand. It was a nice thing, he thought, that she was here, in the desert, that she had taken up her life and followed him here, on his wild errand. He couldn't imagine himself ever doing a thing like that for anybody. It would never even have entered his head. And as he got into the car, Dr Oppenheimer did a thing he had not done in a very long time. He thought about his wife without thinking about himself.

5

The boy had not slept soundly since before he was melted. In the soft straw and the gently rattling dark he took the opportunity to sleep, and passed westward across the United States in perfect unconsciousness.

By the time his crate arrived in the Hunters Point Naval Yard in San Francisco, the sun was coming up again and shining through a few narrow slits in the wood. He heard voices and the wave-wash of the sea and the seabirds and he felt the crate swaying. A bell was ringing.

'Stand by,' said a distant voice. 'Fall out.'

A huge battleship lay at anchor in the water. Among its high gray turrets and gunmounts and funnels and masts and towers and antennas, hundreds of men scurried in the white hats of the U.S. Navy. A crane hoisted the crate high into the air and placed it down onto the quarterdeck. Then the crate was moved into a large hangar on the port side. The doors of the hangar were closed and locked and two armed guards took their posts in front of the doors. Captain de Silva and Dr Serber then came aboard, having come from Los Alamos with the boy, and were introduced to the ship's captain, a friendly affable man, with a toothpick in his mouth and a pair of dark aviator sunglasses.

'Welcome aboard,' he said. He looked at Dr Serber, who was wearing a military uniform. 'Your insignia's upside down, soldier.'

The ship cast off without delay, and soon the wind was howling along the decks. It was a fine day—the new-risen sun shone bright on the San Francisco Bay and on the Golden Gate Bridge as the ship steamed under it. The green waves of the sea came vaulting to meet the ship, and it sliced them clean through, in a sparkling spray.

The boy was leaving America. And as he charged westward, he felt an urge, an urge that was not quite his own—to turn and plant his eyes on it again, the land he had so long resented, from which he had drawn nothing, the land of his institutions, of the beatings, the showers, the exercises, the plummets, the fires. He had not taken the last look he ought to have taken, and he wanted to get out of the crate, turn round and look at America once more. But paralysis prevented him. Paralyzed he had come, and paralyzed he had left, and there had been no point to any of it. The huge turbines and boilers roared in the deep of the iron body. The four propellers turned and burbled and left fading ghosts of white foam, rocking steadily behind the ship, like pale bruises, slowly spreading on the water.

The ship was arranged, structurally speaking, in a manner most favorable to the boy. The men's sleeping quarters, in which their hundred sleeping-racks were crowded, lay directly under his hangar. So that in the evening hours of that journey, the clamor of sailors' voices drifted up through the floor.

The men on the ship were soldiers—real soldiers. They had seen battle. They had supported the raids on Tokyo. They had bombarded Iwo Jima. They knew all about the shells going overhead, and the way everybody crouched, all at once, by instinct, and they had been in the Battle of the Philippine Sea, doing something or other, and they had been at Saipan, with the smell of the bodies coming across the water from the beach, and the flies, and they had shot down six planes at Okinawa, and they had been blown up by a Japanese suicide plane. It had come right through the main deck and the mess hall and they had lost two propellers and nine men. All that life and danger had filled them up with a wild restlessness and they talked at night like it was their last opportunity to do so. And the boy just lay there and listened to them, and though he understood just a fraction of what they said, he picked up a great deal.

They talked long into the night sometimes. Their topics were extremely varied. They talked about the captain, and the course of the war, and the new Japanese weapons, and the mainland, and the food in the mess hall, and the food in the officers' mess hall, and their hometowns, their brothers, their dogs, the Ziegfeld Follies, the 1939 World's Fair, the 1938 Kansas State Fair, and the matter of who had whose shaving brush and who had whose cigarettes, and various girls, and the different types of girls, and the types of girls they wanted to marry, and Rita Hayworth especially, and the Good Book, and the zodiac, and the concept of the Sacrament of Penance, and the benefits of football compared to the benefits of tennis, and so on.

He began to acquire a sense, as he lay there, of what a soldier was, and it seemed to him something very exciting and admirable. He began to wonder if the reason he had never found anybody really interesting before, was that all the interesting men were soldiers, and all the real soldiers were overseas. There was nothing at cross-purposes between these men. There was no pretence. They did not bother about codes and arithmetic, like the doctors. They spoke freely, in a way the boy liked. They were not competing, they were not analyzing each other or comparing themselves to each other.

He listened at night to the thumping of their boots, and the creaking of their sleeping-racks, and the opening and closing of their lockers.

'We're going thirty knots, best speed all the way. Classified mission.'

'No kidding?'

'Must be churning up quite a wake. Hope they don't see us.'

'What do you think we got on board?'

'Don't know. Gauges or fuses or something.'

One of the men began complaining at length about the officers.

'They sure know how to bust your balls. They're experts at ball-busting. Three months—K.P. and guard duty—and dog watch at that. Rates are few and far between. My division was meant to be a fast-rating division. What a lot of baloney that was.'

'Guard duty won't seem so bad when they send us to the mainland. I tell you what, you'll be wishing you were back in this tin pot.'

'I doubt that.'

'Oh yeah?'

'I'll be thinking about Tucson. Just like I do every god-damn day. You know I'd probably be married to Barbara right now if it wasn't for the war.'

'Sure, and then what?'

'What do you mean and then what?'

'Once you get married, what do you do then?'

'Then you get a job and you fuck like rabbits and you get old and die.'

The boy considered this for a moment. He thought about marriage, girls, women.

'Man, I'd take guard duty over any office job. At least it's real out here and it's doing something. You know, helping somebody. You know what those Japs'd do if they ever got to Tucson and got their hands on your little Barbara.'

Nobody made any reply to this remark.

'Why do you pick at your socks like that?'

'Did Smith come in yet?'

'Smith? Oh no, he's in the brig. Five days.'

'What for?'

'Beats me.'

A lot of this of course went over the boy's head. But he understood that they were going to war, going to fight. They talked about it constantly—the mainland—the place where all soldiers must go to fight.

'There's no doubt about it,' one of them said one day. 'We are all to be sent to the mainland. Not next week. Maybe the week after. But it's gonna be something else, yes sir. Remember that suicide plane that tore up our mess hall? Guy I know in the Third Fleet says they've got ten thousand more. And plenty of those underground tunnels too. They're moving all their soldiers in from China. And they've got all the housewives and everybody trained up over there on the mainland, not just soldiers. Everybody wants to kill an American—for the Emperor, you know. They want to die doing it. They actually want to die. They're like Chesty Puller, they don't quit. They'll be out in the streets with rakes and shovels and kitchen knives and goddamned bamboo sticks. Old folks. Kids. They'll strangle you with a garden hose. Oh, it's tooth and nail on that mainland. Worse than Okinawa. If you can believe that. They say if we send a million men into Kyushu, there'll be five hundred thousand dead, no doubt about it. Not counting the Japs. And the wounded. They're making the Purple Hearts already.'

The boy was fond of the sailors. After nine days on the ship, he felt he knew them quite well. He had grown used to the sound of their voices. And when the ship arrived at its destination, he was sad to leave them. As his crate was moved off the ship, he heard them celebrating—cheering and clapping their hands. They had made the journey in nine steaming days, which was a record for a service vessel, and they were crying out at the top of their lungs that the U.S.S. Indianapolis was the fastest ship in the Navy. The boy did not even think of his destination, did not even consider that he was here at last, in a place he knew nothing about, that he was being carried ashore, and that he was now inches from the war. Instead he was caught up in their joyous, uncaring spirit, and he felt that he was on the verge of a life just like theirs, and he yearned more than ever to have the power of speech and movement so he could spring from his crate and celebrate with them.

6

Dr Szilard had written his petition and begun to circulate it. Among his own small team, it had acquired some modest support, which, rather than pleasing Dr Szilard, had filled him with a greater sense of the justness of his cause, and thus a greater sense of urgency. He had encountered difficulties in conveying it to the institution in Los Alamos. He could not go there himself, of course, nor could he telephone them directly. With few options left to him, he had sent the document to Dr Teller, and had received in reply an assurance that his old colleague would telephone him that afternoon.

So he awaited the call, pacing his hotel room in a state of the greatest unease. Time was dribbling away. He was certain that the Army was reading the doctors' mail, and he feared that they had censored his petition. He had been all morning in the bath. His baths were his time to think, but there was no longer anything to think about. He had thought it all through, from beginning to end, countless times. The prosthesis disgusted him. The whole thing disgusted him. It was now almost August. He wished the Japanese would surrender. Perhaps they were trying to. Nobody was communicating. All he could do was lie there shriveling in his bath with the terrible knowledge that something was about to happen, that the boy was to become public knowledge and his idea was to be an idea no longer.

Back and forth he went, in his hotel room, in his blue bathrobe. Drafts of his petition, written and rewritten several times, none exactly right, none even remotely right, were heaped on his desk. There were letters and memoranda and pages of equations that he had not touched in several weeks. A scrunched piece of paper lay on the floor beside his chair, which he had not put in the trash, telling himself he did not have time to do so until after the urgent matter of the boys was resolved. For several weeks it had lain there.

Nothing mattered to Dr Szilard that did not relate to ending immediately the problem of the boy. Picking up papers from his floor did not matter, polishing his shoes did not matter, shaving his chin did not matter. Friendships did not matter to Dr Szilard, to say nothing of affairs of the heart. He had been, for some time now, for the sake of the boy, a man without a personal life. There were too many things to do. Day by day, his motivation for a few more commonplace tasks vanished and the rubber balloon of the boy expanded a little more in his cerebellum, pressing upon the walls of his skull. He got up in the mornings, straight into his robe, unable to expend the mental energy necessary to decide which clothes to wear. He took his meals in the hotel. He kept no strict hours anymore, slept when he could, woke when he could. He made no long-term plans. It was too late for that. Every deadline he had set himself to solve the problem of the boys once and for all, every date which he had told himself would be the last possible date upon which it would be physically possible for him to endure the thought of the boys, had slipped past him—and still he thought about them. He was fighting a losing battle, he knew this, he knew the odds were against him, knew he would probably fail, fail at the eleventh hour, but his flesh cried out to help the boys. To keep trying.

In only the briefest instants did Dr Szilard dare to think what he would do after the boys had been steamrolled out of him at last. His suitcases were by the door. Packed. The keys in the locks. Old friends. When all was done, they would flee again, together, like they always did. He saw himself standing in the doorway, picking them up again, and setting out, bound for somewhere else, somewhere no different, another hotel room, identical in every fundamental particular—another mad sprint into another abortive life. Start anew, he would say to himself. Strike another match. Keep staving it off. He would think no more of the boy at last, at last know the sensation of thinking of something else. He would go into a different field, turn his mind to some other pursuit. Perhaps he would even begin to live his own life. That would be a real novelty. What deliciousness—to be done with the boys. To have the boys behind him. But he could not think of this now. Why was he thinking of this now? He was wasting time.

At two o'clock the telephone rang.

'How are things, Leo?' said Dr Teller.

'Things are as they always are,' said Dr Szilard. 'Have you got the petition?'

There was a shuffling sound at the end of the line.

'Yes,' said Dr Teller. 'I received it the other day.'

'They didn't censor it?'

'No.'

'Marvelous. Well, how many signatures have you got?'

There was a pause.

'I have forwarded it to Dr Oppenheimer,' said Dr Teller.

Dr Szilard considered this for a moment.

'That's wise, I suppose. We must be open about all this. We have nothing to hide. But you know Oppenheimer himself won't sign it. And he won't pass it on either. That's why I have sent it to you. You must show it to the other doctors, that's the main thing.'

There was another pause.

In his office, in Los Alamos, Dr Teller sat before his desk, hunched over as ever, the receiver pressed to his ear. From below his desk came the metallic tapping of his prosthetic foot, striking against the chair leg.

'I have considered this carefully,' said Dr Teller. 'And I wish to give you my reasons.'

He straightened a few pens and pencils that were laid before him on his desk, and began:

'I do not feel that there is any chance to outlaw any one invention. Our only hope is to get rid of war itself. And there's no way to do that unless the people really know what the boys can do. That's our only hope, really. They need to see it.'

Dr Szilard was surprised by these arguments, and

replied, 'Surely you are aware, Teller, that we can demonstrate our abilities quite well without sending the boys to war. People are not so stupid that they cannot have things explained to them.'

'Ah, but you would not say that if you had seen it yourself.'

'Teller, you are not saying—'

'Allow me to give you my reasons.'

'Very well.'

'It must be the decision of the people,' Dr Teller went on, as though responding to Dr Szilard, but in fact continuing with statements he had prepared in advance. 'Not the doctors, but the people as a whole. This must wait until after the war. If we start making announcements about the boys now we would compromise our situation. The secrecy will be lifted as soon as the war is over, of course.'

Dr Szilard did not know what to make of this. He paused for a moment and said, 'You really believe this?'

'It's my understanding.'

'I see.'

'I know this may seem to you quite wrong.'

'Well,'—Dr Szilard laughed weakly—'It does. It seems terribly wrong. It's a crime. We don't do this to children.'

'I feel,' Dr Teller said carefully, 'that I would be doing the wrong thing if I tried to say how to tie the little toe of the ghost to the bottle from which we just helped it to escape.'

Dr Teller thought this rather well put. But as usually happened when Dr Teller said things which he thought were rather well put, his interlocutor paid it no attention whatsoever.

A fresh wave of panic had broken upon Dr Szilard. All his days of empty talk, all his idling hours, had risen up before him at once. He had known them to be idle and empty, had felt their emptiness, yet something within him had always believed that at their conclusion, after an obscure lapse of years, something would be accomplished in accordance with his will. But this belief now crumbled out of him, and he saw that he had done nothing.

'At the very least, we must go on record,' he said. 'At the very least we must let it be known we said this was not right.'

Dr Teller made a snorting sound. His voice continued speaking quickly, distorted by the telephone.

'Let me say this, Leo. I know I have no hope of clearing my conscience. No amount of protesting or fiddling with politics—'

'Teller, listen to what you are saying. When you do something like this with—with humans, you do something very wrong. You cannot ignore the responsibility we have here.'

'It is not our decision to make.'

Dr Szilard knew his arguments well and was prepared to go on repeating them until somebody saw reason. So he did just that, and began laying out his points to his old friend as clearly as he could.

Dr Teller listened. And as he did so, he turned to his window, and gazed out over the Technical Area and the gray expanse of the pond, and his mind began to wander.

Ten new boys were to arrive, the general had said, by the end of October. Ten new boys, in little lead boxes. And after that maybe three or four more a month. That meant forty-eight more in a year, if one was optimistic. Not to mention the possibility of speeding up the methods of processing, of which Dr Lawrence was supremely confident. And once Dr Oppenheimer was replaced by somebody of better judgment, somebody with a better understanding of the Russian situation, the Advanced Design was sure to emerge as the primary prosthetic focus of the institution.

As he reflected on these facts, a feeling of grandeur spread through Dr Teller with a subtle smoldering fire. The smile, which he had worn habitually since the moment of the test, settled once more upon his face. He imagined the boys assembled before him, in their gleaming new prostheses. How could he explain to Dr Szilard what he had seen in the desert?

It is easy from afar, Dr Teller thought, to condemn the manifestations of the grandeur of thought. Men condemn what they do not understand. He turned from the window and looked at the map he had pinned over his desk. Small black dots signified the cities. He turned his attention methodically, as his old colleague spoke in his ear, to certain of these cities. Moscow. Leningrad. Berlin. Prague. Each of these neat-printed dots contained several hundred thousand human souls. And he thought of the people there, setting off to their day's work, returning to their homes, going to sleep. He thought of them lying in their beds. Like fatted calves. He thought of them sitting at their tables. At their desks. He heard their little voices, babbling through their city streets. How easily he could reach out, if he wanted to, and cover them over, with his little finger. Just a jerk of the finger. That was all it would take.

'Japan must be given the opportunity to surrender,' Dr Szilard was saying, 'before we even think of sending the boys out there.'

'Japan has the opportunity to do that now,' said Dr Teller gently.

'Yes, but they must be told about the boys. They must be told, at the very least.'

'When it happens, they will not need to be told. Hirohito will find out and word will spread and Stalin will find out and they will all see.' Dr Teller's voice had fallen oddly quiet, and he went on, almost in a whisper, as though speaking aloud to himself:

'Didn't we always know it? Didn't we always know it was terrible? I must say, I have gotten much more trouble than pleasure out of all this. I worked on these problems because—because they interested me. That's all. I am sorry. I must go. It is against regulations even to be speaking to you about this.'

He was all hunched over, his foot was still tapping, obsessively tapping, on the leg of his chair. His eyes, beneath their enormous brows, flickered about his office.

'If you wish to dissent,' said Dr Szilard, 'very well. I have made my case, and respect your decision. But I ask you to put the arguments to Dr Bethe, at least. And Fermi. I am not sure what Fermi thinks. If you can give him and some of the other doctors more or less an impression of the ideas of the petition—'

But he realized as he was speaking that Dr Teller had hung up.

7

The boy had been brought to an island. All about this island's edge, tall palms swayed in the seawind. On the bright pink sand the breakers rolled, shattering and receding with low foaming scornful sighs, and the sea came gurgling in and out of hollows in the caves and cliffs. In the green hills, the sun gleamed on twisted axles and twisted propellers and ruined tanks and rusted wheels and tons of spent ammunition.

The island was small—no more than eleven miles long. Most of its surface had been levelled into runways and taxiways. There were hardstands and hangars and quonset huts and control towers and mess halls. The air was full of airplanes, day and night. All the buildings were military buildings, all the vehicles were military vehicles, the clothing was military clothing and the food was military food. There were no women on the island. The last civilians had thrown themselves from the cliffs. A mood of passionate camaraderie predominated, and there could be no doubt that the war was somewhere in the vicinity. It was an environment in all respects conducive to the present stage in the boy's development.

His quarters were in the north. It was an area called North Field. He had been brought there in an army truck, in his crate, on a long straight road of pulverized white coral. The assembly building, as it was called, was simple, green, with large double doors rather like his shed in Africa, and no windows. Almost immediately upon his arrival, indeed less than an hour after his crate had been placed on the concrete floor, and pried open, and he had begun to look out at the enormous airfield, and the hundreds of airplanes, and to sample of the gasoline-scented air, the men reached in and began to assemble his body.

The men were mainly S.E.D. men. Admiral Parsons was among them, but most of them he did not recognize.

To describe the prosthesis they had made for him, to put into words the body so long anticipated by the boy, is no easy matter. For the doctors, in designing that body, had departed freely from anatomical conventions in favor of the principles of simplicity, efficiency, and the purgation of superfluity. And what had inevitably taken place was the gradual eradication, theoretically speaking, of the body as ordinarily understood, with its lumps, its limbs, its bristles, its pendula and other embellishments.

The body had been reduced to a single cylinder, a long hollow pipe, six feet in length and roughly ten inches in diameter, with a head at one end and a tail at the other. These two terminating elements—the head and the tail—were themselves rudimentary in appearance and streamlined almost beyond recognition.

The head was a broad steel cylinder, domed at one end, with a diameter twice that of the pipe. It had no facial features, with the exception of two small circular points, upon the dome. These were the eyes.

The tail was, at its foremost point, the same diameter as the head. But it differed from the head in several important respects. It tapered backward, like a funnel. On its sloping surface, four triangular fins were mounted at equidistant points. And these in turn were enclosed within four flat square panels, comprising, when viewed from the back, an arrangement of the utmost geometrical harmony, with the edges of the four panels in profile forming a square and the back of the pipe forming a circle in the center, and the four fins stretching outward from their four equidistant points on the circumference of the circle along the diagonals of the square and meeting the square precisely at its four corners.

'Very nice,' said Admiral Parsons, as the tail was removed from the crate for the first time. And it was not clear to the men, or to the boy, whether he was commending them on their work, or remarking on the beauty of the appendage.

The head having been screwed onto the front of the pipe, and the tail having been screwed onto the back of the pipe, two feet of naked pipe remained exposed in the middle. But it was not long before the men gathered about his skeletal frame and began to affix his organs. These intricate components—each representing years of meticulous medical development—were removed one by one from the crate.

They were all contained in boxes, which the men bolted carefully into place on the prosthesis. One rectangular box, wrapped in gray felt, contained six spring-wound clocks, nestled in a jumble of wires, capacitors, transistors and microswitches. Four others contained radar units—these boxes were heavy and black, and were connected in turn, by cables, to small white batteries. Then the six little aneroid organs, these too in little square compartments, were affixed in turn—everything as neat, rigid and simple as humanly possible. All were positioned around the pipe and bolted to brackets. From these boxes emerged numerous black cables, which led back towards the breech.

Where, one may ask, was the boy himself, the midst of this elegant mechanism? Where, that is to say, was the gray ring-shaped piece of matter which had attained its shape in the flames of the furnace and which the boy had hitherto thought of as himself?

The answer is simple—he was in the pipe. His nine rings had been placed there by one of the men at the beginning of the assembly, and pushed to the back of the pipe, in the tail-section, where he was firmly held in place by steel stoppers. There he had been, in the back of the pipe, when his head was screwed on, and his tail was screwed on, and when the boxes were bolted on, and when the wires and cables were threaded and plugged—there he had been for all those tedious hours of screwing. The pipe was the perfect size for these rings, and they could have slid smoothly up and down its length, had they not been firmly held fast, in place, at the back, by the stoppers.

Had he been permitted to slide forward to the front of the pipe, he would have discovered there a cylindrical rod that fit perfectly into the hole in his rings. But it was not permitted. The stoppers stopped it. He could only look at it afar, gleaming in the dark of the pipe. When his eyes were connected, by an obscure network of contacts and cables, then he ceased to look at it. For as soon as his eyes were connected, his vision changed. As though by magic, he was no longer looking at the interior of the pipe, but out—forwards, at the doors of the assembly building, and the legs and bodies of the men moving about him. For when we speak of his eyes being connected we are speaking of the two eyes on the front of the dome, the eyes on his rings having exhausted their practical purpose.

But he went on thinking, in spite of this alteration, of that little rod. He went on yearning for his rings to slide down the tube and for them all to fit together nicely, rings and rod. The image reminded him, naturally, of the tall apparatus in Los Alamos, his old plummets, when he had slipped down perfectly through that hole in the platform, and the strange thrill it had given him. The thought of things sliding perfectly into other things, of bores being filled, vacant cylindrical spaces being filled by concentric cylinders of exactly corresponding size, of shapes passing through corresponding shapes, becoming one—such thoughts contained the promise of an immense satisfaction which he did not entirely understand. Evidently this sliding and inserting mechanism was fundamental to the operation of his prosthesis. He assumed he would understand it, in time.

His body was not yet quite complete. He lay in the center of the assembly building, his innards exposed, as though upon an operating table. The wires had all been wired and threaded through the requisite holes, the boxes had been mounted, the connections had been established, and all that remained was to seal him up. To this end a series of curved panels were bolted onto his prosthesis, each connecting the tail, at the back, with the head, at the front, and completing his outer shell. Another feature that was added at this time was a small sturdy handle on the boy's back, just behind his head.

The boy was dark green from head to tail. It was a nice green, not olive drab, which he had seen to excess in Los Alamos, but a dark, midnight green. It was nicer than any green he had seen before. He stared ahead of him, through his eyes, feeling very strange indeed. He felt long and smooth and heavy. The men toiled about him and bent over him and crawled underneath him. He had a special stand that he lay on. It had wheels with thick rubber tires. Admiral Parsons observed everything closely. He passed a casual remark to one of the S.E.D. men as the last bolt was bolted in. The boy could not make out what was said exactly, but it was some words of congratulation.

It took two days to assemble his body. It was the screwing that took the longest, the alignment of the threads, the turning by several men of the long leather belt that hung from the ceiling, and the application of various greases and powders. And then the wiring, which was done with the utmost care. The S.E.D. men were well-practiced. It occurred to the boy that whenever he had seen the S.E.D. men at Los Alamos, whenever he had watched them from windows, coming and going with pipes and boxes, rarely interacting with him, they must have been rehearsing for this moment, perhaps with these very body-parts, or perhaps with prototypes, in their own separate buildings, with the admiral. So they worked now in perfect calm, with efficiency and without confusion. And Admiral Parsons, though he watched them closely and murmured a few words from time to time, seemed not to force them or direct them in anything. When some of the holes did not line up correctly, and had to be re-drilled, he simply nodded his head and said, in his faint calm voice, 'Well, go ahead,' and they re-drilled them.

When the work was done, the men passed out of the assembly building, and piled into a canvas-topped army jeep. There were too many of them for the jeep, and a few of them hung off the sides. They drove off down a white road, out of sight of the boy, headed for the western edge of the airfields. They came to a cove on the shore. There they took off their clothes and swam in the clear water. The evenings were silent on the island, because the insects and the birds had all been exterminated. They swam for a while, then they got out of the water and dried themselves and sat on the rocks, and gazed out over the Pacific Ocean.

8

The door of the assembly building remained open, and the boy could see the sea in the distance, a flat blue line beyond the airfield. He could see also a few green tent-like buildings, some power lines, and the runways stretching away for miles on the right side, with the airplanes landing and taking off. Clouds were gathering in the sky.

He thought about his new body. The overwhelming sensation was still one of strangeness. A precarious, poised feeling. Having a body, he thought, was going to take some getting used to. For one thing, it was not what he had expected. He looked nothing like anybody else. He had always wanted to be six foot, but not like this. To be green and pisciform, symmetrical, low to the ground, still without arms or legs, was unsettling. There was a great dissimilarity between his body and those of other men, and between his body and that which he had envisaged for himself.

He distracted himself by gazing out through the doors. It was an incredible sight—flat runways for many miles. And airplanes—hundreds of airplanes, everywhere he looked, their silver bodies and tails gleaming. He saw the little pilots climbing into the airplanes, heard the engines and the spluttering propellers. For the next few hours he watched them approaching, points of silver in the marbled sky, getting larger and larger and louder and swooping down, teetering, onto the runways. And he watched them take off, and he did not know which he liked better—the takeoffs or the landings.

He knew they were warplanes. Though he did not know the details of their operations, he assumed rightly that they were going to and returning from missions. He imagined that they were going to the mainland. He had heard brief mention of the 6th Bombardment Group, the 9th Bombardment Group, the 504th—or was it the 505th? He knew the S.E.D. men were members of a special group all of their own, and Admiral Parsons was their commander, and he knew that they were engineers. Was the boy too an engineer? Was that the way it worked? That was the problem—nobody had ever told him the way anything worked.

All he knew was that he was near the war. But he was not yet in the war. In the war, things would be different. He was getting ahead of himself. There was no use speculating on the merits and deficiencies of the prosthesis until he had been taught how to use it.

Presently it began to rain. The weather had been fine when he arrived on the island. But less than an hour after the completion of his prosthesis, the clouds gathered, and the heavy rain and thunder began. The sea grew colorless and blended with the sky, and the trees swayed violently, and the tent-like buildings shook across the way, as though made of sticks. It was a fat, dense rain, different to other rains he had known. It fell at a diagonal, soaking the earth.

It interested the boy to observe that the airplanes continued to take off from the runways of North Field. A whole contingent was taking off in spite of the bad weather. Their bravery amazed him. He watched them roaring along the runways at great speed and going up into the air, and he feared for them. The rain moved in dim masses over the enormous flatness. For some time he watched them.

And as he lay there watching them, he contemplated the pilots, blinded by the rain and going blindly up into the sky, into that gray turmoil, for their country—into the war, where they could be shot, where they could plunge into the sea or spiral to the earth. He thought of how fearful he had been, throughout his life. All the time he had spent in institutions, sheltered from the world, when in reality there was no greater threat to him than the institutions themselves. The airplanes went on rising, one by one, before him, through the turbulent sky, storm-tossed, as though on invisible strings, one after the other, like pulses of electricity along a wire.

He too would go out into that world. Out—among the wild keeling palms, and the rush and roar of battle, and the carrion beaches, and the dim gray skyward-heaving columns of the sea. Soon it would happen. He had spent his whole life in his head. All his life, like a fly in a jar, he had rattled in the crock of his head. And soon he would be out there.

Night fell. He saw headlights moving on North Field. Men came in out of the streaming dark with drops of water on their faces and running down their clothes, and mud on their boots. They stood around him and seemed to be doing something to him. He couldn't see what they were doing. The boy heard them say it was a typhoon. Nothing could be done, they said, nothing could be done yet. They must wait. So he waited.

9

Admiral Parsons stood in the rear of the assembly building, near the boy's tail, talking to Dr Serber, a black-haired soldier named Colonel Tibbets, and Captain de Silva. It was morning, not long after the reveille. For seven days the rain had rained on the island, pounded the roof and deranged the trees, and still it rained.

Dr Serber lay like an odalisque, shirtless on an army-green stretcher bed, his smug face observing the conversation through his thick spectacles. The others stood about him, all in variations of the same shade of khaki, glancing from time to time at the boy, and out through the doors over the airfield. They were concerned, because a few airplanes had crashed upon takeoff.

'It's the B-29s,' the admiral was saying. 'They're

unwieldy to begin with—'

'They're not easy things to fly,' said Colonel Tibbets.

'Long wingspan,' said Dr Serber.

'Look, I don't want to get superstitious about it—' began Colonel Tibbets.

'Then don't, for Christ's sake,' said Captain de Silva.

'Well, alright.'

His point remained unstated. Colonel Tibbets moved round with measured steps in front of the boy, his hands in his pockets. Then turning once more to the doors, he gazed out thoughtfully over the island.

'The essential problem is that the boy is heavy,' said the admiral. 'That could cause all sorts of problems.'

'Put it this way, if a fire starts, we could lose the island and every blessed thing on it,' said Captain de Silva.

'Make a terrible mess,' said Dr Serber.

'Surely would,' said Colonel Tibbets, scratching at his widow's peak.

'I think we ought to arm him in the air,' said the admiral.

The boy's curiosity was sparked. Was he to have arms? Unable to see the men, he listened to their deep American voices.

'That would take away the danger of take off.'

'Would you have enough time to do it in the air though?' said Colonel Tibbets.

'Oh, I could do it in a few minutes, I suppose,' said the admiral, resting his hand lightly on the boy's head. 'Five minutes, with practice.'

'You don't have long to practice,' said Captain de Silva. 'Groves wants this kid in battle last week.'

The wet wind blew on.

'Well,' said Admiral Parsons brightly. 'I've got all afternoon at least. The rain won't let up til tomorrow at the earliest. That's—well, that gives me this afternoon to practice.'

'If you think you can do it, I have no objection to it.' said the Colonel.

They began, with a quiet but insistent restlessness, to move towards the door. They seemed to have said all that they felt needed to be said about the boy, at this juncture.

'Should have brought an umbrella!' cried Captain de Silva, thrusting one of his pale clean hands out in the downpour.

'There's something I wanted to show you, Admiral,' said Dr Serber, who had risen from his place and was drawing across his scrawny shoulders a crumpled and dirty khaki-colored shirt. 'Come, it's in the other building—with the fat man.'

In the afternoon, as the light dwindled, the admiral returned and began what he called his practice. He had a toolbox and a bundle of soft bags, like sandbags. Setting these down beside the boy, he removed his wristwatch and placed it on the floor. Then he kneeled and looked at his watch, evidently waiting until the second hand had reached some significant point.

The admiral opened a small square tin, like a cigarette-case, and took out two green plugs, which he proceeded to insert into two small orifices located on the boy's back. Then he went around behind the boy to his tail-section. At the very back of the tail, there was a circular plate of metal. Admiral Parsons knelt behind the boy, removed some bolts with a socket wrench and unscrewed this circular plate. Sixteen turns, and it came away. There was some empty space between the end of the tail and the very back of the boy's pipe, where his rings were. Into this empty space Admiral

Parsons now inserted his arms, and from time to time his head. He unplugged a few wires. Then he took his four heavy bags and placed them into the space. They were soft bags, made of fine silk. The admiral arranged them carefully. He reattached the wires with care, closed off the back of the tail once more, screwed it in, ensured it was tight, then went back to his watch to check it.

This complete, Admiral Parsons undid all he had done, removing the bags and the plugs with not as much haste as he had employed in putting them in. Once he had returned the prosthesis to its initial state, the entire procedure began again.

He tried variations. For instance, on one occasion, he placed the bags on top of the boy as he worked, and on another he placed them on the floor. On another occasion he placed the bolts, as he unbolted them, into his breast-pocket, and on another in the pocket of his trousers. On some occasions he bolted the bolts in a clockwise fashion, on others in an anticlockwise fashion. With these and other variations, Admiral Parsons experimented. But the insertion was always the same, and the checking of the wristwatch always closed the procedure. His speed seemed to improve over time.

The boy was long past the age at which he would have attempted to ascertain the meaning of such an exercise. He was also beyond the point of feeling any special contempt for it. This procedure, though not pleasant, was nothing compared with the agonies of the furnace and various other prior degradations. His hope to get away, to get up and moving, commence his life, to be done with treatments and training of all kinds and with the whole deceitful muck of his interminable boyhood, could not have grown any greater than it already was.

Instead he contemplated Admiral Parsons himself. He observed, when able to see him, his calm inconspicuous face, his balding head, his long slender efficiently-moving body. The boy had never before given any significant amount of thought to the admiral. Indeed, all the men who had accompanied him to the island from Los Alamos were not men he had considered before at any length. Dr Serber, Captain de Silva, the S.E.D. men, the admiral—it was as though they had been selected especially for their bland-ness and insignificance. Admiral Parsons was particularly unassuming, in spite of what the boy now realized to be his position of considerable authority. He realized that it was perhaps Admiral Parsons more than anyone who determined how the prosthesis was to operate on a practical basis, and what it was to do and where it was to go.

Over the next few hours, a certain intimacy sprang up between the boy and this most unexpected of caretakers. One minute you think nothing of a man and the next minute he is plugging your orifices. The boy began to gain a renewed understanding of certain small details of the admiral's conduct, such as the way he kept the assembly building swept and neat and tidy. There was the place for the boy, in the center, on his wheeled stand. There was the white shelf where the toolbox and the bags were kept, along with the record-books and documents. There were the surgical tools, neatly arranged. There was the stretcher bed for the men to sit on. Everything had its approximate place.

The admiral was an ordered man, that was what he was—ordered. Everything about him was ordered, but not to the point of obsession. No, for the truly ordered man cannot be ordered to the point of obsession, because obsession is a kind of disorder. And Admiral Parsons was an ordered man, a tidy man, in the truest sense. Which meant that his uniform was always correct, but not perfectly starched in the manner of some men's uniforms. It meant that he was reticent, but not silent, that he was affable, but not comical, that he was serious, but not stern, that his posture was straight, but not rigid.

The boy considered carefully, in his peculiar way, these aspects of the admiral's character, which he had never considered before.

Even when he talked about his earlier life, as he did from time to time, in his conversations with Captain de Silva, it seemed that the Admiral Parsons had never been led by anything other than a calm, disciplined sense of duty.

Admiral Parsons had opinions of course, but none of them were particularly extreme. He was a man of science, he tended towards skepticism in his personal beliefs. He was very fond of Dr Oppenheimer, though he found him pompous, and he did not like Dr Teller. He did not talk about the war, as some men did, as though it were a personal ailment, or a mandatory scheduled event, or a game, or an insect colony, or a scientific experiment, or a religious ceremony, or a country fete. In fact there was only one occasion upon which the admiral gave expression to any specific opinion concerning the war, in the boy's presence. It was when relating to Captain de Silva a short detour he had made—on official leave, of course—to San Diego, just prior to leaving for the island. His young half-brother had been injured, and the admiral had visited him briefly in the Naval Hospital.

'He was at Iwo Jima,' the admiral explained to Captain de Silva. 'A mortar had gone off, and a rock caught him. Smashed up one side of his face. The family was all there to see him. He could talk fine. He had his wits about him, but he didn't particularly want to talk. His face was all sunken in. They'd wired his jaw together. And he had a pink plastic ball in his eye-socket. Everyone was there and he was all—he was not the same as before. Terrible thing for a kid of eighteen. To have the face messed up like that.'

He had been wiping his hands as he spoke, with a rag, and he paused a moment to examine the ends of his fingers. The sound could be heard of the fitful rain on the roof, and the wind howling across the airfield. Then he resumed his anecdote:

'I thought about it on the way back and I thought that really is bad luck. The face, I mean, why did it have to be the face that the rock went through, and not the shoulder or the—or the air above the face? I thought how he probably has no idea, not even now, of what that's going to be like, of what the rest of his life is going to be like now, because of that. It'll take him years to understand it and he may never understand it.'

'He was lucky to get out,' said Captain de Silva.

'Twenty-six thousand guys did not.'

The boy thought about this for some time, after the men had stopped talking. In particular he thought about the pink plastic ball.

10

That night there were four more plane crashes. Four in succession, all during takeoff. For a while it seemed to the men that every airplane was henceforth going to crash, and no more missions would ever be able to continue from the island.

The boy watched them lift, wheel skyward, spin, and in a flash of flame, strew themselves across the ground. One of the crashes looked almost gentle, a kind of extended skid. Down, thump, a distant boom, and then the fire, hissing in the rain, and the stench of burning gasoline and the column of black smoke. They all burned for twenty minutes at least. With as many as eight hoses on them— they would just go on burning.

They interested the boy, and he came to realize by

the third crash that he was not as affected by them as he may have expected to be. One would think the boy would have been averse to fires of any kind, in light of his recent experiences. But it was not so. He found, rather, something almost appealing in the sight of this raging fire, and the beautiful airplane that was so perfectly formed and so shiny and perfect, slowly turning into a big gnarled mess of black smoke, its beautiful propellers twisted, its windows smashed, its smooth body torn and dented, and the people running over like ants from all directions and the firefighters unrolling their hoses and everybody utterly possessed with panic, though it had happened before and would probably happen again, all behaving as though it was the only time it had ever happened, some raising their hands to their heads in helpless, hollow gestures, and some instinctually ducking their heads at the sound of the blast.

What was attractive to the boy was not so much the fire itself, but the thought of himself, watching it. And as he watched the long white arcs of water pouring onto the fires, and the smoke mounting into the wild wind, and the wind shuddering out over the trees on the shore and the darkening indifferent sea, he wondered what it would be like to be perfectly indifferent—not merely to say to himself that he didn't care, but actually not to care. To be unaffected by fear and pain and hurt, free of suffering, his emotions silent, his emotions dead, his heart still—or even better, without a heart, heartless, neither kind nor cruel, neither happy nor sad, refined out of all weaknesses—disciplined.

It would mean of course forgetting all that flimsy whimsy about Miss Piles for good. But he was already halfway to doing this, and it would be no great difficulty.

He had long ago washed his hands of the entire business of Miss Piles and her sting, long ago let slip the face and the eyes and the golden neck and the charming bow legs and the curves of the arms of Miss Piles, who had accosted him so unpleasantly, and there were merely a few scraps of that feeling left, a few scraps, which could with a little effort be swept out. And what better place for such a sundering, he thought, than here on the island where there were finally no women, literally zero women among the population?

For all they had ever tried to do was to mock him, he said to himself, to meticulously take him to pieces, and to acquaint him in various ways with his own ill-adaptedness. To weaken him, in order to justify their own weakness. It was time for him at last to put this aside, to let it go, and to welcome into his soul an entirely new feeling—the cold, firm, strong, slightly-unhinged feeling of being a soldier. They had merely to give him the chance to do it. He was ready. They had merely to give him the chance. Why must it be raining?

At nine o'clock some news arrived about the sailors. Somebody had informed one of the guards before change of shift and the guard informed the admiral. The boy knew as soon as he heard mention of the sailors that they must be dead, and of course they were. Two Japanese torpedoes had hit the U.S.S. Indianapolis, it had sunk, and sharks had come, and no help had come, and eight hundred and seventy-nine American men were dead.

Whereupon Admiral Parsons, having been interrupted from his practice, had to stop and wait for the second-hand of his wristwatch to reach its point again. It seemed to take him a few tries to do this, and he remained for a time in that motionless attitude, on his knees, looking at his watch, his fist tight around the handle of the socket wrench, then he went on with his practice, for some time, in spite of the hour.

11

The boy looked out blankly at the palms dripping and stirring in the distance. The rain had ceased. It was not long after midnight. The S.E.D. men were all about him again, milling about him, looking at his body, talking over him. He did not listen to them. He felt nothing towards them. He knew his duty. A man with a camera took his photograph. The filament in the flashbulb sparked and burst across his featureless face—blue magnesium light. His two lidless, pupilless, perfectly circular eyes stared ahead of him, fixed in place.

Captain de Silva stood in the space between the boy and the door, puffing on a short fat cigar.

'Weather looks good,' he remarked.

'So I observe,' said Admiral Parsons, peering at the

dark sky and the long white columns of the klieg lights.

'You're a little impatient to get going.'

'Oh, no.'

'Had any sleep?'

'Plenty.'

Admiral Parsons was holding his white rag. He moved it constantly, rhythmically, over his hands, between the fingers, over the palms and the knuckles, without looking at it.

They watched the boy being transferred onto a trailer and covered with a tarpaulin. Presently he was taken out, drawn by a tractor, through the predawn dark, down the long white coral road, to the airfield. The men followed in vehicles. A night breeze blew across this convoy, a single slow shiver of the sea, making its way up from the cliffs, through the trees, through the hair of the men, and through their clothes, and through the boy's tarpaulin.

When they had reached the airfield, the tarpaulin was removed, the trailer was unhitched, and the tractor drove away. An airplane stood waiting to receive the boy. A rectangular section of the concrete upon which the trailer stood descended slowly into the ground, six feet down, creating a pit. The S.E.D. men went on babbling, then hopping down into it, attended to the prosthesis as the admiral paced uneasily. The boy was silent and still as ever, his face to the blank gray pit wall. The airplane had looked enormous in the dark with the sheen on its skin, the huge nose covered with windows, the long silver wings, the black propellers. The camera flashed again, faintly. He heard the engines and the wind and the occasional shouts of the men.

It was time for boarding. Though it was all quite new to the boy, it had been planned and rehearsed to the smallest detail, several weeks in advance. An elaborate method of insertion had been devised to accommodate the paralyzed passenger, and this method, reworked and revised over several iterations, had been approved at last by Admiral Parsons, by Dr Oppenheimer, and even by the general, that is to say by Mrs O'Leary herself. A set of double doors was opened on the underside of the airplane. It then moved forward, casting its vast pitch-dark shadow over the pit, and stopped. The boy was raised up from his trailer, by means of a hydraulic mechanism, passing through the doors and into the bowels of the airplane.

Then swiftly, with their dog tags dangling, two S.E.D. men climbed up and attached him to the interior by means of the sturdy handle on his back. The hydraulic support descended back into the pit. The boy was now hanging from his handle, suspended, his nose pointed slightly downwards, so that he could see, through the doors, the young faces of the S.E.D. men. They closed the doors beneath him.

His compartment in the airplane was cramped, dimly illuminated by four small lights, with walls that appeared unfinished, covered with exposed wiring and screws. Below him were the doors, shiny and silver, shut fast. He heard the propellers on either side of him. They seemed very close. Presently the airplane began to taxi along the tarmac, and the boy felt the sway and bump of movement. This went on for some time.

Then another part of the airplane shuddered to life, and the noise grew into a roar, vibrating through the walls and through every inch of his body, shuddering and trembling—and the whole thing lunged forward at great speed. He swayed and bumped as before. He felt the airplane accelerate, then he felt it lift. The structure all about him

started to float, and to tilt, slightly, to the right. He knew
at once he was off the ground, having seen it a hundred
times. But it felt different from the inside. And when he
tried to imagine himself hurtling out over the cliffs and the
wastes of the sea, up into the high clouds, he could not.

Things had leveled out. The boy had become accustomed
to the drone of the propellers. It is remarkable how one
becomes accustomed to things. He heard footsteps, a
shuffling of movement, and a groan, which was the opening of a hatch behind him. At length, a familiar balding
head came into view.

The admiral gave the boy an impassive glance as he
made his way carefully around him in the cramped space.
He wavered as he went, like a drunken man, clutching
to his breast his silken bags and his toolbox in the other
hand. He set them down and glanced at the boy again.
Bending over the boy, he placed the green plugs into his
orifices. Then, picking his steps with as much precision
as could be expected under the circumstances, he went
behind him. He unbolted and unscrewed the back plate
of his tail, as before—sixteen turns—he disconnected the
wires, then he placed his bags in carefully behind the back
of the boy's pipe, reconnected the wires and replaced the
back plate. He had reached the point at which he normally
looked at his watch. But this time he did not look at his
watch. He went back to the boy's head, tottering, removed
the green plugs, and replaced them with two red plugs.
The green plugs went safely into his pocket.

As he was reaching again for his toolbox, the airplane
dipped and tilted. Admiral Parsons, stumbling, moved
abruptly forward and wrapped his arms around the boy's

body. For a moment the side of his face was flat against the boy, his ear and his cheek and his jaw, fleshy and clean-shaven. Nobody had ever done this to the boy before. The admiral then let go, took up his toolbox, and went back the way he had come.

The hatch was closed behind the boy, and all went quiet again. The quiet drone, the faint dim rattle of motion, the small space. He watched the doors—the neat juncture, a straight line. Soon he would be in the war. It was close, it was on the other side of a threshold, long-promised, long-awaited. The propellers droned—dull thick droning throbs.

After a while, the doors parted, quickly and smoothly. The compartment was flooded with a bluish light. He saw, still dangling from his handle, with some surprise, the sea. It was dark gray-blue, and still, like ice. Terror seized him. He was a thousand miles above it, moving over it, leagues were disappearing beneath him. His handle creaked on its hook.

He saw tiny boats on the sea, their white wakes trailing behind them. Then they were gone and it was the coast he saw, the three-pronged coast, merging into a vast dun slab, and the forests, the small green stirring canopies, rows of brightening hills, hollows, the long broken slopes, squares of fields, roofs of houses. The airplane, droning, banked to the left. Somewhere, he thought, in this maze of insignificant habitations, there were two great armies, the Americans and the Japanese, gathered for battle. But now all he could see was houses.

The fear nagged at him, but he forced it out of his mind. He knew that what he feared was the loss of himself, and he knew that he must not fear it. For it was inevitable. It had happened already, on countless occasions. He had left himself again and again by the wayside, without realizing it, he thought, as he gazed down grimly at the thousands of rooftops. And he thought of how far he had come, heedless of the days, and what little he had held onto. His life had spun out from under him. Though he had done nothing it had unfolded itself all around him, and though it had not touched him, he had changed. It had turned him all awry. A series of infinitesimal gradations of change had been secretly applied to his body, his cells being replaced by others, of similar appearance. Now the long cruel joke of childhood was almost over, he was years and miles from where he had begun, and still he understood no more than he ever had, and still was in utter perplexity, and still this wild voice was chattering in his head, urging him obsessively to begin his life. Begin, it said. Commence—do it—be done with it—do the thing, it said, the thing—spurring him on, as ever.

The day glowed full upon his face. There was a stirring in the region of the hook. That is to say, of the handle. Briefly the thought crossed the boy's mind, terrible and stark, that once you have begun, there is no returning. And this thought having hardly formed itself, in his intelligence, the lurch came—a great sickening involuntary enteric heave—and he dropped through the open doors.

A falling body with zero initial velocity is subjected to two physical forces—the gravitational force, which is its mass multiplied by its gravitational acceleration, and the air resistance, or drag, which is contrary to the gravitational force, and proportional to the velocity of the body as it falls.

Yet for the first time in his excessively long childhood the boy felt no force upon him. In his immediate vicinity, all was still. He felt no stir. In a matter of seconds, the airplane was a dot, far above. He was alone. He was young and he had been set loose at last on the world. It was all before him—a vast gentle curve, bordered by whiteness, then miles of cloudless blue. In the depths of his prosthesis, the six clocks had begun ticking—tick tick, as ever. Birds were calling far away, over distant fields, but he couldn't see them.

He saw the long winding line of a river, branching southward into two distributaries. He saw a bridge, unusual in shape, a building with a beautiful dome, he saw a tram stopping on one side of the bridge, and rows of houses and gardens spreading out from the banks, rows upon rows, in rigid lines, and cars heading in various directions through the streets, and trams and horse-carts, and bicycles, and little people walking, standing, riding, embarking, disembarking. It was eight-fifteen in the morning. People were beginning their day's work, and children were coming out to play on the school fields.

Little Boy
By John Smith

First published in this edition by Boiler House Press, 2022
Part of UEA Publishing Project
Copyright © John Smith, 2022

Original Design by Emily Benton Book Design
Cover Design and Typesetting by Louise Aspinall
Proofread by Clare Kernie
Typeset in Arnhem Pro
Printed by Imprint Digital
Distributed by NBN International

ISBN: 978-1-913861-06-3